Remember My Love

Elise Dee Beraru

Hard Shell Word Factory

To Maria Carbajal, who was the first person (after me) to fall in love
with Blair Carroll.
To Josette Valtierra, who understands more than anyone how hard it is
to write and run a law practice simultaneously.
To Los Angeles Romance Authors and Romance Writers of America,
for showing me how to get through the door that separates dreaming
about being an author and becoming one.

© 1999 Elise Dee Beraru
Trade Paperback
ISBN: 0-7599-0053-1
Published July 2001
Ebook ISBN: 1-58200-099-9
Published June 1999

Hard Shell Word Factory
PO Box 161
Amherst Jct. WI 54407
books@hardshell.com
http://www.hardshell.com
Cover art ©1999 Mary Z. Wolf
All electronic rights reserved.

Chapter 1

SUNLIGHT PEEKING in from a crack in the drapes assaulted Blair Carroll's senses like a knife to his flesh. His head splitting like he had been struck with an ax, he slowly opened his eyes and tried to focus on his surroundings.

He was in his bedroom in San Francisco. He recognized the dark wood paneling, the dark blue wallpaper and curtains, the heavy oak furnishings. A fire blazed in the fireplace opposite him. How he got there he had no idea.

He glanced down. He was covered nearly to his shoulders with a fine percale sheet and silk counterpane of the same dark blue as the walls and drapes. His long arms at his sides were encased in the sleeves of a nightshirt on top of the coverlet. For a brief moment, it didn't seem right.

The blanket should be more colorful, not so smooth and dark. But that's ridiculous; I've had this same bedding for years.

At the bottom of the bed, a pair of stocking feet rested, crossed at the ankles. Blair followed their trail up to reveal the form of his brother, who sat in a chair beside him, dozing, an open book in his lap. Stephen was wearing his trousers and shirt, with his suit vest unbuttoned. A lock of his raven hair fell forward over his forehead. A couple of days' growth marred his usually clean-shaven face, yet he still managed to look boyish in slumber.

A sharp pain in his temple jolted Blair and instinctively he raised his palms to his forehead to find a padded bandage wrapped around his head. The pain subsided and Blair lowered his hands, seeing them in focus for the first time.

"My God!" he cried in anguish and anger, jarring Stephen awake so quickly that his book slid off his lap as he brought himself upright. So strained was Blair's cry that Stephen forgot to be glad that his brother was conscious for the first time in days.

"Blair, what's the matter?" Stephen blurted out.

"Look at my hands. What happened to my hands?"

Blair stared at his hands like they belonged to someone else. His right little finger was completely missing, both hands were tanned brown, rough calluses coated the palms and the pads of his remaining fingers, tiny scars from small nicks and cuts were evident. His fingernails were roughly pared and stained, as were his ragged cuticles. Small, black dye-filled needle pricks covered the tips of his left index and middle finger. On his left ring finger was a horseshoe nail forged into a ring.

"What's today?"

"Saturday."

"No, I mean the date."

"December sixteenth. You've been unconscious for nearly four days."

"I arrived home December twelfth?"

"Um-hmm."

Blair frowned and held out his hands again. "How could I have done this much damage to my hands in a month?"

Stephen started. "A month? What do you mean a month?"

Blair looked at his brother. "I left you in Milwaukee on November eighth. I was trying to ride to some goddamned depot in Wyoming because the track was out. I was held up—a couple of seedy bastards. They cold-cocked me. I'm sure it was November tenth or eleventh. Somehow it took me a month to get home. You just said I got home December twelfth. Unless I crawled home from Wyoming on my hands and knees, I couldn't have done this much damage to my hands in one month."

Stephen stared at his brother's face. The older man's gray eyes were dark with confusion and anger. The younger one's similar eyes were filled with dismay. He quietly asked, "Blair, what date do you think it is?"

"You just told me, December sixteenth."

"No, I mean the year?"

"Are you crazy?" Blair spit out angrily, "December sixteenth, 1873."

"Eighteen seventy-*five*," came the clear, quiet response. "You've been missing and presumed dead for over two years."

"It's not possible."

Stephen reached beside him to the floor where he had dropped the morning paper after reading it while sitting at the bedside. He handed it to Blair, saying, "Today's *Chronicle*."

Blair looked. There was no doubt. The numbers 1875 were clearly printed on the masthead. If he suspected a gag, the look on Stephen's face quickly relieved him of that notion.

"Blair, where have you been for the last two years?"

Blair leaned back on the pillows and closed his eyes. "I have no idea...." He squeezed his eyes tighter shut and put his palms to his aching head. "God damn it, I can't remember."

A long, silent, painful moment passed. Then suddenly Blair yanked the covers off and lurched to get out of bed. Stephen rose to aid his brother, but Blair pushed him off and walked over to the window, yanking the drape aside. The afternoon sunlight streamed into the bedroom, stabbing at his throbbing head. He then lurched over to the full-length mirror that stood beside the closet door. He pulled off the bandage on his head and looked in at his silvered reflection.

A stranger stared back. The face belonged to the hands, but neither belonged to Blair Carroll. His eyes and nose were the same, but there the resemblance ended. The stranger's hair was black, but below shoulder length and thickly wavy. He had two weeks' growth of black beard and his mustache was bushy and long, the ends covering his closed mouth. The skin was bronzed from hours in a hot sun, although there were dark circles beneath the eyes. A yellowing purple bruise and some scabbed-over lacerations decorated his left temple, but there was also an older scar running across his forehead from above his left eyebrow and into his scalp. In the bright sunlight, he could detect the evidence of tiny stitches on the older scar.

None of this was familiar. Blair never allowed himself to become shaggy or tanned. Except for a well-trimmed mustache, he was normally as shorthaired and clean-shaven as his brother.

For a minute he looked at his right hand. The same tiny stitch scars were present where his little finger had been. Whoever had stitched him up had done a really careful job.

The silence of his exploration was punctuated only by the steady breathing of both brothers. Ignoring his brother's presence, and feeling his nightshirt binding him across the shoulders and chest, he reached down and pulled it over his head to stand naked before the mirror.

If his face was a stranger's, his body shocked him even more. He was massive; previously broad shoulders made even larger by well-defined musculature. The bulging muscles of his forearms, biceps and pectorals were defined as if sculpted. His stomach was ridged like a washboard, covered with a pelt of familiar black hair; perhaps the only familiar sight he recognized on this stranger in the mirror. From the waist up his skin was nearly as tanned as his face. From the waist down his flesh was white, but his thighs and calves were thickly muscled and his buttocks firm and hard. There was not an ounce of fat on him; not that there had been before, but he had been slender, impressive physically only in height, bearing and demeanor. He stared at himself for long minutes, analyzing, not admiring, turning slightly to get a full picture of his metamorphosis.

"I look like a stevedore. Wherever I was, I must have been working like one."

Stephen nodded. Since he had bathed Blair and dressed him in the nightshirt, he had already seen the radical physical changes to his brother's body.

Blair strode back to the bed and sat down heavily, pulling the nightshirt back on for privacy sake, even though it clung to his massive form like an uncomfortable second skin.

"You must have been looking for me all this time. The last thing I remember is one of those fucking bandits aiming the handle of his gun at my head. What did you discover?"

"About a month after you disappeared, your ring and watch were discovered at two different locations in the Wyoming and Colorado Territories. I've got them now. Did you have them on when you were robbed?"

"My watch was in my vest pocket, but I had already given it to the bandits. My ring was under my gloves when the leader cold-cocked me."

"You always had trouble getting that ring off, didn't you?"

"Yeah," Blair affirmed.

"Well, when I put you to bed, I noticed that the scar on your hand and the one on your head had been stitched up."

"Yeah, I just noticed that myself...I'll bet those bastards couldn't get the damned ring off and cut off my finger to get it."

"And probably left you for dead. Only someone found you and stitched up the two wounds. Can you remember who found you?"

"Not at all. I haven't any clue."

Stephen brightened. "Maybe there's a clue in the clothes you were wearing when you arrived."

"Somehow, I have the feeling they're not my usual style."

"I'll say." Stephen brought a bundle over to the bed.

On top of the bundle was a large pair of worn, scuffed, brown leather work boots with worn leather laces. The boots had been cleaned and polished by a servant, destroying any evidence of their origins.

Putting those down on the floor, Blair looked at the clothes.

The leather gloves had once been a butternut color, but were water-stained and work-worn. The right little finger was stuffed with cotton batting and tacked to the ring finger with tiny stitches; obviously so it would move with the finger, giving the illusion of a complete hand. The shirt was handmade of cheap muslin, but he could tell it had been made by a skillful stitcher or tailor by the careful, even stitches and the elegantly worked buttonholes. Blair thought for a moment that the stitcher must have really taken pride in her work, even if she had to use the meanest quality fabric.

The vest, on the other hand, was of good quality black broadcloth and lined with silk. It was also carefully made, but he noticed a seam down the center back of the vest. A normal vest back was usually made of a solid piece of fabric, but a suit jacket would have a center back seam. The trousers were made of the same fabric. He saw that the legs had been extended with the same black broadcloth. It dawned on him that this vest had been someone else's jacket and that the tailor had pirated the sleeves to extend the length of the pants' legs. The silk lining had come from the original suit jacket and had been cut down with it to make and line the vest. These clothes, as well made as they were, were makeovers from the wardrobe of a much shorter man.

The sheepskin jacket was the only commercially-made garment, but it bore the label of a well-known manufacturer in Chicago. One could purchase a jacket exactly like this one right here in San Francisco as well as just about anywhere west of the Mississippi River. No help there.

"Stephen, was I carrying anything? Money, papers?"

Stephen had not heard Blair sound so desperate since the day they met their father's mistress. He was actually worried about Blair's state of mind.

"You had a few dollars, mostly in coin, and a pocketknife." He handed his brother the pocketknife. It had a horn case, well worn, but no distinguishing marks or initials. "Nothing else except the ring you're wearing now."

"This isn't a ring. It looks like a nail."

"Well, I had it off for a moment and your skin is white and smooth under it, so you've been wearing it like a ring for quite some time, I'd guess. What do you think it means?"

Blair shrugged. "I've never worn a ring on this hand. If a woman were wearing a ring on this finger, I'd say she was married. Shit,

Stephen, you don't think I managed to get myself married."

Stephen gestured helplessly. "Well, it's certainly within the realm of possibility."

"It figures some bitch would get her claws on me while I was out of my mind...."

"But why a horseshoe nail?"

Blair picked up the clothes and dropped them in disgust. "Wherever I was, there couldn't have been much money. We probably use better quality cloth than this shirt for dustrags. I'll wager whoever she was married me hoping her scrimping days were over."

"You never sent for any money. If you knew you were Blair Carroll, or she knew you were, one of you would have wired or written, don't you think? Do you think you knew who you were?"

"I don't know. The time is gone as if it never happened. I feel like Rip Van Winkle. Stephen, if it's true—if I'm married—can I get out of it?"

"I'm not sure. It's not exactly my field of law. Let me check on it and let you know. In the meantime, I suggest you stay out of any romantic entanglement until we resolve the problem."

"Believe me, the last thing I want now is a *romantic entanglement.* Speaking of entanglements, does Julia know I'm back."

"It's possible. Rumors fly. I haven't told her myself, but it wouldn't matter much. She's been married for over a year—to Gerald Rafferty."

Blair leaned back on the bed, exhausted. "Rafferty, huh? Son of a bitch always wanted what I had. I hope he's happy now. What other little surprises do I have in store? Do I still have a business?"

Stephen looked perturbed. "Of course, damn it. I'm not you, but I'm no idiot. We're as rich as we ever were."

"Dad still in Europe?"

Stephen shrugged. "Got a letter from him a couple of months ago. He was mildly concerned about your continued absence, but not enough to come back home to take up the reins again. I guess as long as his allowance keeps coming he's willing to let us run the business while he plays the man of the world; even if it's been just Winslow and me for the last two years. I doubt he'll ever come home."

"Let him stay away. I don't miss him any more than he misses me. I think I want a bath and then to sleep. Also can you get a barber and manicurist in here?" Blair added, rubbing his bearded face, "I think I'm going to need a lot of help returning to normal."

"Of course, I'll send Lopez to get Giovanni and his daughter for a haircut and a manicure later this afternoon and I'll get someone to fill the bathtub for you right away." Stephen turned to leave, then turned back, "One more thing I forgot."

"And that is?"

"Cherry Leval died three weeks ago. Your son should be arriving in San Francisco in about a month. His name is Joshua, in case you care."

Chapter 2

November 1873
Milwaukee, Wisconsin

"The woman is nothing but a goddamned whore. If she had the bad judgment to get herself pregnant, then she has less sense than most. But I'll be damned if I let any son of mine be dragged around from theater to theater all over the country."

Blair Carroll paced the confines of the richly-appointed Milwaukee hotel suite like a caged lion.

"Are you sure the boy is mine?"

"You know there is no way to be a hundred percent certain, Blair." Stephen Carroll walked calmly to the bar and poured himself a small whisky while he responded once more to the barrage of angry questions thrown at him, then returned to an armchair near the fireplace. He sat down, crossed his long legs and held the glass up to the firelight, turning it slightly in his long, graceful fingers. At 24, Stephen was four years younger than his brother in years, but decades younger in outlook. "Our investigator says his August '69 birth date corresponds to December '68, when she was playing in San Francisco and you were— um—intimate with her."

"We got good use out of each other."

"Yes, if you must be vulgar about it. Miss Leval is a blue-eyed blonde. The investigator says the boy has black hair and gray eyes. The Carroll looks, if you will."

The Carroll looks that seemed to defy dilution by any spouse for generations. Both brothers were over six feet tall, with Blair six foot four and Stephen two inches shorter, lean of build with broad shoulders, large hands and feet. They shared the same wavy black hair, gray eyes, aquiline noses and strong mouths and chins. They both had arrestingly good looks that made them favorites among the well-bred ladies of their native San Francisco, and neither would lack for female companionship if they chose.

Blair's upper lip was adorned with a well-trimmed black mustache while Stephen was clean-shaven. Their differences were as striking as their similarities, and that was the least of the differences. Blair's eyes were the gray of forged steel, hard and stormy, as he was. In his well-tailored suit he looked every inch the hard-driven executive he was.

Stephen, on the other hand, had eyes like gray velvet, gentle and sympathetic. He smiled often, revealing straight, white teeth. Had Blair ever smiled, he might have looked more like his younger brother, but Stephen could never effect his brother's deadly gaze.

Blair took a deep drag on a cheroot, then tossed it angrily into the burning fireplace. He never seemed to finish one before he tossed it away. He turned that steely gaze on his brother. "Stephen, I don't care how you do it, but I want you to get me custody of the boy."

Stephen noted that Blair never called him "Steve" anymore. It was indicative of the loss of the easy intimacy they'd had as boys. That intimacy had been riven ten years before and Stephen's recent extended absence while away at school hadn't helped matters any.

"If this were a divorce case," he began in the requisite calm, businesslike manner, "that wouldn't be a problem. But assuming the boy is yours, he's illegitimate. You don't exactly present the image of the loving, caring father to get a woman pregnant and then forget about her."

"It's not my fault the bitch didn't tell me she was pregnant until the kid was four years old. Do you seriously think I'd marry the little tramp to make an 'honest woman' of her?"

"No," Stephen responded, "I don't think you would—now."

"What do you mean *now*?"

"Sometimes I think I don't know you anymore. In the six months since I've been home, I don't think I've heard you laugh once. You work seventy, eighty hours a week. You smoke too much, drink too much and order me around like I'm some lackey instead of your brother. Your attitude about women is the worst I've ever seen. You made Julia cry, and the last time that girl shed a tear was when Lincoln was shot."

"What gives you the right to be so goddamned self-righteous? Who ran this company so you could go to Harvard and dear old Dad could go gallivanting all over Europe with Alabama Dodge? That piece of Southern fluff ruined my life and Father never has married her. If I don't laugh, it's because there's nothing to laugh at. Carroll Enterprises is the largest import-export on the Pacific Coast and I don't see you or Father pulling your weights the last few years. And if my *fiancée* is crying, it's because she's afraid I won't let her redecorate the house.

Julia is an ornament. She'll look good at parties and she won't interfere in my life. I've never met a woman yet who wasn't more fascinated by the Carroll purse than the Carroll looks."

Stephen didn't respond for a few moments. He held up his glass and stared at the light playing off the cut crystal. Stephen drank very little as a rule. More often than not he would merely play with the glass. It might take him the entire night to empty the contents.

"What? Nothing more to say, little brother?" Blair mocked.

"Not much. Just thinking. I guess I don't think of women as ornamental. Maybe I still believe in love."

"Then you're more naive than I thought, counselor." His posture ramrod straight, Blair moved over to the door and started to put on his overcoat, top hat, muffler and gloves. "Going out tonight?"

"No, I guess I'll stay in and work on the custody petition and then turn in. I'll have to go to the county courthouse in the morning and familiarize myself with the local rules and fees. I'll need to engage Wisconsin counsel to make appearances. Besides, it's colder outside than a pawnbroker's heart."

"Whatever it takes, you have carte blanche, just get me that boy. I'm going out to get a drink. I'm suffocating in here. Damn!"

"What?"

"Never can get gloves on smoothly over this damned ring," complained Blair, adjusting his glove to fit more comfortably over a large gold engraved signet ring with a small diamond set in it that he wore on the little finger of his right hand.

Stephen looked at his own hand. He wore a similar ring. Both had been presents from their father, Oscar Carroll, on their twenty-first birthdays and were identical to his own. "I never have trouble. I just buy bigger gloves."

"I don't know why I wear it."

"I always remember Mother telling us how Grandfather gave Father a ring like her brothers wore because he had joined the Blair family. It's really the only connection to her anymore."

Blair's response was a frustrated grunt as his glove pulled into place. "Couldn't even budge the damned thing off anymore if I needed to." Then he was gone, yanking the door shut behind him.

Stephen sighed. Until tonight he'd not been so fully aware of the resentment Blair felt about not being allowed to go to college. Instead he was drawn into the business because Oscar Carroll, newly widowed when Blair was sixteen, wanted to get himself out of San Francisco and away from unpleasant memories as soon as possible.

Blair had kept his disappointment to himself, and had even sent Stephen to Harvard on the money he'd saved to send himself to Yale. His letters had been short and business-oriented. If he had a personal life, he mentioned little or nothing about it. Stephen had returned from Massachusetts with the ink on his law degree barely dry and immediately began to act as staff counsel for Carroll Enterprises.

As for Oscar Carroll, Stephen hadn't seen his father since he was fourteen, when he'd shown up back home with that Southern belle he'd called his fiancée. Something had gone wrong with Alabama Dodge's divorce, and Oscar had taken her to Europe via South America and had not been home since. So the now thirty-year-old woman was traveling through Europe as Oscar Carroll's mistress, where such arrangements were not nearly as frowned upon as in the United States. Blair kept his father supplied with a generous allowance and considered it the price to pay for his staying out of their lives.

Having left for college at the age of seventeen, just barely grown into his looks, Stephen also remembered envying his older brother's success with women, when they flocked around his handsome face and vied for his attention. Blair could get anyone he wanted with hardly any effort, if he even cared to.

Blair was right, in a way. Julia Longridge was largely ornamental. A more buffleheaded girl Stephen hardly knew. Stephen had the feeling Blair would be faithful though, if only because he made himself too busy with work to need physical fulfillment. Even Cherry Leval, the actress whose son Stephen was now charged with wresting away—had been a brief affair nearly five years ago.

Oh, Blair would marry Julia and they'd live an opulent if sterile life forever after.

"Not for me," said Stephen aloud into the quiet air. "Blair, I hope you meet someone who sweeps you off your feet and makes you believe in love." He toasted the air with his whisky glass, drained it in one swallow for once, and walked over to the work desk in the suite, where he began to jot down draft notes for the petitions he would need. He worked until about midnight when he hauled himself into bed.

Blair came in sometime much later. He had gone to a gentlemen's club he found through a business acquaintance and spent the night playing poker with other businessmen like himself. He had a few drinks and played well enough to break even. Finding Stephen asleep, he merely hauled off his own expensive evening clothes, draped them over a chair in his room and dropped off to sleep in his own bed. If he had any dreams that night, he wouldn't remember them in the morning.

"MR. CARROLL, why does your brother want to take my son away from me?" Miss Cherry Leval asked plaintively. "All I wanted was some help until I'm feeling better and can go back on the stage."

Stephen looked at the actress. She was gaunt, her cheekbones prominent, her blue eyes slightly sunken and glassy with dark shadows beneath them. Her blond hair was lifeless; her bodice loose enough to make it obvious that she had a more prominent bosom not long ago. She had tried to hide her pallor with a little rouge, but only succeeded in looking like a painted bisque doll. In her nervous, gloved hands she grasped a handkerchief, into which she periodically coughed, although she appeared trying to fight the spasms that regularly rocked her wasted body.

Consumption is a terrible way to die, Stephen thought.

"I believe my brother feels he can best provide for the boy in our own home in San Francisco, rather than just providing a property settlement or support drafts. Having found out about the boy, he wants to do the right thing."

"But Joshua is all I have. He's only four. He needs his mama."

"I understand how you feel, Miss Leval, but I think your own lawyer would agree that you need to consider the best interests of the child." Gritting his teeth against the next statement, Stephen continued, "Surely a fine house on Nob Hill is preferable to a ramshackle boarding house in a Milwaukee slum."

"But he's my baby and I love him." She turned to Blair, who was sitting silently beside Stephen at the conference table in Cherry Leval's lawyer's office. "Blair, can you say the same?"

Blair looked through her, almost as if she wasn't there. "What the hell do you know about love, Cherry?"

"Blair...." Stephen cautioned.

"What do you want from me, Cherry? Money? Is that why you had that scum-sucking manager contact me about the boy?"

Tears appeared in Cherry's eyes. Right now it was hard to believe she was five years older than Blair. "I wouldn't have asked him to write to you at all, except that I've been sick lately...But the doctor says I'll be getting better soon."

"And in the meantime you'll sponge off my hard work. That's quite a price for a few nights of *pleasure,* wouldn't you say, Cherry?"

"Blair," Stephen snapped, "will you shut up and let me do my job? I think it would be better if you left now."

Blair rose quickly to his full height and strode with long strides out the door. Cherry Leval's control broke down and she collapsed into a violent coughing spasm.

Her attorney glanced from her to Stephen. "Mr. Carroll, I think our discussions for today are over. We will contact you tomorrow."

"Please, Mr. Garrett, there are a few things I must ask Miss Leval privately...that is, with Blair not here...Are you all right, Miss Leval?"

Cherry's cough slowly calmed. She folded her handkerchief in such a way as to hide the flecks of blood her coughing left on its white surface. "Blair didn't tell me he had a brother."

"I don't doubt it."

"You look just like him."

"I know."

"And my Joshua looks like both of you."

"That's what I need to ask you. It's my job, you understand, but are you sure that my brother is your son's father?"

The gaunt blonde looked at Stephen through rheumy eyes.

"My baby was born in August of 1869, Mr. Carroll. Regardless of what your brother might have told you about me, I'm no harlot. I'm an actress. I did have lovers, but when I did, it was one man at a time. When we played San Francisco the end of '68, the only lover I had was your brother. The next February I found out I was expecting. I'm no saint, and I certainly wasn't a virgin, but I'm absolutely sure that Blair Carroll is Joshua's father. If you saw him, you wouldn't doubt it. He's got the blackest hair and grayest eyes you've ever seen, and he's already tall for four years old."

"I must tell you that I have instructions to start formal custody proceedings if we don't hear from you by Friday with a voluntary custody agreement."

"Mr. Carroll," said Cherry, "I only needed help because I'm sick. When I get better and can go back on the stage, I'll be able to support him the way I have since he was born. We've been all right together, Joshua and I. I don't want to give him up."

"I understand, Miss Leval, but even though your son is my nephew, I have to follow Blair's instructions in this matter."

"We understand," cut in Mr. Garrett. "Miss Leval is very tired, as you can see. Please go now. We'll be in contact."

Stephen picked up his briefcase and his winter coat and hat and left the offices. He found Blair on the street, angrily dragging on a cheroot.

"You're not coming along next time," Stephen stated flatly.

"You're not telling me what to do, little brother." Blair tossed the cheroot into the gutter, where it hissed out in the snow.

"Do you have to be so hostile, Blair? The woman is dying, for God's sake. Couldn't you see that? She's holding on for dear life because that little boy's probably all that's keeping her alive. I'm sure I can appeal to her better nature. Why litigate if I can negotiate?"

"Who in his right mind can negotiate with a woman?"

They hailed a hack and returned to the hotel.

UPON RETURNING to the hotel, a telegram was waiting for Blair.

Opening it in their suite, he read:

"SERIOUS DELAY IN ARRIVAL OF CHINA GIRL FROM SINGAPORE HAS BACKERS ALARMED STOP NEED YOUR RETURN TO FORESTALL PANIC STOP WINSLOW."

"Guess you got your wish, little brother, I have to get back to San Francisco immediately. Negotiate, litigate, whatever it takes, just get the boy. I'll wire from home when I get there."

"LADIES AND Gentlemen, may I have your attention please," the station master announced to the passengers. "On account of there being unseasonably early heavy snowfall there has been an interruption in train service on this line. We expect a delay of between three and four days. The Central Pacific fervently apologizes for the delay and will assist all passengers in securing lodging here in Rock Springs for all passengers until the track is repaired."

Blair tossed his cheroot out the train window and strode toward the station master. "Look," he said angrily, "I have to reach San Francisco as soon as possible. Is there an alternative to remaining here?"

The station manager eyed the tall man, measuring him up. The look in those steel gray eyes allowed no nonsense. "The only alternative is not particularly pleasant this time of year."

"What is it?"

"We're about seventy miles from Green River, Wyoming Territory. On horseback you could be there in twelve to fifteen hours—

even in this cold—and pick up westbound train the other side of the break. But I wouldn't recommend it."

"Why, because of the cold?"

"Well, that, sir, and bandits. A lone traveler is not safe in these parts."

HE ARRANGED with the livery stable to rent a horse and leave it for retrieval in Green River. The livery barn owner knew of no one who would hire out as an escort in this weather. Blair walked over to the General Store. Once inside, he pulled off his gloves against the warmth the stove gave off in the store and purchased a six-shooter and bullets. He'd never even owned a gun before and certainly had never fired one. Probably the station master was exaggerating. He'd have no occasion to use it.

He pulled his wallet out of his suit pocket and paid cash for the pistol. Blair was unaware of two pairs of feral eyes following him from over near the checkers table next to the stove. He returned to the livery stable, where a roan gelding stood saddled and ready, and tied his portmanteau to the saddle. He left his trunk in the baggage car. He had an armoire full of clothes to wear at home. He mounted and began to ride in the direction of Green River, unaware that he was being followed not too far behind.

THE WEATHER was clear but biting cold, sub-freezing with enough wind to make it seem even colder still. The trees in the forest near the horizon were barren of leaves, looking like skeletal fingers giving an eerie welcome. The sky was a blue-gray with clouds streaking white through it. It was clear now, but snow could fall imminently.

Blair rode along, his mind on where he was going and on controlling the unfamiliar horse in even more unfamiliar surroundings. This was hardly a Sunday ride in Sausalito on a spring day, which was the limit of his horseback riding. He passed farmlands, sometimes sighting lonely farmhouses and barns standing brown and red against the snow, but mostly it was open range, miles and miles of miles and miles. Lulled by the monotony, Blair didn't hear the riders approach until he heard the percussion head click a few feet behind him.

"Throw down yore gun and put yore hands up and ya ain't gonna get hurt," growled a husky voice, muffled by the bandanna and scarf that covered the speaker's nose and mouth.

Blair complied, knowing he couldn't handle his own gun well

enough to defend himself in this situation.

"Git off that horse and turn around."

Blair dismounted and turned to see two masked men training revolvers at him. The smaller of the two dismounted and walked over to Blair.

"Open yore coat and give me yore wallet and watch." As Blair was doing so, the smaller man reached over to untie the portmanteau. As it slid off the saddle, the horse, which by now was nervous and cold, moved, bumping into the smaller bandit. The little one fell, his scarf sliding to reveal his face, nondescript and in need of a shave.

"Holy shit, Rafe, he's seen me."

"Look," said Blair, thoroughly frightened for his life, "you've got my wallet, my watch and my case and my gun. The horse isn't even mine. Let me just ride into the next town, get on my train and I'll be on my way. No one need ever know."

"Do ya think we're stupid?" Rafe, the larger man snarled, dismounting and racing over. He grabbed Blair by the arm and began to punch him in the face.

Blair fought back as best he could, but he was not an experienced brawler. The two men together were too much for him. Both his eyes blackened and his jaw and ribs bruised and sore, he was thrown against the rented horse, which galloped off back toward Rock Springs, reins dragging. The smaller man landed a blow to Blair's stomach, knocking the wind out of him, and he fell to his knees. Rafe then grabbed his revolver by the barrel and struck Blair hard on the side of the head with the gun butt. It cracked the skin near the temple, sending Blair into the darkness of unconsciousness, bleeding from the blow.

"What are we gonna do now, Rafe? Do we have to kill him?"

"He needs to die, Jack, but we're not gonna kill him."

"What d'ya mean?"

"This fool is out riding alone in the middle of snow country. If he falls off his horse and lies unconscious, the cold'll get him. That's what everyone will think if they find his body, if animals don't get it first." He thought for a moment and then added, "Take his clothes off."

"Why do we want his clothes?"

"First, half-wit, they're good clothes, we can sell 'em. Besides, now that I think of it, he'll freeze faster nekkid."

Jack and Rafe worked fast, stripping Blair of his coat, suit, shirt, boots, even his union suit, until their victim lay naked and helpless in the snow. When Jack pulled off Blair's gloves, he spied the large ring on Blair's small finger.

Jack whistled, "Will ya look at that ring, Rafe. It's got a diamond and everything. I'll bet it's worth a fortune!"

"Well, don't stand there lollygagging. Take it off."

Jack tugged at the ring. It wouldn't budge. He twisted at it. It still remained. "I can't budge it, Rafe," Jack complained.

With a snort, Rafe answered, "Ya really are useless, ain't ya." Pulling his hunting knife from its sheath at his waist, Rafe lifted Blair's right hand off the ground. The bandit slid the knife blade between the ring and small fingers and with one stroke severed the little finger of Blair's hand. Blood immediately spurted from the wound as Rafe dropped Blair's hand. With Blair unconscious his hand fell limply into the snowdrift. Rafe pulled the ring off the bloody end of the finger, tossed the severed digit aside and pocketed the ring.

Jack looked aghast. "Why'd ya do that?"

"What do ya care? He'll be dead by dawn anyway. So he'll go to heaven with nine fingers instead of ten. We gotta ride."

The two bandits, loaded down with Blair's clothes and possessions, rode off, leaving their naked, bleeding victim to the mercy of the Wyoming snow, which was just beginning to fall again as they rode off.

Chapter 3

THE LATE morning sun struggled gamely to penetrate the overcast sky and the threat of more snow. Adele Stoddard stood on the porch of her farmhouse, one of her thick quilts drawn around her against the cold. She closed her eyes and let the cold penetrate her senses. *When the snow comes to the range this early,* she thought, *winter promises to be long, hard and lonely.*

Adele glanced toward the barn, where her younger sister, Susannah came hobbling toward the house, a filled milk pail in her hand. Susannah would be sixteen on December 8th and from the ankles up she was rapidly becoming a beauty, petite and curvy. Were it not for a clubbed right foot, Adele didn't doubt Susannah would have been begging to go to dances and parties and meeting local boys. Of course, at twenty miles from Green River, there weren't really many "local" boys.

Adele and Susannah shared the same sable brown hair and brandy brown eyes, but Adele was tall where Susannah was small, slender where Susannah was becoming voluptuous and serious where Susannah was still a child in many ways. Despite Susannah's handicap, she worked as hard as her sister to complete all her chores and was a much better cook than her older sister. Neither young woman was a stranger to hard work.

Susannah may well find a husband yet, thought Adele. *I wish I could say the same for myself.* To her mind, twenty-three was already too old when you had never even been courted.

Adele had never really had much of a childhood. Their mother, Beatrice, had never really recovered after Susannah was born, leaving an eight-year-old Adele to run the household. Eight years later she died in childbirth. Although she deeply loved Tom Stoddard and followed him from Baltimore to the prairie, she had never been suited to life in the wilderness. Like many a pioneer woman, the prairie had drained her strength and soul and killed her by the age of thirty-five.

Adele was made of stronger stuff. She stepped right in and took over running the house and working alongside her father, planting and reaping, building and repairing. Then the cancer that had eaten his life away became too much for him, and Adele became nurse, as well as farmer, mother and housekeeper. Thomas Stoddard died in the spring of 1871 and Adele had been too busy working hard to worry about such insignificant things as courting and marriage.

It didn't help that Adele was five feet ten inches tall, as tall or taller than most of the men she met.

"Mabel was real generous this morning," Susannah's cheery voice broke through Adele's concentration. "We may have enough to make some cheese as well as butter. And the hens laid six eggs," she added, pointing to the bulging pockets of the threadbare, outgrown pinafore she was using as an apron to cover her blue calico dress.

"That's wonderful, Susannah," Adele answered absently.

"Oh, Sissy, isn't it beautiful out? I just love wintertime."

"That must be because it gives you something different to draw."

"I reckon so. On a morning like this you feel something wonderful is about to happen. It's like the air is anticipating something."

"If the air is anticipating anything, it's more snow. I think we're going to get snowed in early."

"Gosh, I hope I have enough paper and pencils."

Susannah was an artist. She had never studied drawing, but almost as soon as she could hold a pencil she began sketching. There was hardly a piece of paper safe in the house. Her old school copybooks were filled with drawings and illustrations of lessons. She had a real eye to line and texture and could draw with almost photographic precision. Where she got the talent, nobody knew. Pa had told them about Mozart once, that he had musical talent when he was a baby and guessed that Susannah was the same with drawing. Tom Stoddard had always regretted that, even if there had been anyone in Green River who could have taught Susannah the fine arts, their money would never stretch that far. The best they could do was try to keep his younger daughter in paper and pencils so she could at least have an outlet for her drawing, which was as much passion as talent. It was only too bad that there was no money in Susannah's skill.

"I was thinking more about enough food," responded the more practical Adele, "I'm going to saddle Esmeralda and go hunting for rabbits or a deer. If it stays this cold, the meat might keep for a while."

"Great. When I'm done churning the butter, I'll get together the fixings for some stew. And even if you don't catch anything today we can always have an omelet." With that Susannah tromped into the house to put down the milk and eggs and drag out the butter churn.

Adele followed. She folded the quilt and put it back on Susannah's bed in the main room. She'd made this quilt. It was a simple pinwheel design, outline quilted, but it was durably stitched. If Susannah was an artist with a pencil, Adele was an artist with a needle, though neither she nor anyone else would have used the term. For Adele was a quiltmaker. The beds in the house were covered with colorful evidence of her handiwork.

Pieces of old garments, feed sacks dyed with homemade dyes, even fabric bought especially for the purpose found their way into the tops and backs of Adele's creations. She prided herself on being able to consistently get ten to twelve stitches to the inch and the old trunk in the bedroom held a trousseau's worth of quilts she had made. Enough to cover the beds of an entire family—the family Adele was sure she would never have. She'd even made a Wedding Ring quilt. It lay in the bottom of the trunk for the wedding night that would never come. Adele also made every stitch she and Susannah wore and just about everything their father had worn as well. Pa had told her once that no tailor in Baltimore or even London ever made better. About the only garments they had to store buy were knit goods like long underwear and lisle stockings.

Adele went into the division of the house whose larger bed had been Thomas and Beatrice Stoddard's but was now hers. Shortly after her father's death she had moved from the bed the girls had shared from the time Susannah was out of the cradle. From the roughly-built cabinet that served as an armoire, Adele selected her quilted petticoat, which she pulled on under her calico skirt and two muslin petticoats and grabbed her father's sheepskin winter coat and felt hat. A scarf and knitted gloves completed her cold weather gear. She had a warm woolen cloak, but it was not as practical for hunting as the coat since it got in the way of her arms and hampered her shot. The coat and hat were too large for her—Thomas Stoddard was a barrel-chested six-footer before his illness—but for several hours in the freezing cold, it was the best she had. Returning into the main room, she took the rifle down from the wall and pulled it out of its scabbard. As she had learned years ago, she checked it quickly and carefully and loaded it with cartridges.

At least Pa bought us a repeating rifle. It certainly makes hunting easier, she thought. Returning the rifle to its scabbard, Adele went outside and tramped through the snow to the barn.

Once in the barn, she saddled their mare, Esmeralda. She was tying the scabbard and a length of rope to the saddle when she felt a familiar rubbing at her ankles. Looking down, she saw a small gray tabby tomcat with a still-living mouse in his teeth.

"Well, Little Gent," she said to the cat, "I see you've had a successful hunt today."

Little Gent looked up with his pale green eyes, then scampered off to tease and eventually devour his trembling prey.

Adele mounted up, kicking her right leg over the horn of the sidesaddle and straightening her skirts around her. As she rode past the front door of the house, she called out, "Susannah, Little Gent is in the barn torturing mice again. I'm glad he kills them, but I wish he would just get to it instead of playing with them first. You may want to get him inside later."

"I'll bribe him with some milk," came the laughing reply. "See you later, Sissy."

THE RANGE WAS biting cold. Adele could feel icy blades of wind trying to slice through her clothes. Even the quilted petticoat and shearling jacket were not really enough. Her nipples hardened against the cold and she shivered painfully deep within.

If it's this cold on November 12th, what's it going to be like by Christmas, she thought, wishing there had been enough money from the crops this year to buy something more substantial than calico for garments.

"God, I'd sell my soul for twenty yards of blue serge," she bargained aloud, remembering that the last time she had gone into Green River she had a choice between the warm woolen yardage and buying cheaper cotton and a new package of drawing vellum and pencils for Susannah. The drawing paper had won out. Maybe if Susannah wasn't so clever with her pencils, it wouldn't be such an easy choice. Well, they would make do. They always did.

Skirting the edge of the forest that bordered the range, Adele had been pretty lucky. Although she was an average rifle shot, she had bagged six rabbits foolish enough to poke their heads out of their holes on this frigid day. If it stayed below freezing, six rabbits could last the two young women nearly two weeks.

"Just as well I didn't see a deer. It's too cold to be dressing venison today," she mused aloud, a steam cloud puffing with her words.

After tying her quarry to the saddle horn, Adele turned Esmeralda toward home. A light flurry of snow was beginning to fall and the late afternoon temperature was dropping even more.

Since the old roan mare knew the way home, Adele pretty much gave the horse her head. As Esmeralda trotted along, Adele concentrated on how she would go about lining the hoods of their woolen cloaks with the rabbit skins. Suddenly, Esmeralda reared slightly at an odd-shaped, snow-covered object that lay in the way, startling Adele out of her reverie.

Adele quickly threw her right leg over the saddle horn and slid down with both feet touching the ground nearly at once. Still holding the reins, she walked over to the object.

Her eyes widened in shock at the sight of blood. The obscured object becoming gradually more and more covered with lightly falling snow was a man! Adele dropped the reins with a tug that said "stay" to the mare and knelt down beside the man. She brushed snow off his face and saw blood seeping from a long deep cut wound on his forehead running from halfway over his left eyebrow into and beyond the hairline of his short, thick, coal black hair. His face was pale and cold; his lips blue beneath a trimmed mustache the same color as his hair.

Adele continued to brush snow off his body, surprised to find his upper torso bare. She sucked in her breath at the sight of a broad-shouldered, lean chest covered thickly with black hair and multiple ugly bruises. As she examined him, she felt the barely perceptible rise and fall of his chest.

"He's alive!" *But just barely*, she added silently.

Continuing to uncover him, Adele was even more shocked to discover the unconscious stranger was undressed below the waist as well. That pelt of body hair narrowed below his waist, thickening into a nest that crowned...well! Adele had seen her father's during the last months of his terminal illness, when he was too weak to clean or care for himself, but even at rest this one's manhood impressed—and embarrassed her.

Stifling an unfamiliar shudder she blamed on the cold, Adele finished brushing snow from the man's long, hair-roughened legs. His feet were bare and the skin under his toenails was also blue.

"Got to get him home. First, got to get him warm."

Without hesitating, Adele unbuttoned her sheepskin jacket and dropped it to the ground. She then rose and, lifting her calico skirt, untied the tapes holding up her quilted petticoat. It was too thick to slide, so she pushed it down to her knees and stepped out of it. Kneeling again beside the body, she moved to his feet and pulled the petticoat up his legs to his waist. The tapes wouldn't tie, of course, but the petticoat, which had been closest to Adele's own body heat, served as a blanket around the legs and hips of the stranger. She then lifted him up at the shoulders, pulling his left arm into the sleeve of the jacket. It was when she reached across his body to do the same with his right arm that she saw more blood; seeping slowly from his hand where the start of his little finger should be.

"God in heaven, who would do such a thing?"

Quickly, Adele pulled her handkerchief from her pocket and tied it around his palm, putting as much pressure on the wound as she could. Mercifully, the man remained unconscious as she pushed his mutilated hand into the sleeve of the shearling coat and buttoned the buttons.

Knowing he could not ride behind her while unconscious, Adele had to think how she could get the stranger home. Certainly in his condition, she couldn't leave him here while she rode home and hitched up the wagon. Between the snow and the dropping temperature, he wouldn't survive. She tried to get him into a standing position, but his dead weight was too much for even a tall, strong woman to lift alone.

"Got to think how...." she growled, setting him down again.

Remembering how she had hauled deer carcasses home, Adele pulled her rope off the saddle and tied it around him under the armpits. Gently urging Esmeralda over, she threw the rope ends over the top of the saddle, looping them around the saddle horn.

"Steady, Esmeralda, steady," she entreated as the pulley-like action raised the man to a vertical position against the mare's flank. Adele then forced his arms above the saddle, careful not to aggravate his wounds any more than necessary. She stooped behind him, forcing her shoulder under his buttocks and pushing him up over Esmeralda's rump. Mounting the sidesaddle she tied the rope ends around her waist and slowly rode towards the farm, hoping her peculiar bundle wouldn't slip or shift. Shivering—as the cold gave no mercy—she could not ride faster without risking the stranger's safety any further.

It seemed an agonizingly long time before she reached home. She was sure that her own lips and nail beds were as blue as the stranger's by the time she reached the farmhouse.

"Susannah! Get out here fast!"

After the sound of uneven footfalls crossed the room, Susannah pulled open the door.

"Oh my, what's that."

"It's an injured man. Someone must have ambushed him and left him for dead. I'm going to pull him off the horse. Stand near Esmeralda and grab his legs as they come over this side. We have to get him into the house."

Adele untied the rope from around her waist and slid out of the saddle. She grabbed the stranger's arms and pulled him over the top of the horse's back. As he slipped over, his legs fell heavily on top of the waiting Susannah, making her yelp. The two young women shifted their burden to a face up position and carried him up the steps and into the house.

"Put him in your bed," Adele ordered. "Pull the quilts and top sheet off first."

Susannah put down the stranger's feet and walked over to the bed. She pulled the bedding off as ordered while Adele pulled him toward the bed. With Susannah's returning aid, they got him onto the bed.

"Now, go into Pa's trunk and get one of his nightshirts and another quilt. Is there hot water on the stove? Good. Got to get this man warm."

Susannah paused at the opening to the bedroom. "Is he going to live?"

"I don't know," was the grim reply, "but we've got to get him warm if there's to be any hope at all."

Susannah brought the nightshirt and quilt.

"Use the bricks we heat when we have colds. Put them in the fireplace and make two cups of tea...."

"Two?"

"Yes. One's for me. I'm frozen near through myself. I've got to get him out of these things and into this nightshirt."

"Can't I help?"

"The ambushers left him naked. I don't think you're ready for that sight yet. I'm not sure I am, but I've already seen it, so I doubt it'll do me any more harm than it has already. Once you get the tea made, bring me my sewing basket and a bowl and the hot water kettle and a towel. I've got to try to stitch up these wounds. Then wrap the bricks in flannel and bring them over here."

Susannah rushed to follow directions while Adele pulled the jacket and petticoat off the stranger's body. She checked his ribcage for broken ribs. Despite the bruising there did not appear to be any. She was surprised to feel a shudder go through her at the touch of his cold skin. There was no spare flesh on the man, and she could see the faint bas-relief of his ribs and collarbone on his pale skin. He was just plain slender, despite his broad shoulders.

Having satisfied herself that his ribcage didn't need binding, Adele got him into the nightshirt, struggling against the dead weight of the unconscious man. *Thank God Pa was barrel-chested,* she thought, *or this would be tighter across the shoulders than it is.* The nightshirt barely covered the tall man's knees, but it would just have to do for now. He was covered, for warmth and modesty sake.

That task completed, Adele pulled the top sheet and three warm quilts on top of the unconscious man.

Moving as fast as her deformed foot would allow, Susannah brought her sister a cup of tea and the sewing basket and hot water. A quick gulp spread some well-needed heat through her. Adele examined the head wound; it was no longer bleeding. The hand wound was still seeping blood, so she quickly threaded some white thread through the eye of a strong needle. She dropped the needle in the bowl and poured boiling water on it, then dipped a corner of the towel in the boiling water and applied it to the wound. She wished she had some whisky, but there hadn't been any in the house since before Tom Stoddard died.

Instinctively, the man jerked slightly at the pain of the contact, but Adele held fast. Using small, tight stitches, she closed the sides of the wound, forcing closed flesh that had never been intended to meet. She only hoped the skin would knit together so the man could use his hand properly and there would be no infection. The missing finger itself was gone for good; even if she had found it she could never have reattached it. Having been covered in snow had probably slowed down the seepage, stopping the man's bleeding to death before Adele found him.

The stitching stopped the bleeding, so Adele moved to the head wound. Cleaning it with boiling water, she forced her needle into the thin, stretched skin of his forehead and scalp and closed the laceration.

Next, the wrapped, heated bricks were placed strategically under the bedclothes, their heat radiating into that tall, lean body that lay so still, chest barely rising and falling.

"Susannah, I want you to lift his head slightly and try to get him to swallow some tea. Wet a handkerchief with the tea and squeeze it into his mouth if necessary, a little at a time. I'm going to put Esmeralda away and bring in the rabbits. Then I'm going to put on some dry clothes and relieve you while you dress the rabbits and make something with them."

THE NEXT SIX days were a challenge and a discovery. The stranger remained unconscious, muttering unintelligible words in his delirium and occasionally flinching as if warding off blows. Mercifully, he never developed the lung congestion that might signal pneumonia.

While Susannah did her chores and cooking, Adele worked hard at keeping the man warm, clean and fed. Using a handkerchief, she slowly squeezed broth or water into his mouth, stroking his throat so he would swallow it. When Susannah was in the barn doing chores, Adele cleaned her patient and would change his nightshirt.

The stranger's breathing became steadier and his color better over the days that followed and it appeared that if he regained consciousness, he might live. Realizing he would need something to wear, one morning when they were alone in the cabin, Adele surreptitiously grabbed her tape measure from her sewing basket and quickly measured his inseam, embarrassed a bit at the personal contact with his maleness, but more surprised at her tingling reaction to the touch. She then chided herself for taking so intimate a measurement first. She took other measurements as well, using them to alter a shirt and lengthen a pair of trousers from her father's wardrobe.

While Adele sewed, Susannah sat by the stranger, her sketchpad and pencil in hand, busily drawing sketch after sketch of his face and hands.

"I wonder what color his eyes are."

"Hmmm?"

"I said, did you see what color his eyes are?"

Adele rose and walked over to the bed. "No, he's never been conscious."

She looked down at the face. The bruising around his eyes had nearly vanished. It was a wholly masculine face, thick black eyebrows and straight spiky lashes, an aquiline nose above a well-trimmed mustache and full sensuous lips. A speculation suddenly flashed in Adele's mind as to how it might feel to be kissed by that mouth. She closed her eyes against the folly of such thought. The man had a strong chin, squarish and only slightly softened by the unshaven black stubble that covered it. Even without seeing his eyes, Adele knew this was the most arrestingly handsome man she had ever laid eyes on.

"If his eyes are anything like the rest of his face," observed Adele, "I'll bet he had to beat the girls off with a stick."

"I wonder where he comes from," mused the younger girl.

The elder lifted his left hand and turned it over. "City, I reckon. Denver, maybe, or Chicago."

"I wonder why he was out on the range."

"If he is from the city, maybe he didn't know any better than to ride alone in the wintertime on open range."

"What makes you think he was alone?"

"If he wasn't alone, maybe he could have fought off whoever attacked and robbed him. I guess we'll have to wait until he regains consciousness and ask him."

"Do you think that will be soon?"

"I hope so. He's getting stronger, but he's not going to live long if we have to feed him one swallow at a time like we've been doing."

THE MORNING OF November 18th was slightly milder than the preceding week had been. After Susannah finished with the barn chores, Adele went outside to the woodshed to chop some firewood while her younger sister sat with their charge.

Susannah was sitting by the bed, sketching the stranger again, when, quietly and without warning, his eyes opened and he stared right at her, confusion apparent.

Susannah stared back for a brief moment, then rose and limped over to the window that gave a view of the woodshed, opening it. "Sissy," she called out.

Hearing the window open, a rarity in winter, Adele looked up. "What's up?"

"Gray," said Susannah. "His eyes are gray."

Resting the ax against the chopping block, Adele ran back into the house and over to the bedside.

Yes, his eyes were indeed gray, dark gray like a stormy sky. "Good morning, stranger," she began with a smile, sliding into the chair set next to the bed.

"Where am I?" came a richly-toned voice that was perfectly suited to the handsome face, handsome despite its pallor and six days growth of beard.

"This is the Stoddard farm. This is my sister Susannah Stoddard and...."

"And you're Sissy...."

"I prefer Adele."

"Hmm. How did I get here?"

"Oh, that was very dramatic," interrupted Susannah. "Sissy found you in the snow all broken and bloody and brought you here all by herself."

Adele shrugged. "Just doing the right thing."

"How did I get 'all broken and bloody?'"

"Well, actually, mister, I was hoping you could tell me that."

The stranger closed his eyes for a hard moment, trying to concentrate. "I can't think. My head is splitting and my hand is so sore."

"Well, you have a nasty laceration on your forehead. I'd have to guess someone beat you up pretty badly and then hit you over the head with a blunt object, like a gun butt. Between that and a fever, you've been out cold for six days, so it must have been quite a blow."

"Did whoever hit me on the head break my hand, too? My little finger feels like it's on fire."

"Well, mister, I don't know how to tell you this except to say it straight out, but whoever ambushed you seems to have chopped off the little finger that's giving you so much pain. Were you wearing a ring or something?"

The stranger lifted up his right hand and looked at it as if it didn't belong to him. He examined the small stitches at the amputation site, as tears formed in his eyes, making them shine like silver. As if angry with himself, he blinked them away immediately. "I can't remember," he responded with a choked, swallowed sound. "I really can't remember what happened to me."

"Maybe it will come back to you," responded Adele, matter-of-factly. "Listen, I don't feel real comfortable calling you 'mister' or 'stranger' all the time. Can you tell me your name?"

The man's eyes flared with terror. He closed them as if trying to concentrate, then reopened them with great pain reflected in them. For the longest time, he said nothing, than when he finally opened his mouth, the response was devastating.

"I can't remember my name either. I don't know who I am."

Chapter 4

THE STRANGER became eerily silent after that revelation, looking away from the women; afraid his frustration would bring tears rather than rage. If he was going to cry, he was going to be damned sure no woman saw it. He didn't know why this was so important to him, but right now it was.

The man is conscious now, Adele thought, *there's work to be done that isn't going away. When he's ready to talk, he will.* Shrugging her shoulders, she walked back outside the house, and returned to the woodshed.

What she didn't see was the stranger's gray eyes following her out the door, nor did she hear the slight catch in his breath. *This Adele is a beauty,* he thought. Her eyes were the color of fine brandy; her hair like sable as it fell in a single braid down her long, slim back ending halfway between her hips and knees. She had dark, arched eyebrows and long curled eyelashes. Her nose was straight, which gave her a serious expression. Her lips were full and a dusky rose in color. Her face was angular with high cheekbones and slightly golden from working outside. The man's fingers itched to brush the tips along those cheekbones; his mouth tingled to see what those lips might taste like.

God damn, I'm barely conscious, can't remember a thing about myself, even my name, and I'm lusting after my rescuer, he thought angrily. *What kind of a bastard am I?* He curled his hands into fists and slammed them down on the bed beside him, groaning as the impact jarred the stitches over the amputation site.

The sounds alerted Susannah, who paused a moment in her cooking. "Are you okay, mister?"

"I suppose so. Just frustrated. It's as if I didn't exist until an hour ago. What date is it?"

"November 18th, 1873."

"Where are we?"

"Wyoming Territory; about twenty miles east of Green River and about a hundred miles west of nowhere. We don't have any neighbors closer than about fifteen miles in any direction."

"Pretty isolated."

"Yeah, particularly when it snows early like it has. We get kind of trapped here 'til spring."

"Is it just you and your sister?"

"There are the animals—but no other people since Pa died—except for you. Haven't had any company since the factor bought our crop back in September."

"The factor?"

"Mr. Duneagan; he's a man who buys crops from small farms like ours, arranges for reapers to harvest them and sells them to someone else. I don't understand it all that well, not like Sissy does, but with Pa gone at least it gives us a chance to get some cash in for our crop."

"What do you grow?"

"Wheat and corn as cash crops. We also have a vegetable garden, a cow and some chickens. I tend the garden and the cow and chickens. I also do the cooking. Sissy doesn't cook that well." Susannah lifted her skirt slightly, revealing the heavy, misshapen boot. "I can't get around well enough to work in the fields. The last two years Sissy plowed, planted and did the cultivating all by herself. She also does all the hunting, since I can't ride a horse," she finished with the sound of regret in her voice.

"Adele hasn't been married then?"

"No. Nobody really ever comes around that might propose to her. The reapers are rovers, and we never spend too much time in town or go too often because it's so far away. Sissy's probably too busy to miss being married, I guess."

"You don't think every girl wants to get married?"

"I guess I never thought much about it."

The stranger looked at Susannah with the same thoughtful assessment he had used on Adele. While there was no doubt these two were sisters, Susannah was far shorter than Adele, at least five or six inches shorter, and considerably younger. She had the same whisky-brown eyes and sable hair, brows and lashes, but she wore her waist-length hair down, pulling only the hair above her ear level back into a small braid. Her face was rounder and paler, her nose slightly turned up, giving her a merrier look. Although she was obviously just emerging into womanhood, she was already showing promise of voluptuousness. Susannah was going to be the kind of woman people referred to as *well-upholstered* when she matured. While the combination might be pleasing to some, the stranger found that her pleasant lushness did not appeal to him as much as the slim, serious demeanor of her older sister.

She wasn't unattractive, just not his taste.

Funny, you remember you have taste in women but not who you are or where you come from.

Her dinner preparations in the oven, Susannah grabbed her drawing board, some vellum and pencils and sat down in the chair by the bed. "Do you mind if I draw you?"

He glanced at the supplies. "Draw me?"

"Yes, I want to be an artist. I draw all the time—um—once my chores are done. Someday I want to paint, too."

"Have you drawn me before?"

Susannah looked embarrassed. "While you were out I did."

"May I see?"

"You want to see my drawings?" Susannah asked in wonder. No one ever asked to see her work; even Adele no longer asked.

"Yes, it occurs to me that I don't remember what I look like."

Susannah went over to the sideboard near the table and came back with a small stack of papers. The man looked at the sketches of himself. The subject's eyes were closed, so it was difficult to determine his true likeness, but he could see real talent. This was even truer of the studies the girl had drawn of his hands. It was as if his hands had character of their own, particularly the mutilated right. "These are quite good."

Susannah smiled. "Thanks. Now, can I draw you with your eyes open this time?"

The man brushed his left hand against his stubbled chin. "I think I'd rather you waited until I can shave. Do you have a razor and mirror?"

"I'm sure we have Pa's razor still, only I don't know how sharp it is. Our only mirror has almost lost its silvering. Maybe Sissy can shave you later. She used to shave Pa when he was sick."

It occurred to the stranger with a jolt that it might be very interesting to have that tall beauty close enough to him to shave him while he was conscious. The idea seemed to warm him down to his groin.

Then he scolded himself again for being a lustful bastard. What kind of man thought of nothing but sex when it came to women? The stranger realized that his only consideration of either Stoddard woman was according to her physical attributes. He frowned. Was he so shallow an individual in that life now shrouded in darkness? If so, he reasoned, he had a chance to be someone else entirely.

He only wished he knew who that someone else might be.

Outside, Adele had finished with the ax and went into the barn, angry with herself for the peculiar thoughts this stranger was putting into her head and the unusual sensations running through her body. Figuring that something backbreaking would clear her mind, she picked up the pitchfork and, climbing the rope ladder into the haymow, she began to pitch hay down into the stalls. Esmeralda, Mabel and the jenny began to eat greedily as the beneficiaries of Adele's sudden industry.

Having worked up a sweat already, Adele climbed back down the ladder and began to rake out the stalls, shoveling manure and trampled hay into a mulch bin. This was Susannah's job and had been done already a couple of days previously, so there really wasn't that much to rake, but the barn was warmer than the outside air and Adele felt safer from her lustful thoughts.

"What's the matter with you?" she chided herself between rakefuls. "Haven't got the sense you were born with? When his memory comes back, he won't want a too tall, skinny farm girl. He'll want to go back to his people."

Leaning against the barn wall, Adele drew her arms around herself and closed her eyes. Immediately an image of the tall stranger holding her appeared in her mind's eye. "No!" she cried, "I can't allow it."

But you want him, her mind played back. "No, it's just the wild imagining of an old maid," she said aloud, thinking if she said it enough times, she would believe it.

She slid down the wall until she was sitting on her tailbone with her heels drawn in and her knees drawn up. Tears filled her eyes and spilled over onto her cheeks. She had never been one for self-pity, but suddenly she was seized with the realization of how lonely it was living alone with just Susannah for company.

Little Gent emerged from a corner of the barn and climbed onto Adele's knees, rubbing his head against her cheek to compel a petting. Adele began to scratch the tabby-striped head and white chin of the little tomcat. "Well at least you'll always love me," she sighed miserably.

A COUPLE OF hours later, Adele finally dragged herself back into the house, having washed with cold water in the woodshed. Susannah had done her chores; the house was spotless, the table set for two, dinner was sitting on the stove waiting for Adele to come in for it. Susannah was sitting on a chair at one end of the table drawing something, deep in concentration.

"We were afraid you had fallen down the privy or something," remarked the stranger with a grin.

He was sitting up in bed. His teasing grin was so devastating it fairly took Adele's breath away. God, even his teeth were beautiful.

By the bedside, Susannah had pulled up a chair. A half-eaten bowl of stew and a teacup lay on the chair.

"You're eating," she observed.

"Well, more or less. I'm afraid I'm having a little trouble gripping the spoon because of the stitches. I'm awfully clumsy with it now."

"I think the stitches can come out in a few more days. It may take a while longer for you to get used to only having four fingers on that hand. Do you want me to help you?"

"I think I can manage the spoon, but you can help me otherwise."

"What can I do?"

"I'm not sure I can handle a razor with this hand yet and would really like a shave."

"Of course, let me have some dinner and I'll shave you later, okay?"

The stranger agreed and again reached for the bowl and spoon to finish his meal. Adele brought the plates over to the stove and served herself and her sister with helpings of the rabbit stew. The savory scent of the stew tore Susannah's concentration from her drawing long enough to join her sister in their simple dinner.

As promised, after dinner Adele retrieved the razor and strop from her father's chest and honed the edge as carefully as possible. She pulled the small, faded mirror from the dressing table in the bedroom and filled a mixing bowl with hot water from the kettle. There was no more of her father's shaving soap, so Adele grabbed the hand soap and a towel from the kitchen sink.

"Why the kitchen soap?" asked the stranger.

"No scent. It wouldn't do for you to smell like roses."

"Roses suit you."

"A small indulgence."

Adele soaped her hands into a lather and began to apply the foam to the stranger's cheeks. His face seemed hot, or was it her hands? She pulled her hands away.

"Something wrong?" came his hoarse inquiry. Her proximity made his heart pound harder.

"No, no," followed her over quick reply. She continued to gently lather his face, feeling the strength in his jaw. He watched her with veiled eyes, barely daring to breathe at her closeness. He wanted to reach up and touch her cheek as she was doing to his, but fought off the feeling.

Adele picked up the razor in her left hand and carefully began to stroke his face with it, thanking God that her shaking insides were not transmitting to her hands. Carefully avoiding his mustache, she removed the offending stubble from his face and beneath his jaw to his neck. On finishing, she washed off the remaining soap with a damp towel and handed him the mirror. He stared at the faded image without speaking for the longest time.

"Do you recognize yourself?"

"No, I'm a total stranger to myself. A complete cipher." He handed her back the mirror and leaned back against the pillows again, his eyes dark with misery.

"Maybe you need a name," piped a voice from the other end of the cabin.

"What?"

"I said, maybe you would feel less like a cipher if you had a name," repeated Susannah.

Angrily, he responded, "But I don't remember my name!"

"Then pick a new one," came the defensive reply.

"That's ridiculous."

"Maybe not," mediated Adele. "I'm not real comfortable calling you *mister* and *stranger* either. We could choose a temporary name for you to use until you remember your real one."

"And if I never remember my name?"

"Well, we'll choose a name you wouldn't mind using forever, if you have to."

Susannah pulled her chair over to the bedside. "What kind of name would you like? Should I get the Bible? We could pick a name from there."

"No, somehow going through life as an Ezekiel or Micah seems too austere."

"What about a saint? Peter or Michael?"

"Somehow I don't think I'm much of a saint," responded the stranger with a shrug, thinking a saint would not be lusting after his hostess like he was.

Adele was sitting quietly with her eyes closed. The stranger looked at her, "Aren't you playing this game?"

"Brian," said Adele, firmly.

"Brian?" he responded. "Why Brian?"

"You look like a Brian."

"Have you ever met anyone named Brian before?" he asked.

"No. I just decided that you look like a Brian."

The stranger laughed. "Adele, if you say I look like a Brian, then *Brian* it shall be. How about a last name now?"

Susannah put in, "We've been calling you *stranger* so much that it feels like part of your name. How about *Brian Stranger?*"

Brian frowned. "No not *Stranger*...but I could live with *Brian Strange.*"

"Brian Strange," repeated Adele and Susannah in turn.

Brian held out his hand to Susannah. "My name is Brian Strange; pleased to meet you, Miss Susannah."

Susannah took his hand and shook it, careful to avoid his stitches. "Glad to make your acquaintance, Mr. Strange."

Brian then held out his hand to Adele. "My name is Brian Strange; I am very pleased to make your acquaintance, Miss Stoddard."

Adele took his hand to shake it, but Brian pulled her hand to his lips and gently kissed the knuckles that joined her fingers to her palm. His mustache brushed the back of her hand like soft silk bristles. Their eyes met over her hand, his grays smoky with desire, her browns wide with the realization that his desire might match her own. Frightened, she pulled her hand away, grabbed the shaving equipment and walked quickly to the sink, where she used the pump to rinse the bowl and razor.

"What's the matter, Sissy?" Susannah asked.

"Nothing. I've got too many things to do to sit around playing silly games. And so do you; Mabel needs her evening milking."

"Evening milking? But I already...." Susannah realized that, for some reason, her presence was not desired. "All right," she grumbled, "I'm going." Susannah grabbed her shawl and a lantern and disappeared out the door into the deepening dusk.

Adele tromped over to the rocking chair and reached down for the shirt she was altering. For a long time neither she nor Brian said anything. The silence was broken only by the sounds of their breathing and the occasional click of Adele's brass thimble against the needle or a button.

"I'm sorry if I upset you," came the voice from the bed.

"I'm not upset."

"I was just trying to be gallant."

"I'm *not* upset, Brian!"

"You're not upset and I've got ten fingers," was the sardonic response.

"That's not my fault. Who told you to go riding the range alone in the middle of a snowstorm so you could run into somebody who'd chop your finger off?" she fairly shouted back.

"I wish I could remember. I'd kill him!"

"It was probably your own stupid idea. You're lucky I showed up when I did or you'd have frozen to death."

Brian was suddenly quiet. "You're right. I was damned lucky. Adele, did you see anything around that would identify me. Clothes, papers, anything?"

"No. You were stark naked and stripped bare. I didn't see anything around, not even a button. Whoever got you intended you to die of exposure even if you regained consciousness. It was snowing when I found you, another couple of hours and I would have passed by without seeing you at all."

"Was there a clue as to who got me?"

"No, the snow obliterated any tracks there might have been, but I was more concerned with trying to get you back here alive than with anything else. Dead men don't need identities."

"Maybe I am dead and you're angels."

"I doubt it. This surely isn't heaven and a skinny old maid and a young girl are sorry excuses for angels." *Besides*, she thought, *you're far too alive to be a dead man.*

"I don't think you're skinny." *No, I think you're just the right size.* "How old are you, anyway?"

"Twenty-three."

"That's too young for an old maid."

"I'm resigned to it." *No, I guess for the first time in my life I'm really not.* "I'm too busy here trying to keep this farm going to go husband hunting. Besides, I'm five foot ten, most of the men I've met are my height or shorter."

"What about your sister?"

"Susannah won't even be sixteen for three weeks. She has plenty of time. Besides she thinks more about drawing than she does about boys. She needs to find a man who'll encourage her art and who won't take great stock in the condition of her foot. And if she's really lucky, she'll stop growing now so she has more choices than I do."

"Adele, come over here."

"I can hear you fine from here."

"Don't resign yourself to loneliness," Brian added quietly. "Look, I don't remember if I have any relatives or not. I don't remember when or where I was born nor where I live nor what I do for a living. Earlier I lay here trying to remember any thread, any flash of my past. It's completely gone. Can you even begin to imagine how lonely that is?"

Adele shook her head.

"It's as if I was born today, fully grown with a man's body and needs but with a child's ignorance. My whole world is bounded by the walls of this cabin. From this bed I can't even see outside. For all I know the whole world consists of myself, two women and a silly little tomcat. You know, giving me a name is an even greater act of kindness than saving my life."

"I don't understand."

"Susannah was right. Even if it's a made-up identity, now that I have one I feel like a person again. You gave that to me. Pulling me out of the cold saved my body, naming me saved my life."

"I just try to do the right thing."

"Do the right thing for yourself as well. You're a beautiful woman. Let someone love you."

Adele put down her sewing and stood up. "I have to go to bed now." The conversation was making her decidedly uncomfortable.

She extinguished the lamps and walked swiftly into the bedroom and changed for bed. Brian lay back in bed in the near darkness. The only sounds in the house were the crackling of the fire in the hearth and the sobbing coming from the bedroom. Brian was so exhausted that he closed his eyes and was already asleep when Susannah came back in from her useless excursion to the barn to take herself into the bedroom.

BRIAN OPENED his eyes the next morning to see Susannah opening the door. He glanced around the cabin.

"Where are you going?"

"Out to milk Mabel."

"Where's Adele?"

"She's out chopping firewood next to the house. See you later," answered Susannah as she breezed out, pulling the door closed behind her.

Alone in the cabin, Brian pushed back the quilt and eased himself upright in bed. Throbbing in his head nearly drove him flat on his back, but he shook it off and sat upright, swinging his long legs over to sit on the side of the bed.

Rising slowly on rubbery legs, Brian locked his knees as his balance threatened to betray him. After over a week in bed, he felt as weak as a newborn colt. Feeling some strength surging back into his limbs, Brian walked slowly over to the rocking chair where it stood near the fireplace. Adele's sewing basket stood next to the rocker. The trousers and shirt she had been altering lay on top of the basket. Sitting down on the rocker, Brian reached for the trousers first. The soft brown wool of the legs had been lengthened to the extent of the fabric. Seamed to the bottoms with tiny stitches were extensions of a slightly different brown wool, which were hemmed with small, secure slip stitches.

Brian smiled slightly, realizing that their father, whose trousers these must have been, had been a good four to six inches shorter than he was. He considered how Adele might have measured the length of his legs and the thought made him start to harden, but he fought it. He pulled the trousers on and buttoned the fly placket, finding them a little too big in the waist and hips. *Well, I've probably lost some weight that she figures I'll gain back,* he thought. Pulling the nightshirt over his head, he then pulled up the suspenders buttoned onto the trousers to rest on his shoulders, which effectively held the pants up.

Brian reached down to get the shirt that lay beneath the trousers. The shirt wasn't quite finished. Adele had extended the length and breadth of the light blue cambric with pieces of dark blue calico. It was obvious from the pattern that Adele didn't keep a stock of more masculine fabrics for herself and her sister but had tried to find the most subtle print she could to alter the shirt. The cuffs had been removed, but the sleeves had not yet been lengthened.

Brian put on the shirt, readjusting the suspenders and rolling up the unfinished sleeves to above his elbows. He was sure he looked as patched together as the clothes.

Seeing no cupboards except in the kitchen area, Brian guessed that Adele and Susannah must keep their clothes in the bedroom. He padded on his bare feet past the cloth drape hanging in the doorway to the room. A quick look through the upright armoire revealed nothing but dresses and other women's things. He turned to the trunk he saw nearby. Opening it he rummaged through looking for socks and footwear. Under the neatly folded quilts and unfinished tops, he found several pairs of woolen socks; one of which he took. He also found a worn pair of work boots. Sitting on the bed he put on the socks and then, crossing his fingers, and wincing slightly at the pull on the stitches in his right hand, he yanked on the boots. They fit very snugly, but they fit.

"Well, the late Mr. Stoddard may have been shorter than I, but thank God he had big enough feet."

Walking back into the main room and towards the cabin door, he took the battered felt hat and the sheepskin jacket off the peg rack by the door and put them on as he headed out the door.

The freezing air hit Brian like a punch. The sky was a bright overcast, like a pale gray blanket. There was no wind.

The only sound he heard was the erratic chopping sound of ax on wood. Brian followed the sound to the side of the cabin to find Adele by the woodshed, ax in hand, legs braced before a chopping block. She wore a dark blue dress of the same calico she had used to patch together his shirt. Her shawl lay on the ground nearby. Her dark brown hair was plaited in its same single long braid down her back that slid enticingly back and forth as she wielded the ax.

As if she sensed his presence, Adele stopped, lowering the ax to rest near her ankle, gripping the end of the ax handle in her right hand.

A big grin lit up her face. "You're up. That's wonderful. How do you feel?"

"A little rubbery, but surprisingly good."

"I'm so glad." Brian could hear genuine sincerity in her voice. He was glad their tense encounter of the night before was no longer present in her voice or attitude. "Privy's around back," she gestured.

"Thanks."

"Where's Susannah?"

"In the barn, milking," he gestured.

"It's freezing out here. Maybe you shouldn't be out here so soon."

"I couldn't just lie in bed like a helpless baby while you chopped firewood."

"You're recovering from nearly being beaten and frozen to death. You don't need to rush things, you know."

"I know, but I feel like all I'm doing is taking from you and not giving back. It's not a fair exchange. The least I can do is chop wood."

Adele raised the ax with both hands on the long handle spread apart and held it out to Brian. He walked over to her and put his hands on the handle. The sides of his hands brushed hers and the air was rent by a sharp intake of breath from Brian.

"Oh, your hand! I'm sorry," exclaimed Adele.

"No, it's okay," he responded, taken aback because the gasp came not from any pain in his mutilated hand, but from a frisson of shock at their physical contact that shot to his core like a lightning bolt.

Adele looked up at the tall male. The eyes that met Brian's steel gray ones seemed to have gold flecks in them he hadn't noticed indoors.

They stood together, barely inches apart, both still holding the ax handle for a time—stopping eternity.

Then Adele broke eye contact. "Have you got it?" she inquired.

"Got it?"

"The ax."

"Oh, yes—the ax. Yes, I've got a hold on it."

Adele released her grip. Her arms felt amazingly weightless.

"Um—bring the ax inside when you're done. No sense rusting our only good ax."

"Of course," came the masculine reply.

Adele turned away and started to step toward the cabin door. Her thoughts raced. *I wanted to kiss him—I wanted him to kiss me. What is it about this man?*

"Um—Adele?" came a quiet voice behind her.

She turned. "What is it, Brian?" she responded in an unnaturally husky voice.

"It just occurred to me—I don't think I know how to chop wood."

Adele saw a strange look of confusion and innocence in Brian's handsome face that made him look boyish. Her response was gut felt, relieved laughter.

Through her laughter, she stated, "I should have guessed from those hands of yours that you've never done a day's hard labor."

Brian shot back in a commanding voice, the look of innocence gone, "Do you have a problem with that?"

"No," she replied, walking over to him and lifting his right hand off the ax handle. Turning the palm up, she pointed with her index finger to his remaining fingers. "Look, you have no calluses; no scars except for the new one." Turning his hand palm down, she continued, "Your cuticles show care. Your nails aren't stained underneath and they're smooth. You're a city man who does city work."

"Is that bad?"

"No, not at all." She opened her own work-roughened hand. "See my hand? I'm a farmer. I chop wood, plow fields, cook sometimes and sew, even do carpentry and masonry when I have to. If I lived in the city, my hands might be smooth and pretty. But bankers and lawyers and teachers and businessmen; their work is important, too. It just doesn't rough up their hands."

Brian closed his hand over hers for a moment. "Well, I guess today this city man needs a lesson in how to be a farmer."

They both laughed. Suddenly, Adele rose slightly on her toes. Placing her hand on Brian's cheek, she pressed a quick kiss on his other one. Then she just as quickly let go and dropped to her flat feet again with a smile.

"Well, city man," she began, "stand with your feet apart and hold the ax handle with your left hand near the blade and your right hand near the end...."

Chapter 5

A FEW DAYS after the wood chopping lesson, Adele took out the
stitches from his head and hand. The scars would never go away, but
her careful work had reduced the disfigurement as much as possible.

While it was clear that Brian had no experience with working on a
farm, he was not afraid to take lessons. He learned to chop wood, fork
hay, shovel out the barn. He milked the cow, fed the chickens, renailed
loose boards on the house and outbuildings.

Adele was constantly surprised to see his intense concentration on
learning each task. Everything was new to him, and he tackled each
chore in a most precise and methodical way, determined to master every
skill. Whether his teacher was Adele or Susannah, he asked intelligent
questions and listened to the answers. If he didn't know how to do
something, he admitted it.

Eventually. Sometimes he would try to do a chore first before
asking for help. Adele chalked that up to his being a man.

As Brian worked, he discovered muscles he had probably never
used before. And those muscles seemed to be expanding—even in the
short time he had been working on the farm it seemed that his shirts
were getting tighter in the shoulders and sleeves. His arms and back
ached with ungodly pain, but he also found energy from the sweat and
exertion. Fortunately, at the end of the day, Adele was present with the
liniment bottle. Her strong fingers kneaded life back into his sore
shoulders, filling him with heat that was both pleasant and unbearable.

One evening he was sitting on the edge of the bed, shirt off, as a
fully-clothed Adele massaged his sore back, when he asked, "Why
don't you wear your hair down like Susannah does?"

"Susannah is fifteen. A respectable adult woman simply doesn't
wear her hair down. I'm no coquette. The only reason I don't wear my
hair all the way up is because I don't have enough hairpins left to pin it
up and forgot to get more the last time we went to Green River. The
braid is the best I can do for now."

"I've been trying to imagine how you would look with your hair
loose about your face."

"I would look silly. I learned to face reality a long time ago,

Brian."

"Which reality?"

"The reality that I'm twenty-three years old, live miles from nowhere and have never been courted. I'm not the kind of woman men fall for. I'm not a soft, delicate little flower like the girls you've known."

"Even *I* don't know what kind of girls I've known, remember? Some men might appreciate a girl who wouldn't faint or throw a fit the moment the going got a little rough. Soft, delicate little flowers suck the life out of a man."

Adele felt his tension. "Do you remember knowing a girl like that, Brian?"

"No," he replied. "I have no idea where that thought came from. I wonder...But we were talking about you."

"Can we talk about something else?" It was so frustrating to her to feel the intense hunger she had for this man and know it was hopeless. "Let's talk about how well you're taking to farm work."

Brian raised his hands to her, palms up. His formerly smooth hands were marked with new calluses that bore mute witness. His nails were clean, but the manicured cuticles were now ragged. "I guess I'm not such a city man anymore."

"No, you might make a farmer yet, but, you know, winter is the easiest time on a farm. If you're still here come spring when we start plowing and planting, then you'll find out what really hard work is."

"I wasn't aware I was leaving."

"Well, you weren't expecting to stay, were you?" Adele asked cautiously.

"Where else would I go? What other home have I?"

"Well, your memory could still return...."

Brian cut her off. "And if it does I'll deal with it then." *How can I leave when I feel about you the way I do?* he added to himself.

Adele responded quietly, "I'm not asking you to leave. Stay as long as you want. It's so pleasant to have you around." *God, I want to put my arms around him so much.* "What I mean to say is it's good to have a man around the house again."

God, I want her to put her arms around me so much, his thoughts raced. The lust he experienced the first time he laid eyes on Adele had changed. He still battled with arousal, but there was a growing warmth inside him that transcended the merely physical urges. Brian did not want to consider the import of these new feelings. A man with no past had business falling in love.

Falling in love? Where did that thought come from?

Brian quickly changed the subject. "Can we go to the site where you found me tomorrow? I want to look around and see if I can find any clues to my identity."

"It's quite a ways. I have Pa's old saddle, but I'm not sure we can ride double. I don't ride astride and the jenny doesn't like to be ridden. She's strictly a plow and cart mule."

"Can we try? You can bring the rifle and maybe you can teach me to hunt."

"If you learn that like you've learned everything else, I won't have any chores left that you haven't taken over. I may have to start cooking again."

"Oh, God," teased Brian, putting the back of his hand over his eyes, "anything but that."

Adele punched him on the back. "Oh hush up. You've never tasted my cooking."

"According to Susannah, that's probably why I'm still alive."

"I should put ipecac in the stew just to get you for that," she responded, punching him again.

Feeling her fist, Brian turned and grabbed Adele by her upper arms. He pulled her close to his chest and pressed his lips to hers. Adele's eyes widened. She tried to pull her arms out of his grasp, but gradually decided she didn't want him to let go and surrendered to the sensations that began to course through her. Brian's kiss became more demanding; Adele could feel his lips part slightly and his tongue play on her lips, demanding entrance. She slid her arms around his ribcage and parted her lips slightly. His teeth nibbled gently on her lower lip, followed by his tongue's entrance into her mouth, where he tasted her teeth and the soft inside of her mouth. His tongue met hers and she instinctively sucked slightly on the muscular intruder, which drove Brian wild. He pulled her closer to him, crushing her small breasts against his bare chest.

Adele's hands slid up his back. She could feel the new muscles move beneath his skin as he pressed her closer to him. She could feel his heat in her hands and through her calico gown. Her fingers ran up his neck and nestled in his raven hair, which was becoming shaggy. His hair was soft, almost too soft. He smelled of hard work and liniment and something distinctly male Adele couldn't exactly define. Instinctively she pressed closer, feeling her breasts flattened against his chest. A growing heat began in her most private core and spread warmth through her body. She felt like she was melting into his caress.

Brian's arms tightened around Adele as well. To him she smelled of roses and wood smoke. He moved from her lips to brush his own against the shell of her ear, teasing it with his tongue and mustache. Her breathing became increasingly more rapid. He sensed that she was squeezing her thighs together from the building sensations. He himself was becoming hard as a steel rod; he was sure she could feel his arousal through his trousers and her skirt and petticoats. He began to slide one hand around her ribcage to touch the underside of one of her small, firm breasts when the mood was shattered by the sound of dropping papers and a gasped:

"Oh, my!"

Brian looked up to see Susannah standing in the doorway staring open-mouthed at them. He loosened his grip and Adele, with a horrified shriek, pushed away from him. She lost her balance and landed seated on the floor. Her face suffusing with red, she quickly righted herself and rushed past her astonished sister out the cabin door.

Brian sat shocked for a moment, then grabbed a quilt off the bed and wrapped it around himself as he pushed past Susannah and followed Adele out the door.

Adele reached the barn and climbed up the rope ladder to the haymow, pushing her way through the hay to the extreme end of the barn. Her breathing was ragged with sobs; tears splashed down her heated cheeks as she sat in the corner of the hayloft, her hand cautiously tracing her skirts over the apex of her thighs, hoping to still the tumult she felt.

"You know, you'll feel ever so much better if I do that."

"Go away, Brian. Please go away."

He closed the gap between them.

"Why are you doing this to me?" she sobbed.

"It's no more than you are doing to me, sweetheart." His voice was gentle and caressing. His big hand traced the line of her jaw and then her mouth. "So soft, so beautiful, so full of passion." He dropped the quilt and drew her to his bare chest. In almost a whisper he told her, "I cannot imagine wanting a woman so much as I want you now. You ignite my senses. You could not have responded to me like you did in there if you didn't feel it, too."

Adele nodded her head against his pelted chest. She was beyond words at first. Upon finding her voice she said, "But it's wrong."

"How can it be wrong when we both feel this way?" he countered. "Please, darling, let me love you now. Let me see you open up your petals, my precious rose. Bloom for me."

Brian separated from her long enough to spread the quilt on top of the sweet-smelling hay. He reached out his hand to Adele and she wordlessly obeyed, moving onto the quilt and into his arms. He quickly unbuttoned the small bone buttons on the back of her bodice and then slid it from her, revealing her clean, worn chemise and corset and her slim, bare arms. With hands not at all clumsy to the task, he undid the many hooks of the corset and pulled it away from her.

Adele took a deep breath as the released corset freed her ribcage.

"Why do you wear that horrible thing?"

"Respectable adult women...."

He stopped her words with his mouth, nibbling and teasing her lips until he could hear her breathing becoming ragged. He released her a moment to let her take a full breath.

The action caused her small breasts to rise most provocatively beneath her chemise. Brian reached for the tapes of her skirt, petticoats and pantalets and released them all. In two motions, he swept the skirts down her hips, then slid her chemise up and over her head until she was clad only in her knee-high woolen stockings and her button-closed shoes.

The big man surveyed the willowy woman who knelt before him. Her breasts were small, but firm and well-formed, tipped with dusky rose aureoles that surrounded her nipples. Her skin was like ivory. He saw the slenderness of her ribcage, the slight depressions of skin between her ribs and the red marks from her stays. Even without her corset, her waist was small enough Brian thought he could span it with his hands. Her slim hips flared slightly sliding into trim thighs whose smooth skin did little to hide the muscular evidence of years of hard farm work. At the apex of her thighs, a small patch of sable whorls guarded her most private place.

For a long moment, Brian stared in awe. "God, you're beautiful, more beautiful than I even imagined."

She looked at him; her eyes glazed with desire. The hard bulge of his own desire was evident through the heavy woolen cloth. "I want to see you."

"First things first," he responded and reached around her neck. He wrapped one hand loosely around her braid and brought it forward to rest like a thick, dark rope over her shoulder and down between her breasts.

As he watched, she slid the braid out of his grasp. Untying the string that bound the bottom she slowly began to unplait its length until her dark hair fell in crimped waves from her crown to just above her knees. Even in the deep shadows of the haymow it shone like fine satin, healthy and glorious.

Her hair down, framing her face, Adele was more beautiful than he had even imagined she would be. Brian felt a surge so strong he feared he might find his release merely from the sight of her. As if they were on fire, Brian nearly ripped his trousers off. The hayloft was too short for him to stand up, so he came over to the quilt on his knees, his large, hard maleness rampant and dangerous as it sprang out from his own black thatch.

Adele stared at him. She tried to keep her eyes away from his groin, but she had never seen a fully-aroused man before and his erection captured her imagination.

"You're so *large*," she gasped.

Brian laughed. "Not too large to fit. God designed us well for this."

Brian slid his arms around Adele and lowered her onto her back on the quilt. His lips met hers in another kiss, deeper if possible than that he had given her in the house. This time he did not have to urge her to part her lips, she did it on her own and slipped her own tongue into his mouth to taste his softness. His response was a guttural groan as he crushed her to him.

Then, he gradually released his grip on her as his fingers began to explore. He brushed them down her throat, then across her collarbone then lower until he circled them around her dusky nipples. Adele gasped in arousal that increased when he replaced with fingers with his lips, suckling and nibbling on one breast until the nipple hardened to attention. Bolts of fire shot through her from breast to core and Adele felt alive with sensation.

Not content to administer to one nipple, Brian turned his attention to the other one, teasing it and coaxing it to hardness in the same manner. As he suckled, he brought his hand slowly down her ribcage and trailed his fingernails across her flat stomach. She contracted with the pleasure.

"Something wrong?" he asked huskily.

"Is there?" she asked in innocence. She was hungry. It was the only word she knew to describe the indescribable feeling she was experiencing. She could not tell what she hungered for, but instinctively knew only this man could supply it.

"Oh, no, everything is right," Brian assured her.

Using his hands, Brian caressed the tender skin on the inside of her thighs. His newly-callused hands created sensations in her thighs that he was sure he had never been able to evoke in a woman before. Delicately, he teased the curls that were becoming damp with the evidence of her arousal. Delicately, he slipped a finger into her most personal zone. She was small and tight and so moist and ready. Adele rose slightly with a shocked noise and closed her thighs.

"No, darling, relax and enjoy what you're feeling." Brian brushed her with his fingers. "Your body is telling me you want me inside you. I doubt there's a perfume in the world that smells better than a passionate woman with the man she wants."

In a gesture so wanton she would later wonder how she'd done it, Adele reached for his hand and slowly sucked each finger, tasting the combination of his skin and her own womanliness. Brian slipped his hand out of her grasp and replaced it within her. His fingers slid in and out of her, sliding over her pleasure center as well. She began to cry out as her arousal grew. She felt as if her breasts were going to explode and felt a fire at her apex. Her cries increased until she exploded in a series of shuddering jerks like live rifle fire.

On seeing the sensual shattering, Brian poised himself between her thighs. He whispered in her ear, "It only hurts the very first time. After that, it is only pleasure," he said, then thrust home, his largeness sliding into her tight sheath, piercing her maidenhead as she climaxed again.

Adele cried out with shock at the pain that accompanied the climax. Tears sprang into her eyes.

"I'm sorry, love," Brian whispered in her ear. "I wouldn't hurt you for the world. I swear it won't hurt like that ever again." He lay quietly on top of her, giving her a chance to become accustomed to the feel of him buried deep inside her.

"I need to move now, sweeting," he crooned.

Her tight muscles held him securely as he began to move in steady rhythm within her. Her arms surrounded him. Her nails raked along his back. He indicated with his hands that she should wrap her stocking-clad legs around his hips. She did to find the sensations increased as she tried to pull him deeper within her, if that was possible, for it seemed she had room for all of him inside her.

Adele stared at her lover. His eyes were as dark and soft as velvet as he continued to pump himself deep within her. When he came inside her, each burst of seed was accompanied by an agonized groan. Fully spent, Brian collapsed exhausted on top of her, his body shiny with perspiration.

For a few moments they lay there as if melted into one another. Finally, Brian rolled off Adele so as not to burden her with his body weight. His action disengaged them and Adele breathed a disappointed sigh as his sudden withdrawal.

Brian smiled, "Miss me already?"

"You felt so right inside me," she said, and then blushed bright.

"Sweetheart, never be ashamed of what your heart feels. If you liked this, there can always be more."

Adele sat up, suddenly panicked. Guilt flooded through her. How could she have acted this way? Brian was a stranger. She barely knew him. He barely knew himself. He would not even have a name if they had not invented one for himself. She was supposed to be a respectable spinster and she had just allowed Brian to...to...She did not even have a word for what they had just done, but it certainly was not proper behavior for a respectable spinster to engage in.

"No, there can't," she declared defensively.

Brian rose on one elbow. "Why the hell not?"

Because I liked it too much to be able to feel good about myself. Unable to voice the truth, she seized upon a convenient excuse. "Susannah."

"I think she already has an idea. She's very observant, your little sister."

"What she must think of me!"

"I really don't think we have to worry about it. Somehow I don't think Susannah will think any less of either of us. We can always come up here again if you really need to keep it a secret."

Adele began to cry. Helpless over her tears, Brian could do no more than hold her while she sobbed. He brushed her wonderful hair with one hand, smelling its rose scent.

"Do you know why you're crying?"

"No," she sobbed, "do you?"

"There's probably nothing more emotional for a woman than her first experience with a man. Strong emotion always brings out tears. Every time we make love from now on you'll cry less and laugh more."

"Laugh?"

"People laugh when they're having fun."

"Fun?"

Brian looked at her, "Yes, fun, darling. Let me show you how to have fun. I don't think anyone ever tells women that this can be fun. I wish they did."

Adele rose suddenly, crawling toward her clothes. Starting with her chemise, she began to yank her clothing back on, wrestling with getting her unbound hair out of her way. "Maybe for men it's *fun*," she snapped.

"Adele, Adele, next time...."

"What makes you think this is going to happen again?"

"The way you responded. I thought you wanted this as much as I did."

"I didn't mean to act like a—a—fancy woman. You got me so confused I lost all control."

"The last thing I think of you as is a whore—if that's what you mean. I've never had any woman react like you did. I've never felt like this before."

She hissed at him, "How would you know? Or with everything you've forgotten you remember that?"

Brian was suddenly quiet. "I don't know what I remember and don't. I can't remember the name or face of any woman I might have known that way, but there are some things I seem to know instinctively, and one of those things is that what we just had was very special and unique."

"Maybe you really don't remember. Maybe you'd feel this way with any girl."

"I don't think so. For instance, Susannah has a pretty face and figure and she's every bit as thoughtful and kind as you are, but I'm not attracted to her."

Adele stiffened. "She's not even sixteen." She was shocked to find she was jealous of her own sister.

"That's not the point. The point is, men react differently to different women. I like your sister. She's a nice girl and very talented and very sure of herself. But I've known you both the same length of time and I've spent nearly equal amounts of time with both of you and I react to each of you differently. I've never ached to touch Susannah like I have for you. I've never wanted to feel her melt into me like you did today. She might as well be my sister as yours. Memory or none, Adele, you're the woman I want, the only one I want and the only one I'll ever want...."

Adele covered her face with her hands. "That's impossible!" she cried. "Nobody wants me."

"Don't be ridiculous, Adele," Brian responded angrily.

"I can't hear any more of this!" Adele screamed at him. "I'm ruined, completely destroyed...*No*! Don't touch me!" she sobbed, when he tried to comfort her. "Please...don't touch me again. I couldn't bear it." And with that, she tore down the ladder and ran back to the house.

Brian watched after her for the longest time, then slowly reached for his pants and pulled them on, muttering, "Women, who can ever understand them?"

Chapter 6

ADELE DIDN'T come out of the bedroom for two days except to use the privy. She claimed she was sick. What she was, was feeling guilty. Brian was frustrated because Adele would not talk to him. Susannah was frustrated because neither of them would tell her what was going on. Susannah was not blind to the sensual tension she had been witnessing develop over the previous few weeks. She hated being excluded from what was going on because it made her feel like she was being treated like a child.

Christmas came and went virtually unnoticed. Susannah told Brian that, when the weather allowed, they might go to the church in Green River on Christmas morning but that their father's tradition was to wait until Epiphany, or Twelfth Night, for gift exchanging.

Brian, of course, had no memory of what, if anything, his family might have done about Christmas, assuming he even had one. He was as willing to adopt the Stoddard family tradition as he had adapted to life on the Stoddard farm.

Now, if only he could get Adele to talk to him.

The day after Christmas, Adele finally decided she could no long hide in the bedroom. She was haggard from crying and lack of sleep and her hair was tangled because she had been too upset to replait it. She insisted she did not want to talk about it and tried to be wherever Brian was not.

For his own part, Brian was making himself scarce, involving himself in some project either in the barn or in the woodshed, coming inside the house for meals and to sleep. He looked dour and angry and neglected to shave, his stubbled face adding to his look of misery. He did not mention going out to the site where he had been found again.

Susannah did her chores and tried to draw. Her attempts at conversation with either house-mate were met with dull, one-word replies, so she gave up. The tension was so thick she could slice through it. For a week she endured the sullen silence until she thought she might scream. There had always been contentment in this house. This much misery was maddening.

If only she understood what had occurred between Adele and Brian. She had her suspicions, but considering it was unlikely she would get a direct answer, Susannah would not even ask the question. No, she would have to discover it for herself.

The morning after New Year's Day, Susannah went into the barn to do her usual chores and found Brian sitting on the milking stool, her father's horn-handled pocketknife in his right hand. She quickly caught him concealing some object under a horse blanket.

Noticing that the hay troughs in front of the livestock were nearly empty, Susannah grabbed the pitchfork and began to climb the rope ladder to the haymow.

Brian looked up. "I didn't know you could climb that ladder."

Susannah was surprised. It was the longest sentence he had uttered to anyone in ten days. "Yes, I can shift my weight to my good foot pretty quickly. Sometimes in the summer I even sleep up here...."

The barn door closed while Susannah was speaking. Brian had walked out, his mind on something else. Susannah was getting used to everyone's absent-minded rudeness. She didn't like it, but what could she do but bear with it? With a shrug, Susannah forked some hay into the feed troughs and was about to climb down when she saw the quilt lying in the hay where it had been for the past week and a half. Using the pitchfork, Susannah scooped the quilt and pulled it toward her. There were traces of blood and something else on it the girl couldn't identify. Dropping to her hands and knees, Susannah crawled over to the corner of the haymow and explored the area. Susannah continued to search around the haystack when she found what she suspected she was looking for.

There in the hay was a piece of string like the kind Adele used to bind the bottom of her braid and a black button that was too large to be from any of Adele's clothes but which could have come from Brian's trousers.

It did not take more than an instant for the farm-raised girl to interpret the meaning of the evidence she found.

"Well, what do you know. I was right," she said triumphantly, her suspicions finally confirmed.

She sat on her haunches and thought about it. They had made love. A part of Susannah was overjoyed because she always wanted Adele to find a man to love. But both Brian and Adele were miserable. They were trying so hard not to have contact with each other.

Susannah reasoned it out. If the experience had been unpleasant for them both, they probably would have shaken it off more easily. But Susannah watched carefully during the week past. Adele could not walk through the main room that Brian's hungry gaze did not follow her. And Adele's eyes were on Brian whenever she thought he was not looking. Obviously, it must have been wonderful for both of them, but since they were not married it was forbidden and now they were both suffering.

Susannah wondered if they would be doing it if it was just the two of them. She chafed at being protected. She was sixteen for nearly a month now; almost old enough to be married herself. She was coming to love Brian as she would an older brother. How could she stand back and let the two people she loved most in the world continue to live with the pain of longing?

"I better do something about it or we're going to all go crazy," Susannah said aloud.

The only question was, what could she do?

WHEN WINTER weather forces people into an enclosed space with limited activity or stimulation, insanity—whether temporary or permanent—often results. Susannah was seeing the signs of cabin fever. The cold weather kept her and the two antagonists at closer quarters than was healthy. Tempers were abrupt. Adele found fault with Brian at every turn; he yelled back that she was too domineering.

Brian finally staked out the barn as his private territory while Adele took over the house. Susannah had no place to go except outside, which was no solution with the temperatures below freezing all day. She felt like she was invading one or the other's private reserves. It was bad enough the days were so short, because the nights were so long.

Adele set up her quilting frame and spent most of the evenings working on quilting a new top, a Snail Trail pattern. She set a lamp up next to the frame and bent over, her precious brass thimble clicking each time she began a group of stitches through the layers.

Brian was sitting in the rocking chair; but then he would jump up to pace like a caged lion before sitting down again.

Susannah sat next to Brian's bed, sketching the sleeping Little Gent, who lay curled in a circle next to the pillow.

Susannah glanced up at the pacing giant. "Brian, what is the matter with you tonight?"

"I'm so goddamned bored I could scream."

"Surely you could find something to do. Maybe you could read."

"Read? Read? You have three damned books in the entire house and I've read them all. I could probably recite them to you from memory."

Adele looked up. "Would you stop swearing at my sister?"

"God damn it, I'm not swearing. I'm losing my mind."

"Look, this pacing you're doing is very distracting. I'm having trouble concentrating on my quilting."

"That's a lie. You could sew with your eyes closed in the middle of a blizzard."

"Stop swearing. I don't like it," Adele warned.

Susannah put in, "Brian, if you think it's so easy, why don't you try it?"

"Are you kidding, Susannah?" interrupted Adele. "If this was so easy, *you'd* have learned to quilt."

"Oh, it's not easy, huh?" Brian observed cynically. "I'll bet I can learn to quilt as well as you can."

"Fine," snapped Adele. "Pull up a chair and get down to it."

Brian grabbed a straight chair from the table and plopped down on it on the opposite side of the frame from where Adele was sitting.

"All right, how do you begin?"

"First you thread the needle," she began, handing him the skein, scissors and a packet of needles. "Cut about 18 inches of thread at a slight angle and put it through the eye—that's the hole in the end of the needle. Then tie a knot in the other end of the thread."

Brian opened the packet of needles, only to have all of them roll out of the packet and fall on the quilt top.

"Would you watch out? If you lose those needles, we do without until spring."

"Sorry," he responded gruffly, awkwardly picking up the fallen needles in his large, stiffly awkward fingers and replacing all except one in the packet. He cut a piece of thread from the skein and held it up to the lantern with the needle. Grumbling and swearing under his breath and recutting the end of the thread several times he managed to get the thread through the eye and tied a knot in the other end.

"Now what?"

"Now you push the point of the needle through the layers, up and down, up and down, and pull it out to the length of the thread."

Brian watched her perform the task herself. He pointed to her hand. "What's that thing?"

"That's a thimble."

"Don't I need one of them?"

"Yes, I guess you do." Adele reached down for her sewing basket. Rummaging through it, she found a smaller brass thimble that had either been hers when she was younger or was their mother's. "I seem to only have one other, and it's too small for me to use, so it's certainly too small for you."

"What do you suggest?"

Adele continued rummaging, to her surprise, she found a piece of some kind of leather; it looked like deerskin, but she wasn't sure. Picking up the scissors, she cut a wide strip of leather and a thin strip. "Give me your right hand," she ordered.

No sooner did she have his right hand in hers then their eyes locked and it felt like a jolt of electricity shot through them. It was the first physical contact they'd had since the afternoon they'd made love. Adele, trying to ignore it and force her hands back to steadiness, folded the wide piece of leather over Brian's middle finger, covering his nail and the pad of his finger. She then used the thin strip like a binding to hold the piece on.

"That should do until I can figure something else out."

With his leather thimble thus secured, Brian began to ape Adele's rocking motion, occasionally grunting as the needle stuck the fingers of his left hand coming through the bottom of the quilt. At first his stitches were awkward and uneven, but the leather thimble kept the needle eye from sticking his top hand and he began to rapidly pick up the rhythm, fairly scooting across the straight lines he was stitching. His underside hand moved in concert until it brushed Adele's own underside hand.

She took a sharp intake of breath at the contact and tried to move her hand away, but Brian slid his fingers around hers and held her hand while he made eye contact. Adele yanked her hand from his and commented, "You're getting better."

"So are you," he responded with a grin.

"I meant your stitches. You learn fast."

"I guess if you can do man's work I can learn women's."

"Work is work," was the snappish response. "If you don't like it, you can go back to pacing the floor."

"You're just upset that I can do it as well as you."

"Can you? We'll see."

Adele bent down over the frame again. Brian rethreaded the needle and jerked his chair over for a more comfortable position. His knees made contact with hers through their clothes and they both looked up again. Adele shuddered and quickly looked at Susannah and back down at the frame. For an hour they worked, inches apart, breathing the same air, stitching in almost the same rhythm.

"Well, I'm going to bed," sang Susannah as she rose and walked into the bedroom. The cloth covering over the doorway flowed back into place.

The older couple watched until she was out of sight. Adele quickly rose from the frame and walked toward the stove, intending to get the kettle.

Brian was up right behind her. He grasped her by one arm and spun her around, pulling her against his length. Adele struggled, but Brian held her by the back of her head and pressed his mouth down to meet hers.

His kiss was hungry and possessive, nibbling at her lower lip, daring her to resist. Adele had no intention of resisting. Her need was as great as his. Her arms slid around him, rubbing up and down his back, pulling him as close to her as she was to him.

Adele's lips parted at his urging. His tongue tasted her soft sweetness as she seemed to draw it further into her mouth. He could feel his desire hardening until he was sure she could feel it through her skirts. Their breathing quickened, as if they were sharing the very air between them.

She broke from his mouth, pressing her cheek against his chest. She could hear the strong pounding of his heart; so strong it sounded like it was threatening to burst right through. Brian rested his chin on the top of her head. His right hand reached up to stroke her cheek, the smooth leather of the thimble adding additional sensation. Brian moved his hand from Adele's face, stroking down her neck and across her collarbone and drifting down to cup her breast through her clothing. Adele felt her nipple hardening beneath his touch and wondered if he could feel it, too. She was wishing she could feel his hand directly on her pulsating skin as he began to work at the buttons at the back of her bodice, grazing the skin at her back as he uncovered it.

"Is everything all right in there?" said Susannah, appearing in the doorway from the bedroom.

The jolt of the interruption caused Adele to push at Brian's chest with both hands as her face flushed bright red. Brian let her go and stared at her disappointed as she moved away.

"Yes," he said thickly through his teeth, "everything is fine, Susannah."

"I'll be in in a minute," Adele added.

Susannah turned back into the bedroom. Neither Adele nor Brian saw the calculating smile on her face. It would not take much.

The next day, Brian built and installed a door for the bedroom.

THE DAY AFTER was Twelfth Night.

Susannah woke up early to bake. Brian went out to cut some pine boughs to scent the house. Adele cleaned up the house and dragged down the box of decorations that had been carefully preserved since their mother was alive. The little crystal bells and angels had survived the trip from Baltimore to Wyoming. Adele even found the quarto of Shakespeare's *Twelfth Night* in the box she hadn't remembered they still had. She smiled, thinking Brian would have something else to read now. She wrapped the book in a scrap of calico and tied it with a piece of string.

By sundown the house was rich with the smells of pine and fresh bread and cookies. The crystal ornaments were hung from the boughs or placed on the table and a crackling fire burned brightly. A young rooster was sacrificed as an alternative to the rabbit and venison that were their usual fare. Stuffed with bread, onions and dried apples, it had made a succulent meal, leaving everyone satisfied.

After dinner, the three pulled chairs around the fireplace to exchange gifts.

Adele gave Susannah a pencil box for her art supplies that she had bought for her sister in town the previous summer and hidden. For Brian she gave him the book and another parcel.

He opened up the parcel to find two brand-new shirts. One was unbleached muslin; the other was made of Turkey red unprinted cotton.

"Weren't you saving that red for a new quilt top?" Susannah inquired.

Adele shrugged. "I can get more fabric in the spring." To Brian she added, "I thought you might like shirts that were made just for you."

Brian pulled off the motley blue shirt he was wearing and slipped the red one over his head. It fit perfectly across his shoulders with room to move and was long enough in the sleeves and length. He didn't tuck it in, but knew once tucked in, it would stay down. "It's perfect, Adele, thank you." He reached over and gave her a quick kiss on the cheek.

Now it was Brian's turn to give. He handed Adele a parcel wrapped in an old newspaper. She opened it up to reveal a delicately carved box with leather hinges.

"Did you carve this? It's exquisite."

"Open it."

Adele did so. Inside the box were a dozen wooden hairpins, each one small and delicate. With a gasp of delight, she reached for her braid and wrapped it into a chignon at the nape of her neck, anchoring it with her new gift. "I feel like an adult again."

"I never doubted it for a minute. Now, for Susannah's present we have to go to the barn."

"The barn?" the women responded in unison.

Brian had already risen and pulled on the shearling jacket. The women grabbed their shawls and followed him out to the barn.

Lighting a lantern inside the barn, Brian went into a stall and led out the saddled Esmeralda. The mare was wearing the sidesaddle, but it had been altered. Near the top of the saddle two holes about a foot apart had been drilled by hand. Through the holes began a rope ladder with wooden rungs that rolled down to about a foot off the ground. The location of the horn and stirrup had not been affected.

"Try it, Susannah. If it works, I will teach you to ride starting tomorrow."

With a squeal of delight, Susannah stepped onto the first rung and, with the same comparative ease with which she got into the haymow she climbed the ladder until she could put her sound left foot in the stirrup and hook her deformed right foot over the horn. Brian showed her a string with a ring end that she could use to pull up the ladder so it wouldn't bang against Esmeralda's legs when riding. The contraption could also be removed for when Adele used the saddle.

"Oh, Sissy, I'll be able to ride like regular people now." She reached out for Brian, who helped her to dismount by putting his arms around her waist and lowering her to the ground. She threw her arms around him. "Oh, Brian, it's the best present I ever had!"

Brian looked over Susannah's head at Adele. He felt his face flushing as Susannah hugged him. His feelings for her were warm, but definitely brotherly.

"I'm glad I could make your life a little easier."

"Isn't he just the best, Sissy?" Susannah released Brian and faced her sister.

"Yes, Susannah, the very best." Adele's eyes met Brian's.

"Oh, gosh, the coffee," Susannah cried out. "See you back inside the house," she called behind her as she left the barn.

Brian quickly unsaddled Esmeralda as Susannah went back to the house. Adele hung back, watching the smooth, strong movements of his large body.

Tears forming in her eyes, she said, "You've made my sister very happy tonight. I would never have thought of what you tried."

Brian gathered Adele in his arms. "You've been mother, father and sister to her for too many years. If I can help it, I want to give you a chance to have something for yourself; something more than a few hairpins and some stolen kisses."

Adele began shivering. Her tears fell unrelentingly, wetting the sheepskin jacket.

"Are you cold?"

"A bit. Oh, Brian, the best thing that ever happened in my life was finding you. I wish we didn't have to go back inside."

"I know, but it wouldn't do to freeze to death in the barn."

With his arm about her waist, Brian walked Adele back to the house.

Susannah was quickly busy cleaning up, saying nothing about whether she was giving any gifts or not. She began to sing some Christmas carols in her reedy voice. Adele joined in with her more controlled alto, Brian in a steady baritone. There was much embarrassed laughter since none of them was a particularly good singer, nor did they remember all the words.

Finally, when there appeared to be nothing else to do or say, Susannah and Adele went into the bedroom and shut the new door. Illuminated only by the moonlight streaming in the window, they dressed for bed and climbed in.

In the main room, Brian also put on his nightshirt and dragged himself into bed. His senses were too alive to sleep, and he shifted in the bed trying vainly to find a comfortable position. He tried to use counting tricks to get to sleep, but all he could envision was Adele's face and sense the feel of her soft skin the one time they had made love that afternoon in the barn. He knew if it hadn't been so cold they might be in the barn right now making love. He wanted her and he knew from her words that she wanted him, too. He sighed in frustration and continued to toss and turn.

Back in the bedroom, Adele was having similar trouble. She hugged a pillow in her arms and turned left and right, stretching and shifting. As she lay on her back, she dredged up memories of Brian's lips on her and the thought made her breasts ache with longing. Not content to lie still, she continued to shift about, until she felt a small fist punch her on the arm.

"What was that for?" she asked Susannah angrily.

"I want to get some sleep," Susannah grumbled.

"I'm sorry. I'm doing my best."

"It's not enough. I'm not going to put up with it anymore."

"What do you propose we do instead?"

Without responding, Susannah rolled out of bed. She opened the bedroom door and walked into the main room and over to the bed. Adele followed her and stood in the doorway.

Grabbing Brian's shoulder, Susannah shook him and said, "Brian, are you awake?"

"Yes, Susannah, I'm awake."

"Then get out of my bed."

Brian was instantly alert.

"What do you mean, *your* bed?" he asked.

"This is my bed. I've been a good sport to let you sleep in it all these weeks, but I want my bed back. So get out."

Brian hauled himself out of the bed. Towering over Susannah, he snapped, "So, where am I supposed to sleep?"

Pointing to the doorway, Susannah replied, "Where you want to be sleeping, in there."

"Susannah!" gasped Adele.

"Well, Brian, don't you want to sleep with her?"

"Do you know what you're saying?" he responded in shock.

"Of course I do. I'm not a child, Brian. Sissy, don't you want to sleep with him?"

Adele stared at Brian. He returned her gaze, filled with a longing they could no longer deny.

"Yes! More than anything," Adele admitted quietly without taking her eyes from the face of the man she had come to love so completely.

"Brian?"

"Yes, more than anything," he concurred.

"Well then, go on. I'm finally going to get some sleep. Oh, by the way, I hope you like my gift. I didn't know how to wrap it," she finished with a giggle before pulling the quilt over her head.

Brian laughed, a deep, lush belly laugh and he bounded toward the bedroom, grabbing Adele and spinning her around in his arms; then shutting the door behind them. He picked Adele up and carried her the short distance to the bed, setting her on her feet.

With one move he pulled his nightshirt off and with the second pulled her nightgown over her head. "I'll never voluntarily wear one of these damned things again—and with any luck, neither will you."

He pushed her onto the bed with the momentum of his body and began to rain kisses on Adele's face and neck. He grabbed for her braid and unraveled it, brushing the softness of her hair over his face, breathing in her woman's scent, mixed with rose soap and pine smoke.

He was like a starving man suddenly thrust into a banquet, trying to touch with his hands what his lips could not reach sometimes stopping and just gazing at her as if afraid to continue to gorge himself for fear that he would be guided back out the door and into the famine. His movements were almost frenzied, his rapidly growing hardness testament to the force of his desire. There would be no gentle teasing, no sweet words, this time. Any measure of control had been stripped from him from the frustration and hunger of the last few days. She was for him to devour, feasting on the sheer femaleness she offered. Had he twenty fingers instead of only nine he could not have touched her enough this night.

Her hunger matched his. Her searching hands feathered over his body, ruffling the thick black pelt on his chest, sliding over the soft-hard skin of his back to cup his buttocks. She left a trail of little bites on his lips, his ears, neck, shoulders and chest as if to make a meal of him. She felt his hand at her apex; she was already wet with arousal. His slightest touch on her skin had done it.

When he pushed her back against the mattress and parted her thighs, she opened more than willingly, demanding, "Take me, take me, please." His response was a groan as he thrust himself into her as a dagger into its sheath. Again and again he thrust home as she cried, "Yes...Yes...More...More." Her nails dug into his back, leaving crescent-shaped indentations. Her words melted into screams as her senses rose like a skyrocket and sent her soaring. When she climaxed, it was as if her belly and breasts exploded over and over again. His own release followed closely, again and again until he collapsed, drained and breathless, a dead weight on her chest.

She barely felt his weight, only his warmth. It was as if they had melted into each other and had in that moment ceased to be two people, but had instead become one entity. She wrapped her arms around his ribcage and within minutes they were both asleep, still joined within her.

THE PALE GRAY January dawn poked its fingers of filtered light in through the bedroom window as a light snow began to fall blanketing the ground with a pristine, ultimate whiteness. The first shafts of light caused Adele to stir languidly. Her nose felt ticklish and she absently brushed at it, her eyes still closed. Her first impression was that Little Gent had curled up beside her, but she soon became aware of a strong arm wrapped around her, the feel of bare flesh warming hers.

Unconsciously, during the night, Brian had rolled off and out of her and lay next to her, gathering her to his side, protected within the circle of his arm and body, his fingers woven through her hair. The quilt covered them both, adding to the warmth and closeness.

Adele cuddled closer to him, moving her leg across his, feeling the roughness of the hair that covered them. She raised her hand and began to teasingly stroke her hands through the hair on his chest, seeking out his flat, copper paps, which she caressed in circular patterns, surprised to see that his nipples hardened with stimulation as hers did. As she played, she felt a promising change in the muscle beneath her, as he began to harden. She moved slightly to replace her hands with her mouth and began to tease the flat nipples with her teeth, suckling on him as he had done to her in the barn.

Brian slowly woke to her ministrations, and his free hand drifted up to stroke her jaw, his callused palm gentle, as teasing as a feather. As his hand drifted near her mouth, she kissed it lightly.

"Good morning," said Brian.

"Yes, it is; a very good morning," was the cheerful reply.

"You know, if you keep playing with me like this, I'm going to end up making love to you when we should both be getting out of bed."

She drifted her hand down and wrapped it gently around his stiffening shaft. "Is that a promise?"

With a groan, Brian pressed Adele onto her back and joined her lips with his. His untrimmed mustache tickled the sensitive skin of her face. She responded with gentle nips at his lower lip and teasing touches with her tongue. His own tongue savored the sweetness of her mouth, then trailed a path down to one bare breast where with mouth, teeth and tongue, he suckled and teased her nipple into proud arousal.

A growing warmth spread from the point of contact through Adele's body. She drifted her hands up his back and neck, lacing her fingers in his coal black hair, feeling its silky softness. Brian's hair had not been cut in the seven weeks since he'd come to them, and curled around her fingers. She mused on the contrast between the soft curliness and her own reed-straight, heavy hair, but not for long.

Brian began to kiss and lave a path down her ribcage, pausing at her navel, where he thrust his tongue home. Adele's stomach shuddered instinctively and she giggled at the sensations.

Brian stopped and looked up. "Are you laughing?"

"Yes, I am. It tickles."

"Are you having fun?"

"Yes, I'm having fun, you silly."

"You've just begun to have fun, my love. Close your eyes and just feel."

Adele complied. Brian kissed her taut belly, drifting down, nuzzling and tickling until he nuzzled his nose in the tangle of sable curls which guarded her pleasure center.

Adele gasped. "Brian!" she gasped as she realized what he was doing. "That can't be proper."

"Close your eyes," he ordered. "Stop thinking about being so damned respectable for once."

His fingers separated the dark curls and began to stroke her sensitive bud. Her desire washed onto his fingers as lightning shot up through her torso, causing her to curl her toes, grit her teeth and grasp the bed sheet with tense fingers. Replacing his fingers, she felt his tongue address the bud, stroking and kissing. The most intense sensations rose from her core, neither pleasure nor pain but both concurrently into a pleasure beyond description, spilling out onto him. Her hips instinctively thrust upward to meet his ministrations and he cupped his hands on her buttocks to raise her hips closer to his mouth.

She exploded in sensation, waves rippling through her as when a stone hits the water. She shuddered, not from cold, but from pleasure so intense that tears sprang to her closed eyes and she cried from the overwhelming emotion of it.

Brian lowered her hips to the bed and re-instituted himself along her body, kissing her deeply.

"Can you taste us?" he asked.

"Um-Hmm," she hummed. "We taste good together."

"Sweeter than wine."

"I wouldn't know. I've never had wine."

"Are you ready, sweeting?"

"Oh, yes, my darling."

He drove his shaft home into her warm damp tightness. He began to move gently, but quickened as his climax neared. She wrapped her long legs around his as if to use them to deepen his thrust within her. He came, depositing his essence deep inside her and then relaxed beside her in the bed.

For long minutes he merely held her, fighting the languor that threatened to put him back to sleep. Adele cuddled against him as if they had been lovers for years.

Reluctantly, Brian began to stir. "As much as I would love to stay here all day with you, I know we have chores to do."

"It never ends," sighed Adele, sitting upright.

Brian kissed her lightly. "I doubt I ever slept so well."

"I know it for a fact." She kissed him back. "I could do this every night."

"I might just be willing to accommodate you."

No winter morning had ever seemed so bright before.

AFTER MORNING chores were completed, Brian and Adele set out on the long-postponed trip to the place where she had found him.

"I doubt we'll find anything after seven weeks," she commented.

"I know, but I'll never be satisfied until I've looked."

They both dressed as warmly as they were able, Adele wearing her quilted petticoat under her skirts and her woolen cloak over her dress, Brian in the shearling. Adele checked and loaded the rifle, showing Brian how to do it. Like everything else she'd showed him, he learned it the first time.

In the barn, Brian saddled Esmeralda with Tom Stoddard's western saddle and Adele tied on the rifle scabbard.

"I guess we'll find out whether Esmeralda can carry us riding double," she said.

He mounted, then handed Adele up so that she sat across his lap behind the saddle horn, her cloak gathered around her.

She felt him start to get hard. "Exercise a little self-control!" she grunted at him.

"Sorry," he replied with a chuckle, "after last night and this morning I guess it has a mind of its own. Your little sister gives a hell of a Christmas present."

Adele giggled slightly and kissed Brian lightly on the cheek. "That's a down payment for later."

They set off towards the range. They were out about an hour when Adele identified the site.

"Are you sure?" Brian asked.

"Not really," she responded, looking around, "but everything around looks to be about the right place."

They dismounted and began to search in widening circles, looking for something that might be familiar to Brian, something that might jog his memory or serve to identify him. Periodically, one or the other of them would brush snow away, hoping to find a paper or any other item.

Jack and Rafe had done their job well. They had ridden away with everything, including Brian's real identity.

The cold was starting to cut through their clothing when Adele gasped, "Oh, my!"

"What is it?" Brian rushed to where she was.

"You don't want to see."

"If it's mine, I do."

Brian reached Adele to see her squatting near the ground. He looked over to where her gaze directed him.

On the ground, black with rot and rough with gnaw marks, a little bit of bone visible, was something that looked for all the world like it could have once been a human finger.

Adele looked at Brian. His eyes were closed; his right hand balled into a fist.

She touched his stricken face. "I'm so sorry, my darling."

Brian laughed bitterly.

"What do you want to do, Brian? Should we pick it up and take it back to bury?"

"No, leave it. It's not a part of me anymore. Brian Strange was born with nine fingers and burying this one isn't going to change things."

"Let's go back home, my love."

Brian sighed. "It is home, isn't it? For you and me both. The only home I have."

He mounted Esmeralda. She mounted in front of him. For a long time they rode in silence.

Finally, Adele spoke. "Who would do such a vicious thing?"

"The kind of man who would strip a man and leave him to freeze to death. I wonder if the ring I was wearing was worth it."

"Do you think he'll get away with it?"

"I certainly can't identify him. I don't even remember being attacked. If he took anything readily identifiable as mine, maybe a relative—if I have any—will press charges if he tries to hock it."

"It doesn't seem fair."

"Look on the bright side. If I don't get ambushed, I don't get rescued by you, and then where would I be?"

"In the bosom of your family, I suppose."

Brian snaked his arms around Adele, holding her close. "This is the only family bosom I want to be in, my love."

Chapter 7

IN THE CITY by the Bay the morning dawned decidedly foggy and gray. For the rest of San Francisco, the overcast was likely to burn off by late morning, but for Stephen Carroll the closeness of the fog matched his gray mood as well as the sky itself echoed his tired eyes. It was barely eleven and he had been in the office since seven, trying to handle both the business and legal affairs of Carroll Enterprises.

Right now he was standing at the open window of his office, in the Carroll Enterprises headquarters on the Embarcadero, gazing out across the bay toward Sausalito, although its outline was barely visible through the fog. His hand was wrapped around a half-empty cup of coffee. Stephen would have sold his soul if he and Blair could be boys tromping the wilderness, speaking of everything and nothing, of classes and teachers and girls and whether there was going to be a war and about the time the Rafferty boys substituted starch for soap on the Chinese laundryman and ended up wearing stiff under drawers for two weeks.

With a brief knock at the door and permission granted, Lester Conlin of the Pinkerton Detective Agency entered. Stephen moved away from the window and sat in a slatted wooden swivel chair behind his desk, directing Conlin to sit in a client chair opposite him.

Conlin wore a khaki duster over a brown business suit. There was nothing particularly notable about the man. His hair was a nondescript brown, his eyes an undistinguished blue, his features regular. Had Stephen ever been asked to describe the man sitting opposite him, he would have had to use the word *ordinary*. For a detective, looking ordinary was probably the difference between life and death.

Stephen turned to Detective Conlin. "Have you anything new to report?"

Mr. Conlin regarded the man opposite him before opening his notebook. Stephen Carroll was dressed in a conservative style that bespoke elegance and business in the same glance. It was clear to the detective that Mr. Carroll did not buy his suits ready-made. He opened his notebook and glanced down at the writing. "We have made contacts in every state and territory between here and Milwaukee. Your brother's ring turned up in a pawn shop in Cheyenne, Wyoming Territory, on November 25th of last year; his watch and chain in a mercantile in Fort Collins, Colorado Territory, on December 13th. I know those items have been retrieved and returned to you. Both of those cities are over 200 miles east of Rock Springs, where your brother was last definitely identified. Even focusing on Wyoming and northern Colorado we haven't found any other identifiable effects or anyone who saw him after he disappeared off the train on November 10th. Your brother himself did not sell either the watch or the ring. This would mean that either he lost them or was robbed. Was Mr. Carroll a gambler?"

"He played an occasional game of poker, but he was always disciplined enough to stop after a few hours. Even if he lost all his money playing cards, he could still have wired here collect."

Conlin's eyes narrowed. "Could there be any reason he wouldn't want to be found?"

Stephen started. "Such as?"

"Have you discovered any irregularities in the books?"

Indignantly, Stephen responded, "Carroll Enterprises is not a publicly held corporation. Blair, my father and I each have equal interests. For Blair to steal from the company would be to steal from himself. It's out of the question."

The detective took that in dispassionately. "Then the only remaining possibilities are either he met with an accident on the road and was found or he met with foul play. If your brother was robbed, it's likely the robbers killed him and left his body out on the range. If it was an accident, whoever might have found his body merely robbed it of any valuables. If nobody found the body and buried it, I would guess animals got it."

Stephen felt intense pain in the vicinity of his heart. He did not want to believe that Blair was lying in some grave in the wilderness or had been left like carrion to rot on the plains.

"Any description of who sold the watch and ring to those shops?" he asked Conlin.

"No, both merchants described the man or men as of average height, average weight, no distinguishing features, but then these types are known to pay bottom dollar and not ask too many questions, nor to have long memories."

Stephen ground his teeth in frustration. "So whoever robbed him is going to get away with it."

"Well," said Conlin, "if anything else readily identifiable as your brother's turns up, it might give us something to go by."

"All of his luggage except one valise arrived in San Francisco when the rail line was reopened. Other than a small amount of cash, a letter of credit only he could use and his watch and ring, Blair wouldn't have been carrying anything of intrinsic value except his clothing. I'm not even sure whether he used a wallet or a money clip."

"Did he have a gun you could identify?"

"Mr. Conlin, what possible use would my brother have for a gun? He's a San Francisco shipping magnate. He didn't even serve in the War. I doubt he's ever even fired a gun. Have your people checked at nearby towns or farms?"

"Most of the roads are pretty impassable this time of year. Some of those farmers don't see strangers from October to March. We'll send operatives back to Wyoming and Colorado once spring comes. If Mr. Carroll is alive, he should be safe enough if he's at one of those farms. It's possible he's snowed in and unable to get a message out."

Stephen agreed. He had to. It was the only hope he had left. "I understand. When it's your brother, you don't want to think of him as lying dead on some lonely prairie a thousand miles from home. Go ahead and send your interim bill to our office, to the attention of Owen Winslow. And let me know if anything breaks."

Conlin made a polite closing remark and left the office, closing the door behind him.

Stephen put his elbows on the desk and buried his face in his hands. Two months and no word from Blair.

Stephen never asked to be a businessman. He'd never even wanted to be the company's attorney. In law school he'd served as a clerk in a legal clinic for indigents. With Blair gone, Stephen's dreams would die.

Stephen did not want to believe Blair was dead.

But then, where was he?

ADELE KNEW she was in love with Brian, even if she had not told him so. She knew Brian had no place to go and was unlikely to set out in the dead of winter, but she did not want to burden him with a declaration when she was not sure it was returned. She was also afraid that when spring arrived, he might just leave.

Brian knew he was in love with Adele, but he had not said the words to her either. How could he confess his love to a woman when he did not know who he was? How could Adele accept in her life a man with no past? Besides, Brian was not certain Adele returned his affection. He did not want to make her uncomfortable with his continued presence when he knew she would not ask him to leave the Stoddard property until the safety of spring.

As spring approached, the farm work became more demanding. The melting of snow meant it was time to hone the plow and uncrate the seed and repair the harnesses. Some nights Brian and Adele were so exhausted that they fell into bed, asleep before they hit the mattress. Other nights they would massage each other's sore muscles until they were languorous and drowsy. Very often, the contact of the massages led to lovemaking.

Their lovemaking had developed into a comfortable, sensuous habit. It was rare for one of them to pass the other within an arm's length without a touch, a caress, a kiss, either quick or lingering. Brian continued to quilt, bending over the frame opposite his lover, but, unlike the first time, when he would reach for her hand she would not pull away. Their knees would make contact, or their hands on each other's thighs or they would play with each other's toes. Adele, who had been plying a needle since she was five years old, was sure that this was the slowest, but most enjoyable way to make a quilt. Unfortunately, she joked, they would never get the silly thing done because the playing usually ended them up in bed, where they would revel in the constant discovery of each other's bodies and in experimenting with new ways to arouse each other.

Brian is right, Adele would think to herself, *this is fun.*

Brian kept his promise to Susannah and taught her to ride using the altered saddle. After her chores in the house were done, Susannah would ride out for short rides as she became used to horseback riding.

Finally, March arrived. For the first time since Tom Stoddard had taken sick, Adele had someone to help with the backbreaking task of plowing the fields. She and Brian loaded the freshly-honed plow, seed and compost into the rickety wagon and, hitching the jenny, hauled it out to the fields.

Hitching the jenny to the plow the first time every spring was always a challenge because the beast would grow accustomed to the winter's inactivity. More than once the mule tried to kick out, but Adele knew her old tricks and got her bridled.

At Adele's instruction, Brian pulled the plow bridle across his back, also narrowly avoiding a well-placed kick from the mule. He left off his shirt to save wear and tear. Commanding with the reins, he urged the mule forward as the plow cut deeply into the still muddy earth. Large puddles from melted snow caked mud on the plow, requiring occasional halts to clean the blades with feed bags and a hoe.

Adele followed along behind the plow, spreading seed into the furrows from a load in her apron and covering them with dirt using her shoe as she followed along.

She watched Brian's back as his muscles worked beneath his skin, which was becoming bronzed, even from the cool spring sun. A sheen of perspiration coated his torso and separated his lengthening hair into damp curls against the nape of his neck.

Day after day this backbreaking work continued, punctuated only with respites devoted to shoveling compost on the previously planted seed. Brian painfully discovered new muscles previously ignored. His respect for his slender lover deepened with the knowledge that for nearly three years she had undertaken this dreadful but necessary task single-handedly. Days later he was still aching deep in the muscles of his back, stomach, arms and legs, while she was nearly pain-free. Never before had her healing fingers on his shoulders and back been more welcome. More often than not he fell asleep right after dinner and slept like a log until morning. But even if his need to be inside her was diminished by exhaustion, his pleasure at finding her cuddled up against him in the morning more than made up for it.

Even without his memory, Brian knew he was working harder than he had ever worked in his life. He could not imagine that whatever kind of job his forgotten self had performed could have made him feel more alive than this manual labor did. He barely noticed the development of strong, defined muscles and bronzed skin that, with his now shaggy mustache and longish black hair, made him almost unrecognizable from the man who had awakened with no past.

While occasionally he made sarcastic remarks whose source he could not identify, in general Brian Strange was a lighthearted man who treated life as if it had begun on the day he gained consciousness.

Brian made the decision not to dwell on his memory loss, but to deal with his past if and when it returned to him. His world was bounded by Stoddard land and Adele's love and yet he was serene and content, with one small exception.

He chose the day the planting was finished to deal with that.

Having finished the last furrows, Brian and Adele stooped over the plow, removing the last of the mud, when Brian suddenly threw a clod of mud at Adele. The mud splattered on her old calico dress and

Adele looked up to see Brian grinning with mischief.

Not to be bested, she grabbed a clod of her own and threw it at him. It spattered on his nose.

Soon they were having a mud battle royal, running to a nearby mud puddle and splashing the murky soup at each other until they were both soaking wet and brown from head to foot and shaking with laughter like a couple of children. Plopped near the side of the mud puddle they clung to each other panting with mirth and lack of wind and trying to scrape the mud off each other's faces. Before long Adele was lying on her back on the muddy ground with Brian lying next to her, groping a muddy hand under her skirts and sliding up her calves and then her thighs. Her pantalets were made without a crotch seam for convenience and she felt him try to slip his fingers into the opening.

Then, abruptly, Brian stood up and began to walk away.

Right on his heels, Adele crawled upright and followed him.

"What's the matter?" she asked, amazed at his sudden withdrawal. They had never started to make love before that they had not finished.

"It's not enough," Brian replied cryptically.

"I don't understand."

"Us being lovers."

"But I like making love with you. It's wonderful, Brian. It's more than I ever dreamed was possible."

"I don't want to be your lover anymore," Brian said as he continued to walk in the direction of the house.

Adele felt as if something inside her had died. "Why?" she questioned as she followed him, voice thick with emotion.

"I want to be your husband."

Adele stopped dead in her tracks. "Are you asking me to marry you?"

Brian turned to face her. "I suppose it's an awkward way of proposing."

Adele stood facing him, arms akimbo. "Why on earth would you want to marry me?"

"Why? Because I love you and I want to spend the rest of my life with you."

Adele felt her breath stop. "You love me?" she choked out.

"Yes, my darling, practical Adele. I love you."

Adele ran into his arms, tears in her eyes that had nothing to do with the mud. "Oh, Brian, I do love you."

For a long time they embraced, Adele cradled in the shelter of

Brian's arms. She could feel his warm breath ruffling loose strands of her hair; feel the pounding of his heart against her chest; smell the strong, masculine scent as she pressed her face against the hollow of his neck.

She paused, a serious cloud passing over her face. "How do you know you aren't already married?"

Without pausing, Brian responded, "I think I would know such a thing. I don't think I'm married. I don't feel like I've ever been married. When I first came here, I caught myself saying some pretty unflattering things about women. Besides, Brian Strange is most certainly not married since he's only five months old."

Adele chewed on that for a minute. "I'll marry you on one condition; that you wear a wedding ring and never take it off."

A shadow crossed Brian's face and his mouth compressed. "I don't know if I want to do that." He held up his right hand. "Seems I already lost a finger over a ring I must have been wearing. Is it that important to you?"

Adele's hand flew to cover her mouth. "Oh, Brian, I wasn't thinking. It's just that you're so handsome I don't want any women to get any ideas they can steal you from me. And, if your memory ever comes back, I want you to remember my love for you."

"As if I ever could forget my sweet Adele," Brian intoned solemnly. "I'll think about the ring. You know, I didn't do this right, did I?" Brian dropped down to one knee and took her hands in his. "Adele Stoddard, will you marry me?"

"I would be honored to be your wife...Brian...."

"Yes, sweeting?"

"You've got your knee in a mud puddle."

THEY DECIDED to marry in May. Adele had been saving fifteen yards of bleached muslin "for a rainy day" that would turn out to be saved for a sunny day instead. She made herself a wedding dress, full-skirted, modestly cut bodice trimmed in self-fabric ruffles from shoulders to waist in rows of V's. Ruffles also trimmed the ends of the long sleeves. The back buttoned with little buttons Brian carved from a venison bone.

She used the rest of the muslin to make Brian a new shirt especially to be worn on that day. If one can express love with a needle, Adele put every ounce of her love into that shirt, wishing deep in her heart it could be of fine linen instead of cheap muslin. The scraps she fashioned into roses that Susannah helped her dye with a wild berry infusion until they were a pale pink. She would wear them in her hair instead of a veil.

She attacked her father's black broadcloth Sunday suit, cutting down the jacket to make a vest and using the sleeves to lengthen the pants. She could not really hide the seams at the bottom of the pants, but since they were of the same fabric the extensions were far less visible unless one looked closely.

There was special emotion in making over the suit. It was the last of her father's clothes. Everything else had already been made over or pieced together for the taller, broader-shouldered Brian. She remembered arguing at the time of her father's death that it was foolish to destroy a perfectly good suit by burying Tom Stoddard in it. Fortunately, she had prevailed over the undertaker who settled for an overpriced shroud.

During plowing, the axle of the old wagon finally cracked from twenty years of wear and weather. This repair was well beyond the skills of anyone on the Stoddard farm. They got the plow back to the barn, but it was apparent that the wagon would not carry three adults a few yards, much less the twenty miles to Green River.

Attempts to saddle the jenny were fruitless. The old mule bucked and battled any attempts to put a saddle on her.

Susannah volunteered to stay home.

Adele protested, "But it's my wedding day. How can I get married without you? You're my sister."

"How can you get married without the bride and groom? Put Pa's saddle on Esmeralda; Brian can straddle and you can ride in front of him across his lap. Esmeralda can handle the two of you."

"The only other solution," Brian offered, "is to hold off the wedding until we can get someone out here to repair the wagon."

Adele looked ready to make that decision, but Susannah stopped her.

"It's okay, Sissy. I'll make the best dinner you ever ate. I'm sixteen. Lots of girls are already married at my age. Surely I'm capable of spending the day at home alone."

Brian put his arm around Susannah's shoulder and gave her a squeeze. "I'll miss having you with us, little matchmaker." Adele felt such a flood of love for this man that tears of joy filled her eyes. How lucky she was to have Brian Strange in her life!

Early the next morning, Brian and Adele set off. Although not the most graceful means of transportation, having Adele sitting across his lap as he guided Esmeralda was certainly the most sensual journey Brian reckoned he would ever take. Dressed in their new clothes, Adele felt almost like a princess.

Because they were riding double, it took four hours to reach Green River, arriving at nearly eleven. Adele only went to town a few times a year since the town had expanded with the building of the railroad. As they approached the mercantile, Adele was greeted by one of the most familiar faces in town, Mr. Duneagan, the factor.

"Good morning to you, Miss Stoddard," the bandy-legged Irishman greeted in his Limerick brogue. "And to you, sir."

"Mr. Duneagan, I'd like you to meet my fiancé, Brian Strange."

Mr. Duneagan reached up his hand to shake Brian's. Brian was immediately self-conscious of his missing finger. No one except the Stoddard sisters had seen him and until now, he had nearly forgotten its lack, but the factor didn't seem to pay it much mind. It was clear that the man had never seen Brian before.

"Well, Miss Stoddard, it's pleased I am to see you're going to have a man around again to run that place."

Adele stiffened. "I've done my best."

Brian interrupted, "Adele still runs the place. I'm just the brawn of the outfit."

"Excuse me; 'twas an unfortunate slip of the tongue. Last year I marveled at the crop there was to buy, considering this little lady put it in virtually single-handed. Her father was a tireless worker until his last illness, and there are just some things a woman isn't physically strong enough to do. It had nothing to do with brains or heart. Miss Stoddard has both of those in spades."

"In that I agree," Brian observed.

"You'd better be prepared to pay a good price this fall, because this year's crop will be even better," Adele bragged.

Mr. Duneagan assessed the large, handsome man. He seemed to be a good catch. He had known Adele for years and could not remember seeing her look this pretty in a long time. Being in love certainly agreed with her. "You know," he said, "if you were ever to decide that you wanted to sell or lease that farm of yours I could find you a buyer on the spot."

Brian responded, "Actually, I'm beginning to like being a farmer."

"Mr. Duneagan, I really don't know anyone else in town that well. I'd be pleased if you and maybe your wife would stand as witnesses for our wedding. We figure to get to the justice of the peace about one-thirty, get married and head on back home."

"Sure, and I'd be pleased to see you get hitched to this handsome specimen. One-thirty it is."

They entered the mercantile. Before shopping for anything else, Brian and Adele asked to see the ring tray. They saw gold wedding bands suitable for both of them, but the prices seemed high.

Brian had decided that he would wear a wedding ring. Chances were that the amputation of his finger was a freak occurrence that would not happen again. Besides, Adele had asked him to do so. Loving Adele was worth the risk wearing a wedding ring might carry.

"Adele, why don't you get the rest of the things on the list while I go to the livery and find out what it will cost to repair the wagon axle."

Brian left, having received directions to the livery, which was next to the smithy. The estimate on the new axle disappointed him. He looked at the money in his pocket, virtually all of the money the Stoddards had in the world, and realized they could have a new axle or wedding rings, but not both, not this year.

Brian looked down at his hands. Brown and callused from hard, backbreaking work, a far cry from the smooth white "city" hands that had newly gripped an ax handle barely six months before. Yet all the work and change hadn't put an extra penny in the coffer, nor could he repair a wagon and keep a promise to his beloved. If anything, his being there had been a drain on the budget rather than a help.

Once outside the livery, Brian kicked the dirt in frustration and let fly a curse to his bad luck. In the flying dirt, he dislodged an object. He stooped down to examine it. It was a bent horseshoe nail, doubtless dragged out of the smithy by the treading of feet and hooves. Brian held it in the palm of one hand, pushing it around with the other. It poked off his palm, the ends falling between his fingers while the bend balanced on one finger.

Quickly, Brian measured the nail against his ring finger, and with a feeling of triumph strode into the smithy, hope replacing the former disappointment.

Meanwhile, Adele bought canned and dried goods, flour and sugar, a couple of extra large union suits, new lengths of green and red fabric to replace the quilt calico she had made into shirts, along with some more muslin and ten yards of blue cambric, packets of needles and—with a grin—the largest brass thimble in the mercantile. She also added new pencils and drawing paper for Susannah and a couple of dime novels for her book-hungry man. She was making arrangements for delivery when Brian came back into the mercantile. He reached into his pocket to pay the shop owner.

"What about the rings?" asked Adele.

"We can't fix the axle and have gold wedding rings. I'm sorry, my darling, but you tell me which is more important."

"The axle. Wedding rings will just have to wait."

"Perhaps next year we can afford gold rings." He pulled her close to him, pressing her head to his chest. "I'm sorry. Will you marry me anyway?"

"Try and stop me."

When they got to the justice of the peace, the clock at the depot had just reached one thirty. Mr. and Mrs. Duneagan were waiting and the judge, who had to hurry because he had afternoon court to call into session, rushed quickly and emotionlessly through the ceremony.

"Do you declare yourselves before these witnesses to be husband and wife?"

"I do," they answered in unison.

"Then by the power invested in me by the territorial government of Wyoming, I now pronounce you man and wife...That's it, folks, in the middle of a trial, got to get back into session." A moment later he walked from his office into the small courtroom.

Mrs. Duneagan observed, "I'm so sorry, my dear. I didn't even have time to work up a good cry."

Her husband put in, "Grace, you needn't cry for the wedding to be a good one. Well, you're good and married now. You, my boyo, be good to this lady, she's had more than her share of managing alone."

"I will, sir. Thank you for standing up with us. We'll see you in the fall, if not sooner. Come on, Adele, we're done here. Let's get something to eat and head on home."

Taking Adele by the arm, he guided her outside. The May afternoon was sunny and mildly warm. They had reached the dining room of the hotel when Adele started weeping.

Brian held her closely, stroking her hair as she cried.

Through her tears, she gasped, "I never thought I...would ever get married, but I always hoped that...if I ever did...I always thought...that my wedding day would be beautiful...Not slapdash...and so short...Like he didn't care."

Brian guided her to a chair at a table and knelt on one knee before her. "He didn't have to care. I care." He reached into his pocket and pulled out a paper-wrapped object. He opened her right hand and dropped it there.

"What's this?"

"Open it."

Adele did. In the paper were two horseshoe nails, forged and welded into circlets. Brian picked up the smaller of the two and slid it onto her left ring finger.

"With this ring, I thee wed. Now and forever, till death do we part. Now you."

Adele stared at her left hand, then picked the other circlet and pushed it onto his left ring finger.

"With this...ring, I thee wed. Now and forever, till death us do part."

"Never forget that I love you," he added, pressing a gentle kiss on her lips before he rose and sat opposite her at the table.

"I never will."

Chapter 8

San Francisco

IT WAS A sunny day in Green River, but in Stephen Carroll's San Francisco, even a sunny day seemed overcast.

Blair was still missing. It had been six months now and the Pinkertons had so far found no trace of him.

The latest report lay on Stephen's desk. The station master in Rock Springs vaguely remembered telling a few people that there was westbound service at Green River, and even more vaguely remembered that a man meeting Blair Carroll's description was one he told. The livery stable owner remembered renting the horse, but reported that it returned twenty-four hours after being taken out, riderless, with nothing attached to the saddle.

An investigator had gone to Green River, but no one recognized anyone looking like Blair. Between Rock Springs and Green River were hundreds of square miles of isolated farms. Some were deserted when the investigators called, their inhabitants away. Others yielded no clues. The report indicated that repeat attempts would be made later on where there was evidence that the owners were merely away and that further reports would follow.

There was also a letter from Blair's fiancée, Julia Longridge, breaking their engagement. It had come with the return of her engagement ring. Stephen didn't want to think of what other gifts she *had* kept.

Stephen was reaching to file the report with the earlier ones when a knock came on his door. Given consent, the door opened and Carroll Enterprises' General Manager, Owen Winslow, came in.

Winslow had been second in charge under Oscar Carroll and had remained so under Blair. The land-loving son of a New Bedford whaling man, he knew ships and shipping, but preferred to send them rather than sail them. Stephen always thought Winslow looked like Ichabod Crane, tall, skinny, angular and bespectacled, but was glad to have the dour old Yankee on board. The young lawyer knew for certain that Winslow's advice and expertise were keeping the company afloat in this crisis—a lot more than Stephen's one year in practice were anyway.

"Mr. Winslow?"

"Mr. Carroll, are you occupied this moment?"

Stephen remembered when Winslow called him by his first name; then the first six months, before Blair disappeared, it became "Mr. Stephen," to differentiate between the two Mr. Carrolls. Without ever asking him to, Winslow began to refer to Stephen by his last name, conferring on Stephen a respect and authority he needed to hold the reins of the company. Stephen knew his hold on the reins was with white knuckles—how had Blair done this at sixteen while at twenty-five Stephen was scared to death?

"Nothing that can't wait ten minutes," was Stephen's reply. "Please ask Todd to get us some coffee."

Winslow looked at the report in Stephen's hand. "Any news of Mr. Blair?"

"None. But no bad news."

"His absence is deeply felt, Mr. Carroll. This company is his more than it was ever the senior Mr. Carroll's, if I may be so candid."

"Certainly more his than it will ever be mine."

Winslow left, leaving the door ajar.

Owen Winslow returned a few moments later, carrying a battered coffee pot. He refilled Stephen's cup. Usually Todd Mason, the young clerk, would perform this function, but Winslow sensed that Stephen would need to talk.

"There was a messenger from Miss Longridge this morning?"

"She finally got tired of waiting for Blair. She's marrying Gerald Rafferty. I'm sure she'll make Rafferty very unhappy, almost as unhappy as I'm sure she would have made Blair. If it were anyone else, I would feel sorry for the man. If she sucks Rafferty dry, it will only be good for Carroll Enterprises. That's cruel of me, I know. Like something Blair might say."

"Mr. Carroll, I've observed that some men would rather be unhappy with a beautiful but stupid girl than happy with a smart but plain one."

"I've noticed that, too. What I wouldn't give to meet someone smart and pretty...even smart and not so pretty... Well, I've got time... Actually right now I don't have time... God, I don't know what I'm saying anymore!" Stephen buried his face in his hands and began to laugh.

Winslow chuckled indulgently. Then, seriously, he said, "Mr.

Carroll, I've known you nearly your entire life. Under the circumstances, I feel obliged to ask you your true feelings in this matter. Do you think your brother is still alive?"

Stephen looked up and was quiet for a moment. A shadow passed over his face. "Mr. Winslow, somehow I think if he were dead I would know it. Right now I have to believe he's alive. I can't see myself holding onto this company for myself, nor for my father's benefit. If I thought Blair was dead I'd sell out to one of the other shipping lines and just hang out my shingle. I'm not cut out to be a shipping magnate. I'm a lawyer. It's what I love most in the world. In trying to do both I'm not doing justice to either."

"If you must know, Mr. Stephen, you are doing a creditable job in Mr. Blair's absence...."

"With your able assistance, but I'm not Blair. I leave here every day numb to the bone. It's a good thing I'm not a drinking man or I'd probably be drinking myself into oblivion every night...."

"Has anything happened about Mr. Blair's son?"

Stephen nodded. "Until Blair is here to tell me differently, I decided to let Joshua stay with his mother as long as she's able to take care of him. Her attorney writes she only has a few months left, a year at most. I'm sending money to support them both, and I'll leave my nephew in a secure home in Milwaukee where he can visit her until she dies. After that, we'll see."

Stephen pulled his watch out of his vest pocket. "I'm going for a walk and get some lunch while I still have some brain left. I'll meet with you at say, two o'clock?"

Winslow rose as Stephen did. "Excellent, Mr. Carroll. Two o'clock."

FUNNY HOW THE ride home seemed to take Brian and Adele less time than the going there. The late afternoon's lengthening shadows cast a soft light on the range, giving everything a fairy glow. Or was it the magic of two lovers, united in life, traveling the familiar path truly together?

They turned onto the final path and the weathered barn and the house beyond it became visible in the growing darkness. They embraced in the barn and again on the porch, clinging closely to one another, communicating although neither had said a word for hours.

For the first time in her life, Susannah felt invisible. Adele and Brian were operating in a small world that today had only room for two.

They picked at dinner, not conversing, but periodically touching each other's faces as if to assure themselves the day had been real.

Fortunately, the girl felt secure enough to know she was not being slighted and jealousy never entered her mind. She had known Adele and Brian would not be able to spend their wedding night truly alone, such as in a hotel, and so had created an aloneness of their own.

On entering the bedroom, Adele gasped and said, "Look, Brian." With a wide smile, Adele ran her hand over the top of the bed. "While we were in town, Susannah put my Wedding Ring quilt on our bed."

Brian looked at the white quilt with its pattern of interlocking rings of colored wedges. "So?"

"Every girl is supposed to make a Wedding Ring quilt to use on her marriage bed. I never thought I would ever be able to use mine." She glanced up at him. "Then I met you and my whole life changed."

"I love you, Adele."

"I love you, Brian."

That night they made love gently, almost silently. Their consummation was marked only by the changes of breathing and the sense of touch. Each had become so familiar with the other's body that no words needed be spoken, they instinctively knew what would flood the senses, spill the warmth. As Brian's manly hardness slid securely into Adele's answering softness, there was first ease, followed by the more rapid thrusting as he reached the point of no return to be met by Adele's shuddering fulfillment as he emptied his essence into her welcoming vessel. They took their cries of pleasure into each other's waiting mouths, jealously guarding their passions to their exclusive keeping.

What followed was a warm, safe slumber, Adele wrapped in the circle of Brian's right arm and side, her hair streaming long over the pillows and quilt and Brian's arm.

As morning broke, Brian slowly opened his eyes, still holding Adele to him. As he looked to the end of the bed, he saw Susannah sitting on a chair, sketching them as they slept. His eyes opened wider and Susannah gave him a mischievous look. Brian nodded and grinned knowingly like a man secure with his love. Susannah finished the sketch and removed the chair long before Adele ever opened her eyes.

Later, Adele saw the portrait; she didn't know whether to laugh or scream. In it, she lay on her left side, covered to just below the shoulders with the quilt, her cheek and right hand resting on Brian's chest, his thick mat of chest hair curling about her fingers. Brian's right arm was wrapped around her on top of the quilt, his mutilated hand realistically drawn. His left arm was draped behind his head and he looked out with a knowing expression, love, desire and contentment mirrored in his handsome features. Susannah had written at the bottom of the vellum, "Wedding Morning—Susannah—May 1874."

Brian would later make a frame for the sketch and it would be Adele's most prized possession.

SPRING GAVE way to summer. They say marriage changes a couple, even if they have been lovers before. So it was with the Stranges. If it was possible they became closer, more physical with each other, less inhibited by their closeness.

Besides maintenance of the crop, Brian set himself to replacing shelves and cupboards with better-made ones now that the weather was warm enough to spend time outside. His carpentry skill was steadily improving. Considering he was starting from scratch, it was remarkable indeed.

It was early August when Adele located Brian finishing a new bureau for their bedroom. He was stripped to the waist and Adele marveled at his bronzed, masculine beauty; at the play of the muscles beneath his work- and heat-dampened skin. She said a quick prayer of thanksgiving to God for putting this handsome, diligent and gentle man in her life. Her heart was so full of love for him that Adele feared it might explode someday. She slid her arms around his bare shoulders and kissed him lightly on the neck. She loved the way he smelled. She inhaled deeply against his skin.

"What's prompted this?" Brian asked.

"Just that I love you."

He turned around to hold her. "I know that. It's my anchor. If I ever thought you didn't, I think I'd shrivel up and blow away. My universe revolves around you, my sweet rock. Whatever strength I have I've received from you."

For a long moment they stood, leaning into each other's embrace. Adele heard the steady beat of Brian's heart deep in his now powerful chest. If she was his rock, he was most certainly hers. She knew that to lose him would be her death—if not of her body then, at least, her soul. But she had news, and so pulled away.

She pointed to the bureau. "What's that?"

"It's a new bureau to hold our clothes so we don't need to use that trunk anymore. It's probably the last thing I'm going to be able to finish before we start harvest."

Adele lightly ran her fingers along the plain, smooth surfaces. The bureau was plain, but well made.

"You're getting so good at this, one would think you were a carpenter in your former life."

"Not with those city hands you were so fond of pointing out to me." He took her hands in his. "My hands aren't so soft and pretty now."

"That's true, but they're hands a man can be proud of. They're the hands of a man who can take care of his family. They're the hands of the man I love, and I wouldn't trade them for all the city hands I could ever hope to hold. Actually, I came out here because there is something I'd like you to make that we're going to need soon."

"What did you have in mind?"

"Well...I was thinking in terms of a cradle."

"Of cours...Did you say a cradle?"

"Um-hmmm."

"A baby?"

"Um-hmmm."

"You and me?"

Adele looked towards the heavens. "No, you and some other girl."

Brian screamed with joy. He picked Adele up under her arms and swung her around.

"When?" he asked.

"My best guess—Spring—March probably—with any luck *before* planting."

"How do you feel?"

Adele grinned. "I couldn't feel better if I tried. I'm so glad you're pleased with the news."

"Pleased! Pleased doesn't begin to describe it. My God, Adele, nine months ago I had nothing, not even a name. Now I have everything a man could want. A home, a loving wife and now a family. I'm probably the happiest man alive."

"Do you worry much about your memory?" she asked cautiously.

"Sometimes I have flashes like lightning illuminating scenes I feel I should know. I see a room with dark walls and a large desk. And sometimes a bedroom with bulky furniture. Everything is dark and oppressively massive. I also see images of a view of a large city. I'm on a hill overlooking the city and there's a large sea or bay."

"Do you recognize the city?"

"I don't think so. Nothing comes to mind."

"Do you ever see any people? Anyone familiar?"

"I see a man who looks a lot like me, but younger and clean-shaven, and very well dressed—a gentleman. I don't know whether the image is myself as a younger man or a relative of mine. If I dwell on it, I will go mad. My world is here. If my memory never comes back, I am well content to stay here with you and your sister and our babies."

"Babies?"

"Well, don't we plan to have more than one?"

"Please, one at a time." Adele laughed. "And if your memory does come back...."

"We'll have to cross that bridge when we come to it."

THE HARVEST was good. Mr. Duneagan gave them an excellent price and the reapers carted away a summer's worth of labor. The Stranges and Susannah rode into town on their repaired wagon to stock up on supplies for winter.

While they were in town, a Pinkerton investigator stopped by. Finding nobody home, he waited about an hour, but when no one returned, he finally made himself a mental note to return the next day and moved on. Returning to Green River, he found a wire waiting for him calling him to Salt Lake City immediately. In his haste to catch the train the investigator neglected to mark down that he'd found nobody at the Stoddard farm and it would need to be revisited. He did not leave a calling card. His experience was that most people clammed up when they thought they were being investigated by the Pinkertons and refused to give any information. The Stranges never discovered that they had been visited.

They had bought some lovely things: soft flannel for baby clothes, drawing paper and pencils for Susannah. Adele thought so as she put them in the kitchen cupboard and the new bureau. She glanced out the window toward the barn.

Thunder, the gray stallion Brian had just bought for himself, was resisting being led into the barn. Esmeralda, still in harness, was trying to sidle away. Adele felt a frisson of fear at the sight.

Dropping what she was doing, Adele hurried to the barn where Brian was just shutting the stall door behind Thunder.

"Brian, I'm afraid of that horse."

"He's not for you to ride, then. We can't spend our whole lives riding double on Esmeralda."

"I know that. But he seems badly trained. Why else do you think he was such a bargain?"

"Just new surroundings. He'll get over it."

Exasperated, Adele commented, "Well, at least geld him. It might calm him down."

"Oh, is that the solution? Cut off his balls?"

"If it quiets him, it's worth it."

"Maybe you should try it with me, too."

"It probably wouldn't calm *you* down!"

"When did you become such a bitch all of a sudden?"

"Me—a bitch?" she screamed. "When did you become such a damned idiot?"

"You're always trying to run things."

"It's my farm."

"You never let me forget it. You know everything, don't you?"

"No, but I reckon I still know more than you do about farms and livestock. You forget I've been doing it all my life."

"Yeah, and I'm just a stranger you took in out of pity. Maybe you should have made me the hired hand instead of some kind of breeding stud."

"Oooohh!" she bit off. "I don't have to stand here and listen to this anymore!" She stormed off into the house.

That night Adele slept on one extreme edge of the bed and Brian on the other. Or at least they tried to sleep. As midnight approached, Brian turned over in bed and whispered, "I was thoughtless."

"I was foolish," came the dismal reply.

"I'll take care of the horse."

"It's just that I worry. I love you so much, I would hate to lose you because of a nervous horse."

Brian reached for her. He turned her onto her back. He brushed his hands on her tender breasts, hefting their weight gently. Languorously he drew his hands down to her belly, just beginning to round with promise. He kissed her belly, his shoulder-length hair and shaggy mustache brushing on her tautening skin. She moaned her arousal, parting her legs slightly to welcome the ministrations of his hands.

"There's only one good thing about fighting," he observed. "Making peace afterwards."

AUTUMN FOLLOWED summer with winter on its heels. Brian

completed the cradle, carving a rising sun on the headpiece to symbolize the new beginning this baby would mean to their lives. Adele sewed baby clothes. Susannah continued to draw every spare moment, her pencils capturing the changes in season and people.

Adele glowed with inner fire. Her abdomen rounded and grew, her breasts were swollen and tender. The babe quickened within her, and it was not uncommon for Brian to spend nights in bed with her, his ear to her belly listening to the activity within. He never allowed Adele to feel fat, ugly or clumsy with her pregnancy and as a result she appeared even more beautiful than when he fell in love with her.

As winter moved into spring, Adele grew larger and more ungainly. The night rails and dressing gown she had abandoned when she and Brian became lovers were all she could comfortably wear. Her back ached and her feet swelled until sometimes she couldn't fit her shoes. She felt like a prisoner in the house and the confinement put her temper on edge and caused her to cry often.

Fortunately, Brian's response was to stay close, touching her and caressing her with kisses and soft words of love. Holding her as she cried in complete confusion at the mood swings, he told her over and over again how beautiful she was, how much he loved her and how much he was looking forward to the coming baby.

Making love finally became out of the question, but at nights they slept, like two spoons in a drawer, Brian's chest at Adele's back, his arms around her. He knew he had never loved her so much as he did now.

MARCH 1875 arrived with warmer weather. Adele was standing on the porch, in her nightgown and stocking feet, wrapped in a quilt, when her labor began.

Soaking wet and shivering from her broken water, she called for help. Brian and Susannah ran in from the barn, where they were getting the tools ready for planting. Susannah was helping for the first time, trying to ignore the pain the heavy lifting and stooping shot through her lame leg.

Brian reached Adele as her knees gave out on her and she slumped to the porch floor, hanging onto the porch rail. He scooped her up in his arms and carried her inside to their bed.

"Lie still," he cautioned, "I'll ride into Green River and get a doctor."

"No!" she cried, real terror in her voice as pain ripped through her, "If I'm going to die I want you to be here with me."

Brian held her close and crooned, "Sweeting, you're not going to die. I won't let you. But we have to get the doctor."

"I can go," volunteered Susannah, "I know the way and I can ride well enough. Besides, Esmeralda can travel faster because I'm smaller."

Brian looked at his sister-in-law. She looked both brave and frightened. She was seventeen now and becoming a real woman. If the right man could see beyond her handicap and appreciate her artistic nature, innate cleverness and genuine heart, she would have no trouble finding a mate, even isolated as she had been.

He turned to Adele, who was breathing heavily and covered in a fine sheen of perspiration. "Darling, I have to go saddle Esmeralda so Susannah can get the doctor."

They turned to leave.

"Susannah, go to Dr. Hogue," Adele said. "He's the doctor who took care of Pa. You know where his surgery is?"

"I can ask at the mercantile."

"Brian, lend her your coat. She probably won't get back till after dark and it's still so cold at night. Susannah, put on your quilted petticoat."

Brian nodded his agreement as he left the house. Susannah took her petticoat out of the armoire and pulled it on under her skirts, then followed him. After Susannah left, Adele pulled herself heavily out of bed and pulled her father's nightshirt out of Brian's drawer in the new bureau. She smiled, thinking of the last time Brian had worn it, knowing its shorter length would be more convenient when her final labor began. She laid her sodden nightgown and dressing gown over a chair and pulled the nightshirt over her head.

She went into the old trunk and pulled out the oldest quilts, ones already ragged whose further destruction would not matter. She stripped the bed of sheets and quilts and laid one old quilt on the tick and two others on it to cover herself. Using her toes since she could not bend over, she nudged the woolen socks she wore off her feet, preferring the secure feel of her bare feet on the wooden floor. She then opened the bottom drawer of the bureau and removed the baby items she had made, small quilt and flannel coverings, and made up the cradle.

Those completed to her satisfaction, she sat on the bed for a moment as another surge of unimaginable pain ripped through her and her body again became damp with sweat. Adele again rose and lumbered into the main room. She filled the large kettle with water from the inside pump and set it to boil on the still lit stove. She pulled out some string and scissors from a nearby cupboard and the sharpest knife from the block and a large mixing bowl and laid them on the table. She took clean towels from the sideboard and laid them on the table next to the other items. She leaned against the table and closed her eyes, trying to remember if there was any other item that had been needed that horrible day eight years ago when her mother had delivered a stillborn boy and died herself not a few hours later. Terror mixed with another pain tore through her and her knees were weakening as Brian returned from the barn to catch her just in time.

"What are you doing out of bed?" he shouted.

"I...couldn't lie...still. Things to do...needed things...in case the doctor doesn't get here in time...I need to walk now...."

Brian slid his arm around her beneath hers, bracing her as they walked in slow circuits of the room. Periodically a labor pain would jar her and only Brian's strength would keep her upright. At some point Adele declared herself hungry and insisted that she and Brian eat some cold bread and meat and drink some tea. For the first time since coming to the farm, Brian felt the sudden urge for a hard drink as his calm exterior barely concealed his own terror at not knowing what to do.

After they ate, Adele expressed desire to return to bed. Brian tried to carry her but she insisted on walking. Another pain, closer to the previous one than before, hit her as she sat on the bed. She lay back and covered herself with the old quilts.

"Have you ever seen a baby born?" Brian asked uncertainly.

"More or less," came the cryptic reply.

"Is what's happening to you normal?"

"I don't know...the only birthing I ever saw killed my mother."

Brian held her. "Oh, my darling. I won't let it happen to you. I need you too much."

"Then, you must be very clean...Boil the knife and scissors...put on a freshly-laundered old shirt...Wash your hands in the hottest water you can stand with lye soap...and keep Little Gent out of here."

Brian knew it was going to be hours before Susannah returned with the doctor. It would be a miracle if the doctor arrived before the baby. He knew for certain that whatever he had been before coming to Wyoming, a doctor was not it. Sheer terror rippled through his gut. It would be a long day and evening for both of them.

Afternoon turned inexorably into dusk. Adele's pains were more frequent. Brian lit the lanterns, rewashed his hands and sponged his wife's face with cool water. Adele was no longer feeling so brave and capable as her labor intensified. Memories of her mother's nightmare last labor haunted her.

"Brian, if I die...and I have a girl...can you name her after my mother...her name was Beatrice. I killed her, you know. I didn't mean to...I was only sixteen...I'd never seen a birthing. There was so much blood. Oh, God, Brian, I don't want to die."

Brian gently sponged off her face, crooning, "You're not going to die. I won't let you leave me. But Beatrice is a good strong name. I like it."

As darkness fell, Adele went into heavy labor. Brian removed the quilts and lifted the nightshirt as she began to push. He helped her part her legs and pull her knees up to aid her efforts. Adele screamed mindlessly and terribly as each push racked through her. Then, miracle of miracles, Brian saw a patch of wet black hair as the baby's head began to emerge.

"I see it!" he yelled. "Keep pushing."

In a matter of minutes, the baby emerged, sliding right into her father's waiting arms, covered in blood and fluid. She was red and slippery—and completely beautiful.

"It's a girl, Adele, now what do I do?"

"Hold her...by the legs...and slap her...bottom so she...cries."

Before Brian could slap their daughter, a lusty, protesting cry pierced the air as Beatrice Strange heralded her arrival into the world.

On Adele's halting instructions, Brian tied the umbilicus tightly with string and cut the cord with the knife. He cleaned his daughter with warm water as Adele expelled the afterbirth.

"Here's your mommy, sweeting," he crooned, placing Beatrice on Adele's chest, snug between her breasts.

Brian was removing the afterbirth and cleaning Adele's legs with warm water when Susannah and Dr. Hogue burst through the door.

He leaned heavily against the bedroom doorsill and announced, "You're a little too late, Doc."

"Adele?" gasped Susannah.

"Has just given you a fine little niece, Aunt Susannah. And mommy is just fine."

Dr. Hogue went into the bedroom to check on mother and baby. He emerged again, nodding.

"You've done well, son. You've got a fine daughter there. You may want to put the linens back on the bed before your wife sleeps too deeply." Gesturing to Brian to come out of Susannah's earshot, he whispered, "I don't want the girl to hear these things yet. Your wife's milk will probably come in a few hours. Also, I would suggest you restrain yourself in your passions for a few weeks. She's bound to be sore for a while."

"Of course. Doctor, how long must Adele stay in bed?"

"Oh, she can get out in a day or two. Other than, um, privately, she'll probably feel fit as a fiddle by the end of a week."

Dr. Hogue accepted some cold dinner and his fee, although he reduced it seeing as how he had arrived only in time to check out the finished results and left in his carriage for the return home, refusing to stay the night even though Susannah offered her own bed and volunteered to sleep in the barn.

When the doctor left, Susannah and Brian carried Adele and Beatrice into the main room and set them down on Susannah's bed long enough to remake the other bed. Susannah helped Adele to put on a clean nightgown and then Brian carried her back to bed.

When Brian came in to go to bed a couple of hours later, Adele had unbuttoned her nightgown and was holding Beatrice to her full breast, where the infant was greedily suckling her first meal of life. Brian sat down on the edge of the bed and reached to touch the soft black hair, marveling at the miracle before him. The baby, momentarily stopped and opened unfocused eyes in her father's direction before rooting around for the nipple again.

"Are her eyes blue?" he asked tentatively.

"I think her eyes will turn gray, like her daddy's. Brian, isn't she beautiful?"

"She's a close second to her mother, my love."

Adele's brows knitted together, "Brian, now that I've had a baby, you won't stop sleeping with me, will you?"

Brian looked surprised. "Of course not. The doctor says for me not to come inside you until you're ready, but I don't think I could sleep if I didn't have you in my arms to wake up to."

Adele leaned back contented and soon her chest was rising softly with the gentle breathing of sleep. Brian lifted Beatrice from Adele and gently holding her in his arms like the fragile wonder she was, carried her to the cradle and covered her with the little quilt. He then undressed and slid into bed beside the woman who had given him his life and then combined with him to make another, even more miraculous one.

Chapter 9

TEN DAYS AFTER Beatrice was born, they put the cradle in the back of the wagon and began spring planting. Adele worked as tirelessly this spring as she had the previous one, halting only when Bea cried to be nursed.

The baby fascinated Brian. He marveled that he could have had any part in creating so miraculous a thing as a child, yet his participation could scarcely be denied. Beatrice had none of Adele's features. She was a miniature of her father.

Unaware that in the outside world fathers paid very little attention to their young children, Brian participated in every part of Bea's care he could. As often as Adele did, he would dress and bathe his daughter, comforting her when she cried, holding her. He could not get over the sweet scent of her; all powdery and milky.

Susannah, too, was doting on her infant niece, whose eyes were indeed turning a soft, velvet gray. She found herself drawing sketches of the baby's every mood and move.

Spring passed into summer and into autumn, marked by the usual hard work and the rapid growth of the baby. Brian and Adele began to make love again around the time of their first anniversary. It was the best anniversary present either of them could think of. They had never stopped sharing a bed, but being able to have Brian buried deep inside her again felt to Adele like she was coming home. To Brian, loving Adele was as natural as breathing. He could not get enough of touching her, tasting her, feeling her contract about him in their shared pleasure. Adele's figure quickly returned to normal with the labor of planting. Life was as good as it could possibly be.

Except Susannah was not happy.

As she approached her eighteenth birthday, Susannah began to become restless. She had long ago reached her full height of five foot four and had developed into a voluptuous young woman.

For the first time that autumn she openly flirted with the reapers who had come to help them with the harvest. Brian found himself admonishing his sister-in-law to show more discretion with the rovers. He was well aware that Susannah was a very attractive young woman and could easily get into trouble.

Also, for the first time Susannah complained that she wished they could go into Green River more often so she could "meet people." She began to resent her club foot since she knew she could never dance. She began to argue more with Adele and Brian and chafe at being treated like a child. It was her misperception, however. Brian's attempts to protect her reputation were never to treat her like a child, but to keep her safe from harm.

Susannah's sketches began to take on a stark quality fitting her moodiness, so much so that Adele even commented, "Susannah, I'm truly sorry the farm is so far from town. I wish there was something I could do."

"Oh, Sissy, it's just that I will never be as lucky as you—to have the man of my dreams drop into my life like a sack of potatoes."

"You never know."

"Besides, who would want a crippled wife?"

"I used to think no one would want a five-foot ten inch woman. I was wrong. Look, we'll try to give you opportunities to get into town more often. You can make the shopping trips instead of me and check on the dates of church socials and such. Winter is coming, but once spring comes again we'll make a point of it."

THE WINTER OF 1875 was a mild one. The snow level was lower than usual.

One morning, Brian and Adele sat over a cup of tea while Susannah had gone to the barn to milk the cow.

Brian began, "Susannah's turning eighteen December eighth. That's just two weeks away. I was thinking that maybe for this birthday I would get her a box of watercolors, but I forgot to buy it the last time I was in town. I was also thinking of taking her into town with us for a real restaurant meal in her honor and maybe spend the night in the hotel so we don't have to rush through eating to get back before dark."

"That sounds like a wonderful treat. Only thing is, Bea's been fighting a cold on and off for a week. If she comes down with it full blown, I'm not going to want to travel for four hours in the wagon in the middle of winter."

Brian hummed thoughtfully.

"Maybe this is the time we pay back for the wedding trip. I could take Susannah and spend the day, just the two of us. We could ride instead of going by wagon but not spend the night."

"That might work. Or you could spend the night and while you're having luncheon, you could drop Thunder off at the vet and finally have him gelded."

"You still don't like that horse, do you?"

"He still scares me. I never know what he'll do."

SUSANNAH LOVED the idea of luncheon in Green River. "Just think what people will say when they see me on the arm of my handsome brother-in-law." Wanting to surprise her, Brian didn't tell her about the watercolors.

Beatrice did come down with that threatened cold, however, by the seventh of December she was well and it was Adele who was still sniffling.

The morning of December eighth was cold, crisp and clear, with no hint of snow. Susannah put on her new gown, a birthday gift from Adele. Made of sprigged muslin, this gown had been copied from a fashion magazine and even included a bustle on the narrower skirt. It was quite the most fashionable garment either woman had ever owned and Susannah felt very grown up in it. She pulled her heavy woolen cloak about her as she mounted on her saddle ladder to adjust herself in the sidesaddle.

Brian wore his wedding clothes—black broadcloth vest and pants and muslin shirt. It was the first time he had occasion to dress quite that finely since the wedding. He pulled on the shearling jacket and the worn felt hat.

Before he headed out to the barn, he walked into the bedroom. Adele, wearing a nightgown and wrapper because of her waning head cold, was nursing the nine-month-old Beatrice. Brian mussed the soft black curls on his daughter's scalp and pressed a kiss on top of her head. He pulled both wife and daughter into the shelter of his arms.

"I wish you were coming with us," he murmured.

"I do, too," Adele sniffed, "but it's not a good idea. This cold's on its last legs. I don't want to chance it getting started all over again."

"You know, Susannah and I don't have to stay over."

"It'll be far too cold to come home tonight. I'm a big girl; I'll be okay alone for one night."

"I was just thinking, this will be the first time I haven't slept in your bed in almost two years."

"I know. But it's just for one night."

"I won't sleep," he warned. "I'm too used to you."

Adele kissed him quickly on the mouth. "And I you."

Brian stood. "While I'm in town, I may just check out the gold wedding bands I've been promising. How would you like that for Christmas?"

Adele looked at her horseshoe nail ring. "Actually, I've gotten so used to this ring, I think I'd feel strange wearing anything else."

Brian grinned mischievously, "If you want to 'feel Strange,' I could come back to bed right now."

Adele laughed and kissed him on the cheek, "Go on with you before you tempt me further. And take good care of my little sister."

Brian took off his hat and swept her a gallant bow. "As you wish, my lady." He turned to leave.

"Brian...."

"Yes, my beloved."

"Never forget that I love you."

Brian's smile faded. "I never will." And he left the bedroom.

He walked over to the sideboard and opened the small cashbox. He took a large portion of the money, thinking to have enough for luncheon, the paintbox and the hotel rooms if he and Susannah actually stayed the night, and to pay the vet. He shoved the cash in his pocket, yanked on his leather gloves and exited the house.

He walked out to the barn and mounted Thunder and he and Susannah galloped off toward Green River.

IT WAS NEARLY eleven, too early for luncheon, when Susannah and Brian arrived in Green River, so they headed directly for the mercantile. Hitching Esmeralda and Thunder to the outside hitching rail, they entered the store.

Brian took Susannah by the arm and led her to the art supplies. "How would you like to begin to work in watercolors?"

Susannah's eyes rounded. "Really? I'd love to. I'd be a real artist."

"You already are a real artist. I just think it's time you had a more extensive palette. Take a look and see if there's a watercolor set that suits your fancy."

She threw her arms around Brian and kissed his cheek as she thanked him profusely for such a special birthday present.

There were a couple of watercolor sets. Susannah looked hungrily at them both. It would be hard to decide but it was so wonderful to even contemplate. Brian grinned as he watched her carefully examine the features of each one while she tried to made her decision.

Meanwhile, outside the mercantile, a couple of schoolboys were teasing a smaller boy with a snake they had found, pushing it into his face and threatening him until he screamed, and laughing at his terror. Their little victim screamed and ran, crashing right into Thunder's rear flank.

With a whinny of fright, Thunder began to buck and pull at his bridle, panicking and snorting. Through the plate glass window, Brian saw the commotion and—forgetting Susannah—rushed outside to try to gain control of his skittish stallion.

He grabbed at the taut bridle and tried to pull Thunder's head down. The big horse lurched his head with a force that pulled the hitching rail off its supports, knocking into Brian's back and dropping him to his hands and knees. In the excitement, Esmeralda's reins came loose when the rail came down and she was galloping down the street and out of town before anyone thought to stop her.

As Brian tried to right himself, Thunder bucked again, then reared. With all the force he possessed, his front hooves rose in the air and a iron-shod hoof cold-cocked Brian just as Susannah came out of the mercantile to see what was going on. Susannah screamed as Brian crumpled to the dirt.

The sheriff and his deputy heard the commotion from their office next door to the mercantile and rushed out. They saw the frenzied, bucking stallion and the bleeding, unconscious man too close to his deadly hooves. Without a second thought, the sheriff drew his revolver and rushed toward the stallion, dropping him with a single shot to the brain. Thunder fell dead, his last jerk catching Brian in the head again.

Susannah was still screaming; she had dropped to her knees and had her head buried in her skirts. The sheriff barely noticed her. He motioned to his deputy and a couple of bystanders to help him. They turned Brian over and saw blood seeping from a laceration on his forehead, not far from the site of a previous forehead scar. The area was already turning purple and Brian was out cold.

"Come on, Charlie, Dennis; we've got to get this man to a doctor."

Charlie, Dennis and two other men picked up the tall farmer. One of them said, "Doc Hogue's office is in the next street. This way."

Susannah heard the familiar name and tried to rise to follow. The sheriff halted her.

"Do you know the man, miss?"

"Yes...he's my...brother-in-law, Brian Strange."

"You're not from Green River, are you?"

"Our farm is about twenty miles east of here."

Susannah rose to follow, but her clubfoot slowed her. She limped after the men in the direction of Doctor Hogue's office. They were already out of sight with their burden by the time she stood up to follow.

The men brought their prostrate charge to Doctor Hogue's surgery door only to find it locked. A sign on the door said, *Gone to Cheyenne. Returning January 5th.*

"What're we going to do with this guy?" griped Dennis.

Charlie answered, "What about that new doctor? Travis, I think his name is. His office is near the depot."

"Hope he's there."

They carried Brian over toward the depot to Doctor Travis's office and were out of sight by the time Susannah managed to hobble over to Doctor Hogue's office and read the sign. She locked up and down the street, completely baffled as to which way to go now.

Meanwhile, the reluctant Samaritans located Dr. Travis' office. The door was unlocked, so they brought Brian in and laid him down on a cot in the surgery. There was a sign on Dr. Travis' door reading, *Out to Lunch; Returning 1:00 P.M.*

Dennis was annoyed. "I got stuff to do. I ain't stayin' around. The doc can figure it out when he gets back." The other men agreed. Leaving the unconscious man on the too-short cot, they went their separate ways.

CONSCIOUSNESS, like a dark fog barely lifting, crept into his brain about fifteen minutes after the men abandoned him. In the darkened surgery, a befuddled lurch shook his body. As if warding off a blow, he came awake with a start.

His first thought was that he didn't know where he was or how he got there. His head ached, the left temple throbbing and his vision cloudy. He glanced around the room and recognized it as a surgery. He surmised that someone must have found him and brought him here, but upon calling out he discovered that the place was deserted.

Pulling himself off the cot, he walked to the half glass front door of the surgery. His first sight was of the depot.

"Must get home," he mumbled and exited the surgery.

He walked unsteadily to the train station. The box office was open and a steaming passenger train stood on the track.

He approached the ticket window.

"Where to?" the clerk asked.

"San Francisco," he responded.

"Train behind you's leaving for Salt Lake City in fifteen minutes. You can transfer through to Frisco from there." The clerk quoted a price. The man searched through his pockets until he found some bills and coin and paid the clerk for a ticket.

"Oh, and it's *San Francisco,* mister. We San Franciscans don't care much for *Frisco,* " he declared as if by rote.

"Yes, sir. You'd better hurry if you want to catch that train. With good weather and clear track, you should be in Fris—San Francisco by the twelfth."

With a nod, he walked away. He boarded the train and leaned back in a seat and drifted off to sleep. He didn't even feel the lurch of the train as it pulled out of Green River and headed on its journey.

ADELE HEARD the sound of horse's hooves far sooner than she expected. She ran onto the porch to see a lathered and riderless Esmeralda, her sides heaving painfully. Putting Bea in her cradle, she ran over to the mare.

Adele saw the dragging reins and immediately became frightened. Did Susannah get thrown? Was she all right? Then she realized, Susannah was with Brian. Even if she got thrown, Brian could ride her home double on Thunder. She led the exhausted mare into the barn, unsaddled and wiped her down and led her to the water trough. She watched carefully to make sure that Esmeralda didn't drink too fast so she would not get a cramp.

For hours she paced the floor in the cabin, sometimes with Bea in her arms, the rest with her arms wrapped around herself. As the time passed she became more and more worried.

As night fell, Adele was surprised to hear the sound of a carriage coming up the path. She rushed outside to see Mr. Duneagan's carriage pulling up with the factor and a pale and shaking Susannah inside.

"What's happened? Where's Brian?"

Susannah burst into tears. "I don't know," she sobbed.

"*What do you mean, you don't know?*"

Through her sobs, Susannah told her as much of the story as she knew, which dead-ended at Dr. Hogue's locked surgery door. "I couldn't locate hide nor hair of him."

"Mr. Duneagan, is there another doctor in Green River?"

"Yes, there's Doctor Travis, but I took your sister to his office and he told us he hadn't had a patient brought in until three that afternoon."

"Did you check with the sheriff, Susannah?"

"Yes, his deputy says...he was one of the men...says they brought Brian to Doctor Travis's office...That was about eleven thirty, but Dr. Travis didn't see Brian, so he must have come to and...left before the doctor got back at one o'clock. Oh, Sissy, what are we going to do?"

Adele, acting calmer than she really was, replied, "We'll just have to find him, that's all. Right at daybreak we'll go back to Green River and take some of your sketches of Brian and walk around town near the doctor's office and see if anyone saw him. My God, he's six feet four. He doesn't exact blend in with a crowd."

Mr. Duneagan rose to leave. "If I can be of assistance to you, you have only to ask. Now I really must be going, it's a long cold ride back to town."

As Adele closed the door behind Mr. Duneagan, she struck a fist against the front door. "That goddamned horse!" she swore. "It's a good thing the sheriff shot him or I'd've done it myself." Susannah could not remember ever hearing Adele swear before. She said nothing because she realized Adele was even more frightened than she was.

The next morning, they hitched up the jenny to the wagon and, with Susannah holding Beatrice, rode into town. They carried a couple of Susannah's most recent pencil sketches of Brian and started combing in concentric circles from Dr. Travis's office. For most of the morning they were unsuccessful, until Adele walked up to the ticket window at the depot and showed the agent the sketch.

He looked at it closely. "Tall man," he asked, "black hair?"

"Very tall, very black."

"Yeah, I remember him. Bought a one way ticket to San Francisco on the twelve fifteen."

"Are you sure?"

"Yeah, I won't forget. He chewed me out for calling it *Frisco.*"

"When does the next train leave here for San Francisco?"

"Next train to Salt Lake City leaves in two days. Transfer there for the westbound. The baby rides free." He quoted her a price for the fare.

Adele passed on the information to Susannah. They rode back to Mr. Duneagan's office and told him about their dilemma.

"Based on what the ticket agent quoted me as a price, Brian would have had to have had almost all our money to pay cash like that. I'm not sure I have enough money left to get to San Francisco and survive while

I look for him."

"This assuming San Francisco was his final destination," observed Mr. Duneagan.

"Well that's a new starting place to look. Mr. Duneagan, you've told me on more than one occasion that if I ever wanted to sell or lease my place, you could help me. We—that is, Susannah and I—own the farm free and clear. The title was clear before I married Brian. I could try to take out a mortgage, but I'm going to need someone to watch the place."

"I don't know if our local banker would give you a mortgage without Brian's signature, even if you swear he has no ownership interest in the property. The farm may have become half his when you married. And Susannah is a minor."

Adele closed her eyes in pain and bit down on her lower lip. "What am I going to do then? Brian was hurt. He may be confused. I have to try and follow him."

"I'm not a bank to have strict rules. I can draw you up a private mortgage of $1,000.00 as against rents. I have a lessee in mind who could do wonders with that property of yours. That's for lock, stock and barrel, including all the furniture."

"I'll need the cradle for Beatrice, and I'll be taking Little Gent as well. That cat is more family than mouser anyway."

"You've got it. I'll draw up the papers for you to sign tomorrow. Your sister can't sign on her own, but you can sign as her guardian. Pack what you think you'll need and bring the horse and cow to the livery stable. There'll be traveling money and a letter of credit waiting for you. You and your sister can spend the night with my family and leave the next morning."

Bone weary, they drove home. Susannah took over the reins so Adele could nurse Bea.

"Sissy, do you think we'll find Brian in San Francisco?"

"I hope so."

"Mr. Duneagan said he might go somewhere from there."

Adele replied, "Brian told me that he dreamed at night of a city on a bay or ocean. San Francisco would meet that description."

They dumped the trunk and filled it with all of their clothes and toiletries and all of Brian's and Beatrice's clothing and necessaries. Susannah insisted on packing all her drawing equipment and numerous old sketches, particularly those of Brian. Adele packed the wedding morning sketch. She also packed her sewing basket and an almost finished sacque suit she was making from brand-new fabric as a gift for Brian. Finally, she packed as many of her quilts as would fit in the trunk. She filled their picnic basket with padding so Little Gent would have a way to travel.

As she folded her Wedding Ring quilt and the one they had worked on together, Adele fought the urge to cry. Swiping her hands across her eyes, she set her jaw. "We'll find him," she declared aloud.

When she opened the cash box she found, as she expected, that it was almost empty. She put the remaining money in a handkerchief and pinned it inside her bodice. She did not even own a reticule, never having need for one.

Together, the women loaded the drayage trunk onto the wagon bed, along with the cradle and the cat basket. They hitched up the jenny and tied Esmeralda and Mabel to the wagon. Baby in arms, Adele picked up the reins. She didn't look back, for she knew to do so would be to begin to weep and never stop. She would need to keep her wits about her from now on.

True to his word, Mr. Duneagan had drawn up a mortgage agreement, which Adele signed for both herself and Susannah. He had taken the liberty of purchasing their tickets for them and gave them $200.00 spending money and the remainder as a letter of credit with Wells Fargo in San Francisco.

"I hope you find that boyo, one way or t'other. I have to think something is seriously wrong with him to have just walked away like that."

On December 11, 1875, Adele and Beatrice Strange and Susannah Stoddard boarded the twelve fifteen for Salt Lake City.

As they boarded the train, Susannah looked around the depot to the town behind it and shivered.

"What's the matter, Susannah?"

"Just a premonition. I don't think I'm ever going to live in Wyoming again."

As the train began to pull out of the station, Adele just held Bea to her. In her deepest nightmares she had never imagined this day. If she did not find Brian, she knew she would just die.

ON DECEMBER 12th, a meeting was going on in a private office set up in a large mansion on Nob Hill in San Francisco. Stephen was sitting in the big leather chair behind a mahogany desk listening to Solomon Pastor, a Wisconsin attorney.

"Miss Cherry Leval died on November 27th past of consumption. The little boy turned six this past August and is currently living with the mother of Miss Leval's impresario, although my information indicates she'd be just as happy to be rid of the boy."

"Well," stated Stephen, "assuming my brother is dead, that makes me the boy's uncle and his closest living relative. I'm sure he would be in better shape living with a blood relative than a stranger."

"I believe the Wisconsin court would be favorable to your petition, Mr. Carroll. With any luck, Joshua Leval could be in San Francisco and in your custody by mid-January."

"Have you met him, Mr. Pastor?" Stephen inquired.

"Yes, once. He's a very sweet little boy and the spitting image of you."

Stephen laughed ironically. "Yes, these Carroll looks. I can see the rumors spreading already that he's my son. Blair had such a low regard for women I was always surprised he was willing to acknowledge— um—Joshua as his, but I guess being told that the boy has the Carroll looks convinced him. Mr. Pastor," he added, shaking the other man's hand, "please proceed with the petition and wire me about when to expect the little boy."

The meeting over, Stephen poured himself a drink from a decanter on the sideboard and slumped in a wing chair, his eyes closed with a fatigue beyond mere tiredness. He sipped the whisky, its warmth spread through him. He was twenty-six years old, but felt like a hundred. He felt completely out of his depth running the company. He was about to become the guardian to his bastard orphan nephew, and he had to accept that Blair was probably dead.

The Pinkertons had not turned up a lead in nearly two years and Stephen had finally had to ask them to close their investigation. It was too much for one day. This was not what he had planned for his life when he enrolled at Harvard. He felt so damned lonely. He was beginning to understand how Blair had chafed at running Carroll Enterprises. If it wasn't so lucrative, maybe he should try to convince his father to authorize a sell out.

"I should write Father a letter today."

He really should. There was no longer any reason to delay. He had already waited two miserable years. His father had barely responded. The estrangement between the father and his elder son was almost total. Stephen wondered if Oscar even cared that Blair might be dead.

Stephen rested the tumbler on the arm of the chair, holding it secure with the flat of his palm. He had almost drifted to a light sleep when a knock on the office door blew the cobwebs away.

"Yes?" he responded to the knock. It was Jennings, the butler who had been employed for about a year.

"Mr. Carroll, I'm sorry to disturb you like this, but there's a very rough looking fellow at the front door demanding to see you. He keeps insisting his name is Blair Carroll."

Stephen immediately sat upright. "What does he look like, Jennings?"

"Oh, quite a ruffian, sir. Sheepskin jacket, muddy trousers, filthy leather gloves and working man's shoes."

"What color is his hair, his eyes?"

"Oh, his hair is black, sir, and his eyes look to be close to yours in color. Otherwise I wouldn't have bothered you."

Stephen was up in a flash and bounded down the stairs. Standing in the entry hall was a six-foot four-inch behemoth dressed as Jennings described with shoulder length, coal black hair, dusty and matted with blood on one side. His face was brown from the sun, but pallid beneath the tan. His mustache nearly obscured his mouth. His eyes were only barely focused.

Stephen stared into the face of this familiar stranger. His voice choked with disbelief, he croaked, "Blair?"

The giant glared back. "Stephen, I have a hell of a headache," and fell straight forward into his brother's arms as darkness enveloped him.

Chapter 10

Four days later

BLAIR GLARED again at his work-worn hands. Two years were gone from his life and his only clues were some old clothes, a bunch of calluses and a horseshoe nail ring. Where had he been that he'd worked so hard to have developed so muscular a body and so used a pair of hands? With whom had he been that he let himself become so ill-groomed and rustic?"

Why was he wearing a horseshoe nail for a ring? He had no answer.

He looked up at Stephen. "Did you say something about Cherry Leval?"

"She's dead and your son will be here in about a month."

He waved Stephen away, nodding. "Fine. Take care of it. I'm so tired all of a sudden."

ON THE SAME morning during which Blair Carroll awoke to find a black hole in the middle of his life, two pale, anxious and exhausted women, a tired, cranky baby and a skittish tomcat clawing at his basket stumbled off a train at the main terminal in San Francisco. Although Adele had actually been born in Baltimore and had come to the prairie as a toddler, for all intents and purposes this was their first time in a large city. Even in the morning the large station was bustling with activity, passengers and freight arriving and departing.

"Gosh, I wish I had my sketchbook out, Sissy. I would love to be putting all this down on paper," marveled Susannah. "Have you ever seen so many people in your life?"

Adele could not help noticing all the activity, despite her tiredness and worry about Brian. "It is quite a crowd. Maybe once we find a place to stay, you can come back here and draw for a while. I know once we find a bed, Bea and I will probably sleep for a week."

After arranging for the station master to hold their luggage temporarily, Adele and Susannah walked out into the chilly San Francisco morning. Of course, a chilly San Francisco morning in

December felt more like a morning in early spring in Wyoming. There was no snow and only a light fog and the temperature was about fifty degrees. Their senses were assaulted with the sight of people of many types; well-dressed American businessmen, ladies of fashion and those of ill repute, dark-skinned Mexican and Yaqui day laborers, the distinctive Chinese in their unfitted garments and queues, working men in their plain, rough garments. It was a kaleidoscope of rapidly moving images.

"Papa always said if we ever found ourselves in a strange town, we should find the nearest church and ask for help," Adele stated.

They had not walked very far when they found a local Catholic church. The priest knew an Irish woman who kept a boarding house in a safe part of town. He quickly penned the address and a short letter of recommendation. "Mrs. O'Bannion keeps a clean house, serves good meals and loves children and animals and her prices are comparable in the neighborhood. I think you and your sister will be all right there, Mrs. Strange."

"She won't mind that we're not Catholics?"

"If you're women of good character, that will be good enough for her. She's a businesswoman first and foremost."

Mrs. O'Bannion was indeed a businesswoman, but with her wiry graying red hair, round face and full figure she looked like the universal mother figure. She listened to Adele's story about Brian's disappearance patiently. She had two adjoining rooms available and quoted a price of $5.00 per week, including breakfast and supper. For an extra fifty cents, she would even agree to keep an eye on Beatrice when necessary and sent her hired man off to the station to retrieve the luggage, which consisted of the cradle, the trunk and a couple of carpet bags.

"Now," said Adele, "have you any idea where I can go to find a job?"

Adele and Susannah had discussed finding work in San Francisco. They agreed that they did not want to draw on the letter of credit if possible in order not to be any more in debt to Mr. Duneagan than necessary.

"If you can read, you can check the *Chronicle* for want ads. Otherwise you can walk around and look in shop windows."

"I can read, Ma'am. I also have enough money to pay for a few weeks' rent until I find something, so you needn't worry on that account."

"If you don't mind my asking, while you're out working, what's your sister going to do?"

"She's going to start searching, asking around for clues to my husband's whereabouts. Mrs. O'Bannion, I don't mean to be rude, but we've been sitting up on a train for four days. If you could show us our rooms, I am taking my daughter and myself to bed."

While Adele and Bea slept, the luggage arrived. Susannah had it brought up to her room, opened it and unpacked her own clothes. Changing into a clean dress, she grabbed her sketchbook and pencils and a couple of sketches of Brian and headed back to the train station. She asked the station master and several of the railroad clerks and personnel if they had seen Brian, showing them her sketches. No one could remember seeing anyone fitting that description in the preceding week.

After about two hours of wandering around talking to people, Susannah's right leg began to throb. Sitting down on a bench, she began sketching the station building and some of the people she saw.

Her activity began to draw interested spectators.

"Hey, that's really good," said one.

"Looks just like the depot," said another.

"Can you draw a picture of me?" asked a third.

"I suppose so, but...." Susannah answered uncertainly.

"Hey, I ain't askin' no favors, Missy. What'cha charge?"

"Um—a dollar?" she responded.

The man reached into his pocket and flipped her a silver coin. Susannah caught it and stared at it like an alien thing. Then she smiled. "Thanks, Mister. Why don't you just sit here while I get out a fresh sheet of paper and sharpen my pencil."

Susannah barely noticed when the pain in her leg went away. Three hours later, as dusk began to descend, she actually hailed a hack for a ride back to the boarding house. As fast as her legs could carry her, she went up the stairs and knocked on Adele's door.

She ran to Adele's bed, crying, "Look, Sissy," and pulled from her pocket eight silver dollars and some change and showered them down on the bed.

"Where did you get that money?" Adele asked anxiously.

"People asked me to draw their pictures—and then paid me for them. I told them a dollar each, and they didn't even flinch...Maybe I didn't ask enough...I don't know, but, Sissy, it was so much fun. I feel like a real artist. If I can keep this up, we won't have to worry about paying the rent while we look for Brian."

Adele raised her hand, "Susannah, I doubt it will be as steady as all that, but it certainly helps, since I don't know what kind of work I will be able to find." She grinned, "My little sister a professional artist. Well, they always did say the West was a land where dreams come true...But if you're going to be a professional, better do things right. You better get yourself one of those artist stands—an easel—and make yourself a sign. And get a couple of chairs for you and your subjects to sit in...Don't worry, we have enough left of the traveling money Mr. Duneagan loaned to us for you to get those things. If it works out, you might just make enough back to pay for everything."

"And," Susannah added, "I could pin a sketch of Brian to the easel with a sign which says, 'Have you seen this man?' Maybe a passerby will recognize him."

"Um-hmm. I asked Mrs. O'Bannion to hold a plate of supper for you. She said just for today."

"Okay, Sissy, but I'm really too excited to eat." Susannah kissed her sister and sleeping niece and darted downstairs to get some supper.

The next morning, Adele rose early, bathed, knotted her long braid into a chignon at the nape of her neck, put on her second best dress—not wanting to wear her wedding dress again until she found Brian—slipped on her cloak, left Beatrice downstairs with Mrs. O'Bannion, and armed with a copy of the *Chronicle*, began to look for work.

By the end of the dismal day, she had found nothing. No experience, no references, man wanted, not a suitable job for a white woman, etc., etc.

Trudging back toward the boarding house, she heard a commotion from a nearby shop. Curious, she walked over to the shop, marked *Donelli—Tailors*, where two men, one in business clothes and the other in his shirt sleeves with a tape measure around his neck, were embroiled in an argument.

"You're drunk again," yelled the Suit.

"You'd have to be to work here," responded Shirt Sleeves. "You're a fucking slave driver."

"I've given you too many chances. This is it! You're fired," said the man in the suit.

"Good! Saves me the trouble of quitting!" Shirt Sleeves whipped off his tape measure and threw it in Suit's face. He charged back behind the curtain in the rear of the shop and emerged a few moments later with his jacket over his arm, shoving his hat on his head as he strode out, nearly knocking Adele over as he rushed by her.

Suit made a fist that he crashed on a counter top. "*Madonna,* what the hell am I going to do now?"

Tentatively, Adele walked into the shop.

Immediately, Suit pulled on a facade of calm professionalism and extended the hand that had seconds earlier punched the counter. "May I help you, *Signora?*"

"I'm sorry. I couldn't help overhearing. Who was that man?"

Suit grumbled, "That was my tailor and fitter. He was a no good drunk, but he could truly make a suit. Well, that's water under the bridge."

"Then you're...."

"Antonio Donelli, at your service," he responded with a slight bow.

Adele responded, "Maybe we can be of service to each other. It appears you need a new tailor. And I need a job."

Donelli looked at tall, beautiful woman. "You're a tailor?"

"Well, I'm a quilter, but I've been making clothes for my father and then my husband for more than ten years. I've also made my own and my sister's clothes for even longer than that."

"Including that thing you've got on? Come here?" he gestured.

Adele walked over. Donelli told her to remove her cloak. He quickly examined the carefully-made cloak and gestured for Adele to turn around. His practiced eye, for he himself was a tailor, noticed the even stitches, the carefully made buttonholes, the excellent fit on the slender body.

"Well, you sew well," he conceded. "Have you got any of your husband's clothes you could show me, Mrs. uh...."

"Strange. Adele Strange."

"Mrs. Strange, how soon can you be back here with an example of something you've tailored?"

"I think the boarding house I live at is about three blocks away. Can you give me half an hour?"

"If your tailoring is as good as your dressmaking, I'll not only give you a half hour, I'll give you a job. Go now."

Adele headed toward the door.

"Mrs. Strange...."

She turned, "Yes, Mr. Donelli...."

"Can you make shirts, too?"

Adele grinned broadly, "Shirts? When it comes to clothes, they're my specialty!"

A half-hour later a winded Adele returned with a parcel clutched to her. In front of Donelli, she opened the parcel. In it were one muslin and three blue cambric work shirts and a brand-new sacque suit on which the buttons and trouser hems had not been finished.

Donelli held up the garments in turn. The same careful workmanship was evident as on her dress. The materials were inferior, but the skill was evident. He put the suit jacket on a mannequin and examined it thoroughly. He had not seen such quality in many years.

"Your husband is a large man," he commented.

"Yes, sir. I was making that as a Christmas surprise for him. It's almost finished. It's the first time since our marriage that we were able to afford fresh yard goods instead of making things over for him from my father's clothes." Her voice caught. "I only hope he has a chance to wear it."

"Where are you from?"

"Wyoming Territory. We own a farm back there."

"Not much money, hmmm?"

"No, sir. Do I have the job, Mr. Donelli?"

"Absolutely." He tossed a bolt of finely woven cashmere suiting to her. Instinctively she brushed the soft fabric against her cheek.

"It's beautiful. The softest fabric I've ever felt."

"I can't wait to see what you can produce if you have quality yardage to work with. Ten dollars a week, starting tomorrow." Donelli paused, wondering how to put the next statement. He walked over to the counter and wrote something down on a piece of paper. "Mrs. Strange, before you come in, here's the address of a shop which sells women's ready to wear. Get yourself some modest, white or ecru shirtwaists and some dark-colored solid or plaid skirts. As nicely as you sew, those calicoes are far too out of date and unsophisticated for San Francisco. We cater to an upper class clientele who expect the best. Some of the most affluent men in San Francisco have their suits made here. Appearances count in this town, or I would not be able to stay in business." He handed her some money. "Here's an advance on your salary to buy the clothes. See you tomorrow."

Adele nearly danced out the door. She walked over to the shop which Donelli recommended and purchased two white tucked shirtwaists and two skirts, one navy blue and the other a blue and black plaid, as well as a blue-gray smock that could cover her from shoulders to knees to keep lint and threads off her clothes.

She saw herself in a full length mirror for the first time in her life. The woman who stared back was tall and slender with a tiny waist and sad dark eyes. The salesclerk recommended a small felt hat and a pair of gloves that fit snugly on her work-roughened hands.

She only wished none of it was necessary.

Chapter 11

THE NEXT MORNING Susannah set off for the depot both to draw and ask around for information about Brian while Adele walked over to Donelli.

Adele was barely out of her cloak and hat when Donelli handed her the garments his former employee left unfinished when he quit the day before. She sat at the worktable, and opened her workbasket. Her breath caught when she found her thimble. It was nested in the larger brass thimble Brian used when they had bent over the quilt frame together on long winter evenings. With a sigh, she slid her thimble out and slipped it on her left middle finger. Threading a needle, she began to work.

The day was mostly devoted to finishing the garments, but was periodically broken up by interruptions to aid in fittings and make alterations. Donelli referred to her as *Mrs. Strange* to customers, although he called her by her first name privately. He had instructed her to call him *Signor* Donelli.

By the end of the day, Adele was tired; more from tension than the work itself. After all, she had plowed fields and repaired harnesses alone in her time. By comparison, this was easy, almost enjoyable work. Her tension came more from the desire to do her job well enough to keep it at least long enough to get a lead on Brian's whereabouts. Jobs for respectable women were in short supply in San Francisco.

Antonio Donelli had no complaints. In fact he was well pleased. His new tailor was skillful and rapid. He was concerned, though, that Adele's attractiveness might cause a problem. He would have to watch closely.

Adele seemed to ignore the more suggestive remarks, other than to quietly remind customers she was married.

It was Christmas Eve Day when a messenger brought a note to the shop. Donelli read the note and quickly went back to the workroom, where Adele was fitting a lining in a suit coat.

"Mrs. Strange, I have a request I've never made of an employee before. Would you object to working on Christmas Day?"

"You mean tomorrow?"

"Yes, I have a special commission." He waved the note. "One of my best customers is back in town after being gone for a couple of years. This note says he needs a complete new wardrobe, from the skin out. New measurements, full haberdashery, the works. And it's a rush job—believe me—we'll both be sewing overtime on this one. This man demands the best."

"But why on Christmas Day? I expected to have to work on Saturdays, but couldn't even a good customer come in on Monday, the twenty-seventh."

"He's not coming in. He's expecting us to come to him. I'll need your assistance with the sample books and measurements. Besides, I'll bet you haven't seen those mansions on Nob Hill yet."

"Mr. Donelli, I am willing to help you tomorrow, but, I would like to have January sixth off instead. That's when my family celebrates the season and I don't want to abandon my sister and daughter our first Twelfth Night in San Francisco. This city is foreign enough without that."

"What about your husband?"

Adele looked down. "I don't know where he is. He disappeared a couple of weeks ago and we haven't found him yet. That's why we're here," she added quietly.

"I'm sorry. I didn't know." Donelli lifted Adele's chin. With her dark hair and eyes, she reminded him of his late wife Angelina, dead for the last fifteen years and buried in their hometown of Sorrento. If she were not a married woman, he could fall for her himself. But, even though he thought her beauty might attract customers, he never expected any follow through. He was, at heart, a religious man, and there were rules for such things.

"That's all right, Mr. Donelli. My problems aren't yours. I won't mention it again. When do you want me to come in tomorrow?"

"Be here at eight. I'm going to dawn Mass, but afterwards I'll rent a carriage and we'll leave from here. Expect to spend the day there. And you may have January 6th off instead."

RIGHT ON TIME the next morning, Adele arrived at the shop wearing her plaid skirt, which she considered dressier than the blue. The streets were nearly deserted. Most San Franciscans were either in early morning services or home with their families and all the shops and restaurants outside of Chinatown would be closed and shuttered all day.

Adele left Bea with Susannah, who agreed not to go out to draw that day since Mrs. O'Bannion was going to Mass and then to the home of her married daughter for Christmas Dinner. Susannah even offered to cook breakfast and supper for the other tenants so Mrs. O'Bannion could spend the full day with her grandchildren.

She and Donelli packed up cards mounted with fabric swatches and illustrations of the latest men's styles, as well as pencils, paper, tape measures and some small sewing notions. After loading up, Donelli handed her up into the carriage and, with a flick of the whip, they set off through the quiet morning streets.

The closeness of the middle-class apartment houses and shops soon drifted into larger single houses as the carriage wended its way up California Street to Nob Hill.

Nob Hill was a revelation to a country girl like Adele. Huge, often garish, two- and three-story mansions, built mostly from gold, shipping and railroad money, covered the hill. Rolling lawns with elegantly sculpted hedges, wrought iron fences and statuary took her breath away. The wealth and excess were evident, even to the gilded Christmas wreaths attached to front doors and gates.

"This is like a fairy land. Can you imagine never having to scrimp and make do? When I got married, my husband and I had to decide whether to get wedding rings or fix the axle of our wagon. The axle won."

"Is that why you wear that iron thing instead?"

Adele looked down at her gloved hands. "Yes." Brian was going to get her a gold ring when he disappeared. But now she was almost too sentimental about the ring she had to want a new one.

The carriage pulled up the curving carriage driveway of a three-story wood and brick mansion, a little older than some of the other houses on the Hill. The house was also remarkable in that it alone bore no Christmas wreath.

Donelli remarked, "This house dates back to the 1850's. Oscar Carroll built it when he made his first killing in shipping bringing goods in for the forty-niners. Carroll Enterprises is the largest import/export company in California."

"So we'll be meeting Mr. Carroll?"

"Actually, the senior Mr. Carroll lives in Europe now. He left the business to his sons, who live here now. Both of the Carroll brothers have been customers for years."

Tying off the reins, they dismounted and began unloading the carriage. The front door was answered by Jennings, the butler, who directed them to a parlor off the hall that was nearly as large as the entire Stoddard farmhouse.

"Mr. Carroll will be down shortly," he intoned and left them.

Adele looked around in awe. "I've never seen *anything* like this before."

"It's quite something, isn't it, Mrs. Strange. And yet, this house is actually quite conservative in decor. Many of the houses on the Hill are so ostentatious you would think an imperial potentate lived in them."

"But the size. We lived in two rooms," Adele breathed. "Two rooms for the four of us. This house probably has room for twenty people."

Donelli chuckled. "Probably not that many. Let's get set up now."

Setting up their samples on top of the piano and settee, Adele slipped on her smock and both tailors draped their tape measures around their necks with the ends dangling down their chests. She gathered up the stack of illustrations in her arms as the parlor door opened.

"Mr. Carroll," said Donelli, his hand outstretched, "so good to see you again after all this time."

"Thank you for giving up your Christmas for this. I expect you will bill me extra for the inconvenience."

Adele turned at the sound of the voice. On seeing the giant who had just entered, she gasped and dropped the illustrations, which floated to the floor at her feet. All color drained from her face.

Donelli stared at her. "What's the matter with you, Mrs. Strange? Come here and meet Mr. Blair Carroll."

Adele picked up the stack of illustrations and, holding them close to her, approached the tall man. His hair was coal black and cut so ruthlessly short that it would not dare to curl. His equally black mustache was trimmed to reveal a scowling, no-nonsense mouth. He had an old scar on his left temple and yellow remnants of a new bruise in the same place. She stared into eyes that were gunmetal gray and just as hard and cold.

She held out her right hand. "Mr. Carroll...I'm pleased to um— meet you. I'm Adele Strange, *Signor* Donelli's assistant."

She looked hopefully into those hard gray eyes. They returned no hint of recognition. *Maybe I'm mistaken*, thought Adele.

Then he took her hand to shake. She looked down at his right hand. The little finger was gone. *I'm not mistaken. It is Brian. It must be. It couldn't be anyone else*. She looked up at him again, still holding onto his hand. As if struck like lightning, he pulled it away and put it behind his back.

"Not a pleasant sight for a woman," Blair declared. "Still getting used to its being missing myself."

"It doesn't bother me, Mr. Carroll. If you want, I can take any gloves you have back with us and fix them so it's less obvious."

"What do you have in mind?"

"I'd stuff the little fingers with cotton batting and tack them to the ring fingers so they move together. It's a very simple thing, but it gives the right illusion."

Blair thought about the worn leather gloves that were fixed in the selfsame way. *Coincidence,* he thought. *How many ways could there be to fix a pair of gloves?*

"Amazing, Donelli, a woman who can think."

Adele started at the venom in those words. Who was this man?

Donelli caught it, too. "She's only been with me a week and she's already the best assistant I've ever hired. I think you'll be pleased with her work."

"As long as she doesn't prattle."

Adele felt her face heating up with anger and tears prick her eyes. *Prattle!* Remembering her position, she bit back a retort. Blair Carroll obviously had no idea who she was. But if he were the same man, Brian Strange would never have made such remarks.

Or would he? Adele remembered Brian making similar remarks rather unconsciously the first week or so after she had found him. Living and working around the Stoddards, the comments had soon stopped as if they had never been made. This man definitely had a painful history where women were concerned that had been wiped away when he lost his memory. If he was himself now, that history was back in his mind.

Ready to take his measurements, Donelli without comment helped Blair remove his too-tight dressing gown. Under it he wore the muslin shirt and black trousers he had arrived in San Francisco wearing. Donelli pulled at the sleeve of the shirt. The style looked familiar to him.

"I know it's cheap garbage, but nothing else I own fits anymore," Blair commented. He laughed ruefully. "I've picked up a lot of muscle in the last couple of years. Wreaks havoc with the wardrobe."

Donelli fingered the shirt. "Looks well made."

"If you like wearing a feed sack."

Adele reeled at the insult. He had been married in that same shirt and didn't call it garbage then. She had to stay calm and professional, even though her knees and hands were shaking and her stomach churning. She picked up a pad and pencil and began to take down the measurements as Donelli called them out. It was mindless work, particularly since she knew the numbers by heart. She repeated the numbers back parrot-like, until....

"Inseam, thirty-seven...."

Automatically, Adele corrected him. "Thirty-eight," she said without looking up.

Donelli and Blair looked back. "What did you say?" Donelli asked.

"Ah, I—um—think that's not—um—doesn't sound right. He looks more like it might be thirty-eight. Measure again, you'll see."

He did. "You're right."

Adele shrugged.

The rest of the day was devoted to selections. Blair chose very little of what could be called casual wear. White shirts, dark suits and vests, all in the finest fabrics. New dressing gowns, a smoking jacket.

"I don't know why I need a smoking jacket. I don't seem to smoke anymore."

"So you don't have to wear your suit coats in the house," commented Donelli.

You smoked? thought Adele. *I didn't know that.*

Overcoat, evening clothes, nightshirts....

"Nightshirts?" asked Adele.

Blair laughed. "She's right, Donelli. Damned nuisance. Guess they keep me from frightening the maid. Shit, she can stay the hell out of my room. No nightshirts."

"Anything else?"

"Yeah, you talk to the haberdasher about hats, socks and underwear. I don't have time to be bothered. What's the soonest I can expect something?"

"Well, I have to draft patterns. You were never a standard size and you certainly aren't now. If we work straight through, we can probably have some things ready by New Years Eve."

"Can't you get me anything sooner? These damned trousers I'm wearing have *extensions* on them, for God's sake! I can't go to the office in these rags!"

"Excuse me, *Signor* Donelli," interrupted Adele. "If Mr. Carroll doesn't mind that the fabric quality is not up to his usual standards, I can have a suit ready for him by tomorrow morning. And two shirts."

"Are you referring to that sacque suit?"

"Yes, I've got a pretty good idea it will fit him. He can borrow it and the shirts until we get these new clothes ready."

"Why would I be borrowing a suit? I'll buy it, even if I only wear it for a week," Blair stated flatly.

"It's not for sale, sir. I made it as a Christmas present for my husband, but I wasn't able to give it to him. You're the same size, so it should fit. But I really want it back."

"You'd give your husband a used suit?"

"Under the circumstances I'm sure he wouldn't mind. It wouldn't be the first time, Mr. Carroll."

"He must be quite a brick...." Blair then noticed that Adele spoke of her husband in the past tense. He stiffened uncomfortably. "Sorry, I misunderstood. Bring it by tomorrow. I'll return it later."

"Thank you for understanding, Mr. Carroll."

Truly, he did not understand it. In fact it confused the hell out of him. She seemed sensible, as women went. Not that women tended to be sensible, even under ideal circumstances. Why she would be sentimental about clothes she made for her dead husband. He was dead; it appeared from her references to him in the past tense—Blair could not begin to speculate. Well, it saved him a few dollars but from the hundreds he would be spending, what difference did that make?

It suddenly occurred to Blair that he wanted to ask Mrs. Strange about it. That shocked him, because normally he did not give a damn about what women thought—if they thought.

The lady was well-named Mrs. Strange, he thought. She *was* strange, compared to other women he knew. She made him feel very strange.

Hungry, almost.

It was a feeling Blair Carroll had already decided he liked not one bit.

ADELE WAS silent all the way back to the shop. She helped Donelli unload and went into the workroom to finish the hem and sew buttons on the suit while Donelli returned the carriage. He returned a half hour later with a bell-shaped bread loaf and some hard boiled eggs. While Adele sewed, he brewed coffee, then pulled out a large roll of paper and began to draft a suit jacket pattern based on the measurements. When the coffee was ready, he poured two mugs full and cut two generous slices of the bread.

"Here," he said. "It's pannetone. It's Italian sweet bread we eat at Christmas time. I have no anisetta to put in the coffee, but I suspect neither of us would do well tonight if we have liquor. We have some long nights ahead of us, it appears."

"Thank you." Adele took a bite and smiled. "It's delicious. My sister couldn't bake better, I'll bet."

"Oh, I buy them at a local Italian bakery. The man's a Sicilian, but he does bake a good pannetone."

Donelli sat down opposite her. "Seriously, something shook you up today."

Adele responded evasively, "No, it was nothing."

"I know Carroll is a real bastard where women are concerned. Something to do with his father, I've heard. You mustn't take it seriously; it has nothing to do with you."

"No, he didn't—doesn't—even know me." Adele dropped her hands to her lap and sighed. "Mr. Donelli, he's going to hate this suit. Did you hear how he was about the clothes he was wearing? This isn't much better."

Donelli picked up the jacket, now finished with all its buttons. True, it was only serviceable black wool broadcloth, but it wasn't unfashionable. He draped it on the mannequin, pinned Blair's measurements on the form and took out his tape measure. The measurements were exact. This jacket would fit perfectly over a dress shirt. He picked up one of the previously finished cambric shirts and measured it. It, too, was perfect.

"Have you met Mr. Carroll before, Adele?"

"The man you introduced me to today was a stranger to me." She put down the trousers, finished. "Mr. Donelli, I know we have lots of work to do yet, but I need to go home and feed my little girl and have some supper. I can be back in an hour and work all night if necessary."

Donelli dismissed her. "Come back in the morning. I'll have at least one of the patterns done. Oh, and Adele, I've decided to waive the advance I gave you for the clothes—as a Christmas present. You've done yeoman's duty today."

Adele thanked him with a shy smile as she gathered up her things to go back to the boarding house.

When Adele got back to the boarding house, Susannah greeted her with a hug and some good beef stew and fresh baked bread from the morning. After supper, Adele went upstairs and opened her shirtwaist to nurse Beatrice. Little Gent jumped on the bed and curled up beside her. She quickly scratched between his ears. There was the comfort of the familiar in this strange and disquieting city, the soft purring of Little Gent, the gentle pull on her nipple by her hungry little girl. Tears began to flow uncontrollably and stream down her cheeks. She had found Brian Strange, but he wasn't the man she'd lost. The man she found was a monster.

Until she knew what to do she couldn't tell Susannah. She began to piece together almost three weeks of mystery as she sat there nursing.

Susannah told her that Thunder had kicked Brian and that he had been carried away unconscious. Blair Carroll had the remnants of a bruise on his forehead. When she found Brian, he had been struck in the head and had lost all memory of who he was. Was it possible that the new injury had reversed the process, returning his lost memory and wiping out Brian Strange as if the last two years hadn't existed?

"It's the only explanation I can think of," she mused aloud. "Oh, Bea, what are we going to do?"

BLAIR DIDN'T sleep well that night. He kept having odd dreams of holding a dark-haired woman in his arms. He could not see her face for the curtain of long hair obscuring it. She was laughing and reaching out to him. But he kept waking from the dream hard as a rock and smelling roses. Who was she? Was she a clue to his missing two years? He didn't know.

And why did he think of that odd Mrs. Strange?

He rose and struggled into his dressing gown. It only wrapped around him from the waist down, gaping open across his broad chest. He stormed across the hall to his office. Going to the sideboard, he splashed whisky into a glass and took a sip. It hit him like a bitter slap. Suddenly, he didn't care for the taste. He slammed the glass down.

"What the hell has happened to me?" he growled aloud. "I don't smoke anymore. Now I can't stand the taste of whisky. I'm having nightmares about women, for God's sake! I'll be a fucking wreck in a month if this continues."

DONELLI PRACTICALLY had to push a protesting Adele into the Carroll carriage the next morning with the clothes in a canvas garment bag and her sewing kit for any last minute alterations.

"I know it's Sunday, but it's got to be done," he insisted.

Once inside the Carroll mansion, Adele handed a large box containing the newly finished garments to a servant to take upstairs.

At Jennings' direction, Adele headed into the parlor to wait. When she looked up, she saw another black-haired man sizing her up from the doorway. He entered the parlor.

His face was gentle and intelligent. Although clean-shaven, reed slender and closer to her age, he reminded her more of Brian than Blair did. She held out her hand.

"I'm *Signor* Donelli's assistant, Adele Strange. *Signor* Donelli told me that Mr. Carroll had a brother. You must be him."

Stephen took her hand and shook it. His handshake was steady, his hands cool and dry. "Yes, I'm Stephen Carroll. I'm a client of Donelli, too. You couldn't have finished something already. You were only here yesterday."

"It's a loan until we finish something else. I'll get started first thing Monday morning."

"Hmmm. You're very pretty, you know."

"Now, Stephen, don't flirt with the tailor. You turn her head with compliments and I'll be walking around half naked." Blair had walked in wearing the suit and a blue shirt.

Stephen and Adele exchanged glances. There was an instant camaraderie established in that look. Adele knew that when the time was right, this young man—her brother-in-law—could be an important ally.

"I was just leaving for the office, Blair," Stephen responded sharply. "I've got to get that motion finished so I can file it Monday morning."

"Bring me back something to do, for God's sake. I'm bored to distraction sitting around idle like this," Blair commanded to Stephen's departing back.

Turning to Adele, he said, "Well, Mrs.—what's your name again?" He actually remembered it, but this was a ploy to make others believe he had no time to remember their names.

"Strange, Adele Strange, Mr. Carroll."

"Mrs. Strange. It seems your husband was pretty close to my size. This thing fits pretty well."

"Actually, it's a good style for a man as large as yourself. More fitted suits might make you look a little squeezed."

Adele walked behind Blair and put her hands at the shoulder seams of the jacket. It was hard to retain her composure and act in a professional manner. "How does it feel through here?" she asked, "Any pulling or straining?"

"None."

"Button the jacket, please...Good, no straining." She knelt down in front of him and tugged on the trouser legs. "How does that feel? Any binding, um, up there? Can you sit for a minute and tell me?"

Blair sat down. "It feels fine. Almost as if you made it for me. Why don't you add one of these to my order?"

"In that moss gray tweed, do you think?" *God help me, I'm discussing fabric selections when I want to beg him to remember me.* "How is the shirt?"

"Passable. Fits fine."

"Good. Then I'll be going. It *is* Sunday."

"Tell Donelli I will come to the shop for fittings. Now that I have this suit, it's not half as humiliating as those rags I was wearing when you saw me yesterday."

Adele had enough insults to her sewing, even if he did not know they were directed at her. Somewhat defiantly, she commented, "I'm sorry, Mr. Carroll, but it looked like those clothes fit you pretty well. I'm sure whoever gave them to you took care, but she must have been very poor."

"Why would you think it was a woman?" Blair asked defensively.

"No reason, just a guess. It could have been a man. After all Mr. Donelli sews and my husband could sew a little."

"Your husband sewed?"

Adele laughed, "He got bored one winter evening, so my sister dared him to learn how to quilt. He got quite good at it after a while. The hardest part was finding him a large enough thimble."

"Were you and your husband poor?"

"We worked hard; we made do. We didn't have much money, but I never felt poor with Brian...Please, sir, I must go. It's really very painful for me to talk about with you."

Adele couldn't get out fast enough. Upon returning to Donelli, she buried herself in the workroom and sewed nonstop until late in the evening, breaking only to go home for an hour to eat and nurse Bea.

For two weeks she was already in when Donelli came downstairs and stayed long after he left. She was averaging three hours of sleep per night and her face became drawn with dark circles beneath her eyes. She celebrated Twelfth Night by sleeping the clock around and waking up early on January seventh to return to the shop.

Blair's order was taking most of the time and attention, but other patrons needed work done as well. Once the bulk of the Carroll order was delivered, the time demands were greatly reduced and Adele began to regain her energy. But she didn't know what was worse; seeing Blair or not seeing him.

Donelli was pleased with the positive comments Adele's work received as well as by the positive comments about his pretty assistant. He was well aware that Adele did not flirt or treat these clients any way except professionally, but he could live with the hint of promise, as long as the trade continued to increase. Her discomfort around Blair Carroll was obvious as was his with her. Yet both denied that anything had been said between them that would have caused the discomfort.

Adele was out on a lunch break when a messenger delivered the loaned sacque suit and cambric shirt from Blair Carroll. Donelli took out the garments and examined them carefully, looking for alteration marks that would have been made when Adele delivered the suit. The tailor had seen the suit on his client and knew it fit perfectly.

There were no marks, no cut threads, no moved seams. There was only one man this garment had been made to fit, and that man had been the one wearing it.

That would explain Adele's behavior—if Blair Carroll were her missing husband—but, if true, it didn't explain Carroll's lack of recognition of her.

"No, it can't be. If I had a wife like her, I wouldn't act like I don't know her," he declared aloud. "Or don't remember her."

He poured himself a cup of coffee. An image of his Angelina appeared in his mind. He toasted the memory.

"Angelina, *mi amore*," he said in the Italian he hardly used anymore. "Watch over this lady for me. If anyone deserves help from Heaven, it's her. I only pray her heart doesn't get broken."

Chapter 12

THE TELEGRAM read:

ARRIVING JANUARY 20 11AM TRAIN STOP RETURN
TRAIN DEPARTS 1230 STOP COLLECT CHILD AT STATION
STOP MUST RETURN IMMEDIATE EASTBOUND STOP
MARGARET FAIRCHILD WISCONSIN ORPHAN SOCIETY.

"Impossible," declared Blair, looking out over the stack of
documents and files covering the desk in his office at the Carroll
Enterprises warehouse on the Embarcadero.

"What is impossible?" asked Stephen as he entered the office with
a thick file under one arm. "The Villanorte contracts are in order," he
added, putting the file down on Blair's desk.

Blair gestured with the yellow Western Union form. "This woman
from Milwaukee. She expects someone to pick up the child at the
station."

"Joshua?"

"Joshua?" Blair echoed stupidly.

"The *child*. Your son. His name is Joshua."

"Oh, yes, of course, Joshua," Blair responded absently. He started
rooting around in the Villanorte file Stephen had just put down.

"When?"

Blair looked up. "When what?" His mind was already back on
business.

"Joshua. When is he due?"

Blair looked down at the telegram again. "Tomorrow at eleven.
It's impossible."

"Oh yes, Winslow told me you have that meeting with Edward
Donaldson and Captain Nels Sorensen regarding the run to Japan and
Singapore. Couldn't you change the appointment time?"

"What, and have Donaldson take his shipment to Rafferty
Brothers? We can't afford to lose his business to the competition. Shit,
it takes every waking minute to stay one step ahead of that son of a
bitch Gerald Rafferty. He deviled me at school and he still does, he and

his brother. Why couldn't Dad have made his money in gold mining or gambling? Molly can just go with Lopez in the carriage and pick the boy up."

At that moment, Stephen wanted to deck Blair. He could feel his hand curling into a fist in his ire. Instead, he took a deep, calming breath and after a pause, quietly admonished, "Your son is coming two thousand miles to a strange city and a strange father and you're going to send a housemaid and coachman to fetch him?"

Blair slammed his hand down on the desk. "What do you expect me to do? One of these days your softheartedness is going to be the ruin of me."

Stephen felt the stab to his pride. Carroll Enterprises had not lost money the two years he was at the helm. In the month since Blair returned, he made it seem as if the younger man had brought the company to the verge of bankruptcy instead of bringing in modest profits in a cutthroat market.

On the issue of the boy, Stephen felt even more anger. In the previous two years, Stephen had maintained a steady correspondence with Cherry Leval's attorney, Orville Garrett, conducting negotiations for custody of young Joshua Leval. He understood Miss Leval's need to keep her son with her even as her health continued to wane. Stephen sent regular drafts to pay her lodging and medical bills and support both mother and child. These were sent through the attorney in order to assuage Cherry's pride. Until the actress finally succumbed to consumption, Stephen made no attempt to remove the boy from her care and company, but in the weeks between her death and Blair's return to San Francisco, Stephen was able to finally arrange for custody of the child he had never actually met. Stephen actually looked forward to meeting Joshua, even if Blair had trouble remembering the boy's name.

"Actually, I think I'll get Joshua myself. An uncle is better than a housemaid and I wasn't going to the Donaldson meeting anyway. I can take care of that short clause matter at the courthouse tomorrow morning and be at the station by eleven with no effort whatsoever."

Blair chewed on that a moment. "You were going to take him on anyway—if I'd turned out to be dead."

"Uh-huh. I would have been his only living relative. It would have been only right." *As it is, I'm the only one who cares.*

"Should I expect you in the office at all tomorrow?" Blair asked dourly.

"No, I don't think so. I think I'm going to spend the day getting acquainted with *your* son. I just wish you'd figure out a way to find the time to do it yourself."

"Damn it, Stephen, he's gone six years without meeting me. What difference will a few hours make?"

"If you don't know the answer to that, big brother, I'm not the one who can answer it," responded Stephen as he shut the office door on his way out.

JANUARY TWENTIETH was clear and cool. Susannah gathered up her drawing things and grabbed the horse-drawn street trolley for the station, arriving about eight. Quickly, with practiced habit, she set up the easel and two chairs. On the top of the easel she hung the sign that had been Adele's gift to her.

YOUR PORTRAIT BY A PROFESSIONAL ARTIST *$1.00*

Just below on one of the easel legs she pinned up a sketch of Brian that was labeled, "Have you seen this man," set up her sketchbook and began to sketch a picture of the elaborate station clock. She had discovered very quickly that she got more customers if she was actually working on something than if she sat idly waiting for someone to arrive.

The morning was decent. By eleven she had sketched three portraits and was in the middle of a fourth and even sold the sketch of the clock. The five silver dollars rattled comfortably in the pocket of her calico skirt and the station master was pretending to look the other way. Maybe the sketch she had drawn and given him had been enough for him to leave her alone.

The eleven o'clock westbound is on time today, she thought as she heard it slowing beside the nearby platform. *God, I'm getting to know the schedules as well as the porters do!*

RUSHING THROUGH the station, his long legs cutting a swath through the foot traffic, Stephen made it to the platform just as the train came to a complete stop. At six foot two he was nearly the tallest man on the platform, but there were still so many people crowding around that he could not get a good look without being bumped and pushed. Finally, he thought he saw who he was looking for.

A stocky woman in her late forties, gray-streaked mouse brown hair under a nondescript felt hat and a look of annoyance on her face, stepped off the next car. Holding her hand was a small, wide-eyed, little boy with tousled black curls poking out from under a straw sailor hat that was completely inappropriate for wintertime but looked entirely endearing on him.

Stephen pushed his way through the crowd. "Mrs. Fairchild?"

"Mr. Blair Carroll?"

"No, I'm Stephen Carroll, his brother."

"Suit yourself," she responded abruptly, handing him a sheaf of papers. "Got to sign for delivery."

Stephen pulled a pencil from his pocket and signed the necessary papers. *God, it's like signing for a shipment, not a person.* He handed Mrs. Fairchild the confirming documents.

The stern woman pushed the little boy toward the tall attorney. "Go on, child; he's your kin. I've got a return train to catch," and without a backward glance she strode across the platform to wait for her train home.

Joshua looked up at Stephen—and up and up. His dark gray eyes were wide with fear.

Instinctively, Stephen, realizing how imposing his height might be for such a small boy, stooped until he was just above the boy's eye level. It only took one look at the child for Stephen to know that the boy was undoubtedly a Carroll. He had the Carroll looks as distinctively as could be. He held out his large hand and took the little one in it. With a warm smile, he said, "Good morning, Joshua. Welcome to San Francisco. I'm your Uncle Stephen."

"You're not my daddy?"

Stephen tried to sound cheerful for Joshua's sake although he was actually fuming inside. Blair's insensitivity did not surprise him especially; he just wished to God something would crack the shell around that heart of his. "No, he couldn't come this morning. He had to work. You'll meet him later. I'll bet you're hungry. When I was your age, I was always hungry."

The boy nodded. Stephen stood up and led Joshua off the platform and into the main terminal.

"Are you a giant?" asked the boy.

Stephen laughed, "Well, I am pretty tall, but your daddy is even taller. You look just like him, you know."

"I know. My mommy told me so." His voice choked.

Stephen picked Joshua up and held him close. "You miss her, don't you? She was really sick, wasn't she."

Joshua nodded with a sniffle.

"Well, she's with the angels now, sweetheart, and she isn't sick anymore."

"Do you think she misses me, too?"

"I'm sure she does. But time passes quickly in heaven and she'll happily wait until you're a very old man so she can see you again."

Putting him down and keeping a hold of his hand, they began to walk through the station, Stephen shortening his stride awkwardly to match the little steps of the six-year-old, when suddenly Joshua changed direction and walked toward an easel that was set up in the terminal.

Stephen followed him toward the easel. He stopped short, for sitting down before it was the most beautiful girl he had ever seen, drawing a portrait of a customer.

She had hair like a sable stole, worn pulled off her face above her ears, but down in a straight curtain to just below her waist. In her slightly sun-kissed, heart-shaped face, her eyes were large and clear, amber-brown like fine brandy, her nose was slightly upturned and a couple of even, white teeth nibbled on her lower lip as she concentrated on the portrait she was sketching. Even the modest dark-blue calico dress she wore couldn't hide her voluptuous figure, a full bosom and softly curving hips made her waist seem small. It appeared the only flaw in her perfection was a pair of work-roughened hands, one of which gracefully rested on the easel while the other gripped her pencil as she worked. Apparently she did not always make her living as a sketch artist. Stephen thought of his own large hands and then imagined how hers would feel in his. A shot of lightning blasted through him.

He must meet her. He looked down at Joshua and an idea formed. It would be worth $2.00 for a half-hour with this nymph.

Susannah finished her current project and looked up at the lean, towering figure standing before her. Her amber gaze met eyes smoldering like a storm cloud. A jolt of electricity from deep within her forced her upright. Her breath quickened as she took in the slender frame, firm jaw, midnight hair and aquiline nose. He was dressed in a black frock coat, dark gray striped trousers and vest. His shirt was of spotless, white, finest cotton shirting, flawlessly starched, with a gray silk paisley bow tie. He wore a top hat, which added to his already impressive height.

My God, Susannah thought, *he looks just like Brian!*

Instinctually she looked at his ungloved hands. Large, white, city hands. His left hand was clapped on the shoulder of a small boy who looked like a miniature of him. His right hand—with a slight sigh she saw the hand was whole; on the little finger was a gold signet ring.

"Sketch your portraits, sir? Only one dollar each," she said huskily, as if the words were in a foreign language and had never before been uttered.

"What do you think, Joshua? You game?" said a gentle voice to the little boy.

The child nodded.

Stephen sat on the chair behind the easel and lifted Joshua onto his lap. Stephen took off his topper and laid it on the floor beside him. The light reflected off his shiny hair like black moiré.

Susannah's right hand was shaking slightly. She steadied it with her left. It was not Brian Strange, but whoever the man was could easily be a relative. The resemblance was that close, as was the child's.

"You have a handsome son, sir," she commented.

Stephen grinned. "I knew this was bound to happen. Actually he's my brother's boy."

"Then do you want a separate sketch of him from the one of you? It's the same price either way," she added hastily.

"Probably an excellent idea." *Twice the time to look at you, to imagine being even closer to you.* Stephen took off Joshua's hat and brushed a quick hand through his black curls.

That domestic little gesture shattered Susannah. How many times had she seen Brian do just that to Beatrice's hair? Nibbling on her lip, she began to concentrate on sketching the child.

"Have you been doing this long?" Stephen asked.

Mostly concentrating on her work, Susannah responded, "Uh-huh. I've been drawing forever, but I've only been in San Francisco for a few weeks."

"Oh? Where are you from?"

"Wyoming. My sister and I have a farm there."

A farm girl. That would explain her hands. I wouldn't have it any other way.

"Why San Francisco? It seems a far cry from Wyoming."

"We're looking for my brother-in-law. He was last seen heading for here." She looked up. "His picture's pinned to my easel. Maybe you've seen him."

Stephen saw the paper, but could not discern the likeness. "It's at a bad angle. Remind me to look at it when you're done. What's your name?"

"Susannah Stoddard."

"I'm Stephen Carroll. And this is my nephew, Joshua Carroll."

"Joshua Leval," protested the little boy.

"Joshua Leval Carroll," Stephen conceded. "Joshua just arrived here today from Milwaukee."

Susannah looked up again. "You came here from Milwaukee all by yourself?" she said, impressed. "That's even farther than Wyoming."

"No, Mrs. Fairchild came with me, but she's going home," replied the boy. "I'm going to live with my daddy now."

To Stephen she said, "You can tell me it's none of my business, but did his mother pass away?"

"How did you know?"

"I just can't imagine sending a child two thousand miles with a stranger if his mother is still alive."

"Uncle Stephen says my mommy is with the angels now and she's not sick anymore."

"That's right, honey. My Ma and Pa aren't sick anymore either. I wasn't much older than you when my mother died." To Stephen she continued, "If it weren't for my sister, I don't know how we'd have managed. She held us together."

Susannah finished the sketch of Joshua and set to work on one of Stephen. Her pencil seemed to be bewitched, as if something she was feeling inside was manifesting on the vellum. The simple pencil sketch seemed as alive as its subject. The last sketch that had this much life was one she did back in Wyoming of Brian lying on her bed in the main room with Beatrice lying sleeping on his chest while he read.

Finished, she handed the sketches to Stephen. "Two dollars, please."

"These are fine," Stephen commented as he paid her, then looked more closely at the portrait of him. It was stunning. He stared at her. This was no cheap sketch by a street corner artist. It looked like the expression of a lover. "More than fine. Outstanding."

Forcing his heart to calm down, he turned to Susannah and said, "We were just going to get some lunch. Would you care to join us?"

I shouldn't, thought Susannah, *but God knows I want to.* "If you care to wait while I shut down."

I'd wait for you forever, thought Stephen. "Let me help."

As he approached the easel, he saw the sketch of Brian Strange. His mouth dropped open as his mind flashed back to a vision of five weeks ago when a man with those looks collapsed into his arms in his entry hall.

"This is your brother-in-law?" he said tightly. "What's his name?" She had not recognized his last name when he introduced himself. Carroll was unusual enough a last name that it should have been familiar to anyone who knew Blair well.

"Brian Strange. That's not his real name. We made it up for him because he couldn't remember his real one. It's kind of complicated to explain. Good-looking fellow, isn't he?"

Stephen frowned slightly. *Strange. Where have I heard the last name* Strange *recently?* Aloud, he commented, "Looks dangerous. Like a desperado."

Susannah giggled. "That's just because his hair is long and shaggy, I reckon. Looks can be deceiving, though. A kinder, gentler man I never met in my life. And such a loving father. Seeing you with your nephew reminds me of Brian with Bea. That's my niece. She's very sweet. Her coloring is very much like your nephew's."

Not surprising, considering they're probably brother and sister, Stephen realized. *But it sure doesn't sound like Blair she's talking about.*

"Seems kind of funny that someone you describe that way would abandon his wife and child." That did not sound like something Blair Carroll would do either. Even if he was in a marriage he despised, Stephen could not imagine Blair walking out and leaving a wife and baby with no means of supporting themselves.

"That day was very confusing. There was an accident. He was hurt. Kicked in the head by a horse. I saw most of it happening, but couldn't do anything to help. I don't think he knew what he was doing, but the man at the depot said someone matching his description bought a ticket for San Francisco, so we packed up our bags and followed his trail. Unfortunately, the trail came to a dead end here. Nobody remembers seeing anyone fitting Brian's description get off the train in San Francisco. It's as if he disappeared off the face of the earth."

As they walked out of the terminal, Stephen noticed Susannah was limping.

"Are you hurt?"

"Oh, no," she replied, "I'm crippled." She raised her skirt slightly. "Club foot. I was born that way."

She looked at his face for any sign of revulsion. It wasn't there.

"Does it hurt?"

"Actually, my foot and ankle really never hurt much. But if I walk a lot my knee and hip ache something fierce. And I can't do really heavy farm work. My only regret about it is that I could never learn to dance. It would have been nice to go to dances," she added sadly.

Stephen and Lopez, the driver, loaded Susannah's things into the boot of the carriage, along with Joshua's pathetic little carpetbag. They went to a local family restaurant.

"...SO WHAT ARE you and your sister going to do?" Stephen continued the conversation while they ate.

"You mean about finding him? I really don't know. I guess we'll keep looking until we run out of money. We're both working, so we can hold on for a while."

"Has your sister heard anything?"

"If she has, she hasn't told me, but the last few weeks she's been working twenty hours a day at her job. She gets home so tired that she falls dead asleep. I doubt I've said five words to her in days."

"Tell me the truth. Do you think he's still alive?"

"I have to think that. I think we'd both go mad if I didn't. He's a good man and they were so much in love."

"How long were they married?"

"A little over a year and a half. May will be two years. He lived with us for six months before they got married."

That would be November '73. It's too uncanny to be coincidence, Stephen thought. *She has to be talking about Blair.*

"I've been thinking about it. I may know someone who might have some information. Do you think I could meet your sister? Maybe you and she could join me for dinner, say tomorrow night."

Susannah smiled, "I'd love to. I'll try to get her to come along." Suddenly, her smile faded, "Oh, maybe not."

"What's the problem?"

Susannah swept her hands down from shoulders to hips. "I'm just a farm girl. I don't have any really fancy clothes. And my prettiest dress is a ball gown compared to anything Sissy has."

"What does she wear to work?"

"White waist and dark skirt; very practical—kind of like she is."

"Fine. I'll take you someplace where it doesn't matter. Have you ever had Chinese food?"

"No. Is it good?"

"I like it. And it'll be fun to teach you to eat with chopsticks. Just make sure you convince your sister to join us. I wouldn't want a scandal."

"Scandal?"

"Yeah," Stephen said with a laugh, "I can see the headline now: 'Well known San Francisco attorney in *tête-à-tête* with Wyoming farm girl.' It could ruin your reputation."

"Of course, if it read: 'San Francisco attorney seen dining alone with *artiste*' it could make my reputation instead."

Soon they were both laughing heartily. Suddenly, Stephen leaned over and kissed Susannah quickly on the lips. She pulled back, touching her fingers to her lips in wonder. Her gaze met his.

"I shouldn't have done that. I'm sorry," Stephen spit out.

"Don't be. I'm not," came the surprising reply.

Smart and pretty. Just what I always dreamed of.

People don't really fall in love at first sight, do they?

STEPHEN DROVE Susannah home in his carriage. "Tomorrow night. Eight o'clock."

"We'll be ready," she said, waving at him as Lopez drove the carriage away. She carried her gear up the stoop into the boarding house where she put it all into the front hall closet.

Mrs. O'Bannion was wiping her hands on her apron as Susannah came into the kitchen, as close to dancing as she was capable.

"You're in a good mood, Susannah. Did you have a good day?" asked the landlady.

Susannah threw her arms around Beatrice, who was playing in her cradle. "Yes, I had a wonderful day. Don't tell Adele, but I just met the man I'm going to marry."

BACK IN THE carriage, Joshua was looking tired. Stephen looked at him.

"Did you have a nice day, Joshua?"

"Yes, Uncle Stephen. That was a nice lady."

"Yes indeed she is." Then he whispered, "Don't tell your daddy when you meet him, but I'm going to marry that very nice lady."

JOSHUA DIDN'T tell his father, because he was long ago tucked in his bed in the nursery and fast asleep when Blair, more than the worst for whisky, came lurching into the house at one that morning.

Trying as hard as possible not to make any noise, Blair was of course noisier than his pickled brain convinced him. He lumbered upstairs and was almost past the open office door when an angry voice assailed him.

"Do you know what time it is?"

Grabbing the doorsill, Blair hung in the doorway. His eyes were rheumy and his tie and half his vest buttons were undone.

"Who gives a damn? You're not my father."

"No, I'm your goddamned brother." Stephen sat in a wing chair, a barely-touched tumbler of whisky balanced between his palm and the chair arm. "I'm the man who had to put your son to bed and try to explain to him why his father didn't care enough to come home and meet him."

"Seems to me you took on that responsibility on your own. I didn't ask you to fetch him."

"You're completely soused. That's what that kid needs, a hungover welcome in the morning."

Blair glanced at the chair arm where Stephen held a full tumbler of whisky. "That's the pot calling the kettle black."

"This is the only one I've poured and I've been sitting here for hours trying to convince myself to drink this damn thing. I couldn't get angry enough to do it."

"Fine." Blair lurched over to the chair, grabbed the tumbler from Stephen's fingers and downed it himself. "Now you don't have to convince yourself."

"Sometimes it amazes me that we could have been raised in the same house. You disgust me, Blair."

"Look, I didn't tell that *actress* to get pregnant."

"No, your tongue wasn't the organ that did the persuading."

"I'll do my duty by the kid, but don't expect me to like it or him. What possible use would I have for the prattle of children? About the only thing worse is listening to women chattering. But I'm not worried; he'll have his Uncle Stephen to spoil him rotten."

"And to think I just heard you described today as the kindest, gentlest man someone ever met." Stephen laughed bitterly. "And a wonderful father, too. Ha! I guess appearances *can* be deceiving. Good night, big brother." Then Stephen stormed out of the office, slamming his bedroom door behind him.

Blair settled heavily in the wing chair. He frowned. Who could he have been a father to that someone would have said that of him? "Who would have told him that?" were his last words before he passed out in the chair. The next morning, he woke up where he had fallen asleep, remembering that he had argued with Stephen but with absolutely no memory of the content of the argument.

The dark-haired woman came again to him in his dream, weeping into her hands, her long hair sweeping over her before she disappeared. He never saw her face, but then he never did.

Who was she? Blair was not sure he wanted to know.

Chapter 13

"SUSANNAH, I CAN'T go to dinner tonight," Adele declared. "This is the first time I haven't had to work into the night in weeks. Give your young man my regrets."

Susannah was dressed in her sprigged muslin birthday dress. She had put her hair up and curled the ends into ringlets that fell past her shoulders. Adele could not help noticing that her little sister was becoming a grown woman.

"Sissy, he insisted," Susannah countered. "He's a real gentleman and insisted on meeting you and on our being chaperoned. Besides, he said he might have some information on Brian for you."

This *maybe* was the first lead Susannah had managed in all the time they had been in San Francisco. Considering Adele already knew what had become of Brian, she was suspicious of any clues her sister's gentleman friend might know.

"Are you sure this fellow knows anything? It could be a trick of some kind."

"I don't know, but he said maybe. If he meant me harm, why would he have insisted that you accompany us tonight?"

"You have a point. All right, I'll go with you. After all, I've never had Chinese food either."

Adele reached into the closet for her plaid skirt and a clean blouse and laid them on the bed. She unbraided her hair and brushed it out. From braiding it wet, its normally straight length fell in crimped waves to her knees. Having smoothed out the hair at her crown, she rebraided it and pinned it around her head in a coronet.

Before dressing, she nursed Bea and put her to bed for the night. Bea had a couple of teeth now and it was becoming a little bit painful to nurse, even once per day, but Adele needed the closeness of the ritual. Her first birthday would be time enough to stop. That was only a couple of months away.

As the clock struck eight, Susannah was buttoning up the back of Adele's shirtwaist. "I'll meet you downstairs," she said, grabbing their cloaks and floating downstairs.

Adele was as anxious as if this was her date instead of Susannah's, but then, she had never been courted herself and this was all new to her. "Oh, Ma, would I be in this position if you'd lived longer?" she prayed aloud.

She bent down to kiss the sleeping Beatrice and headed downstairs. Mrs. O'Bannion had promised to look in on the baby periodically during the evening.

As she reached the bottom of the stairs, she held out her hand to Susannah's beau. "I'm Susannah's sister, Adele Strange."

The young man turned. Adele paled and her knees gave out from under her. She was kept from falling by two strong arms holding her up.

"Yes, Mrs. Strange. It's Stephen Carroll. It took me a bit to make the connection after I met Susannah this morning. We have a lot to talk about, I should think."

IN THE DARKLY lit Chinese restaurant, Stephen told the waiter to surprise them and then taught them how to use chopsticks to pick up the meat, vegetables and rice. They laughed at their clumsy efforts at first, but soon became proficient.

During dinner, the three became better acquainted with each other and with the history of events as each perceived them.

"It's obvious that Blair has absolutely no memory of anything that happened from the time he was robbed until he showed up at our house six weeks ago. It's as if someone cut a hole in his brain and took the entire period out. I wonder if it's retrievable," said Stephen.

"When Brian—um—Blair was living with us, he used to have dreams. He used to see dark rooms with heavy leather furniture. Sometimes he would see a man whom from his descriptions would seem to be you, although he didn't recognize you. Is he having dreams now?"

"If he is, he won't tell me. But then it hasn't been his way to confide in me in personal matters in years. He seems more distracted than before, but when I asked him what was going on with him he said it was none of my damned business."

"So, have you figured out how I can get him back?"

"That's just the problem. The man you describe as Brian Strange is the kind of husband any woman might want. I don't think it's Blair Carroll you want back. Blair hasn't been that kind of a man since he was eighteen or so. My brother is a nasty, meanspirited, woman-hater who hasn't even taken the trouble to meet his own son yet. I'm not sure *I'd* live with him for more than a day or two if it weren't already my home."

"I've seen this," Adele concurred, "and it frightens me, but I have to believe the man I fell in love with and married is in there somewhere waiting for someone to help him get out again. I want that someone to be me."

"It isn't likely to be anyone else," Stephen said. "The only woman in San Francisco Blair was ever serious about married his business rival about a year ago. Joshua's mother was a casual affair whom Blair barely remembered when her lawyer wrote to us advising Blair he had a son by her. I've seen no evidence since he's been back in town that he's had anything to do with any woman. Then again, he was wearing a horseshoe nail ring on his left ring finger. He conjectured that he might have married during the lost years, but he cannot remember."

"But he was married—*is* married. To me," Adele protested, her voice thick with agony. She held up her left hand. "I'm wearing the same kind of wedding band. In all the fittings he's never noticed or remarked about it. It's like I'm invisible. Half the time he asks me for my name again, as if I'm not important enough for him to bother to remember." She dropped her head in her hands. "What am I supposed to do?"

"Believe me, Adele," Stephen said, "he remembers your name. It's his way of creating a distance between himself and the world. He started doing it when he first started running Carroll Enterprises because it set people off balance enough to forget that they were dealing with an eighteen-year-old. It's become a habit."

"One he didn't use in Wyoming. Of course, we didn't see many people."

Susannah put in, "Stephen, don't you think we've got to do something to get them close together as often as possible so maybe he falls in love with her again. It worked the first time."

"How are we going to do that? He's got all the clothes he'll ever need and I'm hardly part of your social circle," added Adele with a sigh. "Besides, he thinks women are stupid, useless creatures. He accused me of *prattling*. I had to find a dictionary and look it up. It means *idle, useless chatter*. I wouldn't know how to prattle if I tried."

Stephen brightened. "*Blair* may have all the clothes he needs, but Josh doesn't."

"Huh?"

"Joshua showed up yesterday with barely a change of underwear. He's going to need an entire wardrobe—as you say, befitting his new social circle. And I know just what tailor shop is going to get the commission—and what tailor's assistant."

Adele frowned. "Nobody buys clothing for children from a custom tailor shop like Donelli."

"You do if you're a Carroll and nothing is too good for your son. At least that's the approach I'll take with him. Blair doesn't know a thing about children. The last child he had anything to do with raising was me, and that was a long time ago."

"He was always good with Bea," Susannah said.

"With your help, Stephen, at least I'll have a chance." Adele felt more hopeful than she had in weeks.

Susannah raised her teacup. "A toast—to the plan."

"What plan?" asked Adele. "We don't have a plan."

"We'll just have to figure it out as we go along, like I did after I found the quilt in the hayloft. We can do it!" Susannah threw her arms around Stephen's neck and kissed him on the mouth. He returned her kiss, slipping his arms around her and pressing her close to his white shirtfront. He began to take command of the kiss, plunging his tongue deep into her willing mouth. She responded with gusto. For a moment they were oblivious to where they were.

"In my official capacity as chaperon, may I remind you that you'd be better off finding a more secluded place for that. And I'd better not find any blankets where they don't belong," she added, feeling a flush suffuse her as she realized now how Susannah had discovered that she and Brian were lovers.

Stephen and Susannah broke apart. "Where did you learn to kiss like that?" he asked breathlessly.

"From watching your brother," Susannah replied.

Stephen laughed and said, "I wouldn't have thought he had it in him."

"You'd be surprised," Adele remarked.

STEPHEN DID manage to convince Blair to hire Donelli to outfit Joshua, but when Adele came for fittings, Blair was never there, even on the weekend. Blair gave no reason for avoiding Adele, but he still managed to be absent. He told himself it was because it was not important enough a task for him to supervise personally, but a nagging voice inside him told him over and over that he was lying.

Adele did manage to fall instantly in love with Joshua, who seemed all alone in the big house. She saw the wariness in his eyes when Blair was mentioned and the love when Stephen's name came up. Adele tried to convince the little boy that his father would come to care for him given time.

"How will he ever care for me if he never talks to me?" Joshua protested.

"He's just not used to having a little boy around. A lot of men are uncomfortable around small children. You just have to show him that you are a polite, well-behaved boy and he'll come around. It's probably because he hasn't seen you grow up. You're as much a stranger to him as he is to you. He doesn't know how to behave."

"But Uncle Stephen talks to me and plays with me and he wasn't used to me. He isn't even my father."

"Maybe your father will take lessons from your Uncle Stephen."

It was a big *maybe*. Blair Carroll was not the physical man he had been in Wyoming. He never touched or allowed himself to be touched unless it was absolutely necessary. He was a brittle as a dried leaf. Adele wondered if deep down he was afraid that if anyone got inside him he would shatter like so much blown glass.

The governess Blair had hired was a humorless soul who insisted that too much attention was being paid to dressing a six-year-old. While Adele actually agreed with her, she wished the woman would declare it more gently.

Stephen was the only person in the house who treated Joshua like a human being with feelings. Stephen was the only one who would let Joshua talk about his mother. The boy confided to Adele that he almost never saw his father. The very few times Joshua was in Blair's presence it was made very clear that the name Cherry Leval was not to be mentioned within his earshot. The governess was of the school that the surest way to get over grief was to act as if it did not exist. That this approach was ineffective for adults and even more damaging to children would never have occurred to the governess.

Adele promised to talk to Blair about it, but she didn't see him herself. Stephen told her that Blair was working eighteen hour days as if he was trying to make up for two years of absence in a few months.

"MR. VAN DUSEN, I'm sorry, but I can't check the alterations properly if you don't stand still."

Adele gritted her teeth as her fingers clenched around her measuring tape. Van Dusen might be one of the wealthiest man in San Francisco, but the portly, middle-aged man was a continuing trial to her.

It was bad enough to have to fend off his suggestive comments, but he smelled of a heavy cologne he used to mask the odors of tobacco and unwashed skin so much she was almost nauseated to stand near him.

Van Dusen took a step forward, forcing her to take a step back toward the wall of fabric bolts.

"You don't have to be a seamstress, Adele...."

"Mrs. Strange."

"Mrs. Strange with no Mr. Strange, I'm sure. I could set you up in a nice little house."

She took another step backward. The man had her trapped against the shelving. He had a sixth sense when Donelli would be out of the shop. "I'm not interested in being anything except Signor Donelli's assistant."

Van Dusen reached up to stroke her cheek with the back of his hand. She cringed inside at his nearness. "You're so beautiful, Adele. I'm sure you know how to make a man really happy."

"Please, Mr. Van Dusen, let me go." Adele's voice quavered. "I'm married. You're married. I love my husband. I'm sure you love your wife."

"That harpy?" He held her chin. Adele tried to push him away and turn her head, but he was stronger than she was. He bent his head towards as she tried to scream, and muffled the scream with the start of a sloppy, kiss. She pounded at him with her fists as his other hand cupped her breast, squeezing none too gently.

Adele saw red, then black around the edges. She felt his tongue inside her mouth and in a moment of defiance she bit down hard.

Van Dusen pulled back. "Damn, you bitch." He reached back to slap her as Adele fell to her knees, breathing hard.

A moment later he was gone. Adele looked up to see the broad-shouldered, towering figure of Blair Carroll holding the shorter, fatter man by his coat collar.

"The lady said no."

"They always say no at first, Carroll," Van Dusen countered. "They usually come around."

Adele looked into the stormy eyes of her husband. She could see rage and arrogant indignation.

Blair pushed the older man toward the door. "This lady won't 'come around' to you or anyone else. I can't tell you to leave and never come back, but only because I respect Donelli and his right to do business. If I ever hear that you've forced your affections on Mrs.

Strange again, so help me, I'll ruin you."

"Ruin *me*?" a red-faced Van Dusen spit out.

Blair's eyebrow rose. "You think I can't do it? Think again. All it would take are a few well-chosen words. Now, get out of my sight."

"The clothes I came here in...."

"My coachman will deliver them to you later."

Van Dusen glared towards Adele, who had regained a standing position. "Don't think this is over, *Mrs. Strange.*"

"As far as the lady is concerned, it's over," Blair growled back as Adele stood silently.

Conceding defeat, Van Dusen turned and walked out of the shop.

Blair turned back to Adele. She stood, back to the fabric shelves, her arms wrapped around herself, visibly shaking, her face noticeably pale. Blair approached her.

"Are you all right, Mrs. Strange?"

Adele nodded stiffly. "I will be. Thank you."

"Has he done that before?"

Adele shrugged. "Not quite so aggressively, but he's not the only one. I reckon they think a working woman is fair game...I better fold his suit so your coachman can deliver it."

Blair had a peculiar look on his face. But just as quickly it fled. He closed his eyes for a moment.

Adele approached him. "Are you all right, Mr. Carroll?"

"Yes, just for a moment...never mind. Get the clothes."

Adele disappeared into the dressing room. She appeared a few moments later with two paper-wrapped, string-tied parcels.

She handed each in turn to Blair. "Mr. Van Dusen's clothes...Joshua's finished clothes."

"Joshua's?"

"Some of the clothes for your son that I've finished. That *is* why you came in here today, wasn't it?"

Blair shook his head as if to clear it. "Yes, of course, thank you. It was on my way." He turned to go.

"Mr. Carroll?"

"Yes, Mrs. Strange?"

"Thank you. It's been quite a while since anyone was protective of me. Why did you do it?"

Blair frowned. "I don't know. I really don't know."

IN MID-FEBRUARY, Adele came into work after her lunch break to see a woman whose bearing identified her as a leading doyenne of Nob Hill Society talking haughtily to Donelli. She wondered whose wife this woman was. Ever since the episode with Horace Van Dusen, she had been even more cautious of defusing the suggestive comments made by so many of the customers. This was so commonplace; she realized how isolated she had been from the rest of the world all her life.

It made her grateful that, despite their obvious attraction, Stephen was acting like a gentleman with Susannah, only giving her the attention she was willing to accept, not forcing unwanted attention.

The grand lady pointed her umbrella in Adele's direction. "Deal with it, *Signor* Donelli," she declared as she stormed out of the shop.

"What was that about, Mr. Donelli?"

Donelli's dark face was deadly serious. "Come into the workroom, Adele," he responded. "We need to talk."

Adele suddenly felt cold. She walked in and sat down, shaking with uncertainty.

"Mrs. Van Dusen tells me you are flirting with her husband...."

Mrs. Van Dusen.

"It's not true. Mr. Van Dusen very nearly had his way with me on the showroom floor and was about to slap me for resisting him if Blair Carroll hadn't come in when he did. I just do my job. I tell them I'm married. I am always completely businesslike, but I can't do my job without touching clients and asking them how the garment fits or feels. I don't give them permission to touch me back. You've got to believe me. I don't encourage them at all."

"I believe you, but this city is like a small town. The wives of my other clients will believe harpies like Mrs. Van Dusen. I've received a number of visits from these women and their henpecked husbands telling me if I don't hire a male assistant in your place they will take their custom elsewhere."

"But that's so unfair."

"Adele, you're the best assistant I've ever had, but I can't survive strictly on the custom of Blair and Stephan Carroll and the Barbary Coast saloon owners who couldn't care less for society gossip. My business is predicated on being a society tailor. I'm going to have to let you go, effective today."

Adele was in tears. "What am I going to do?"

"I will write you a letter of reference. I'm sure you can get a job with a good dressmaker. It's infinitely safer."

"If that's the case, I'd be better off back in Wyoming. At home I owed nobody and only the elements were my enemies. Why should I have to make dresses for the very women who've cost me my job?"

Donelli walked over to the worktable. "This is the only other thing I can do. Take the patterns and all the fabric and notions for the clothing for the little Carroll boy. You finish this commission keep the payment for yourself. I'll pay you a week's wages in lieu of severance pay. By the time you finish and collect, maybe something else will turn up."

Donelli began to wrap things up.

"Adele, tell me the truth about something," he began again.

"About what?"

"I've been trying to put this together since Christmas. This order for the Carroll boy: I know it came from Stephen Carroll, but none of my clients order clothing for children this young from me. I'm far too expensive for garments that will be outgrown in a few months. I've seen the way you look at Blair Carroll when you think nobody is looking. Is he your Mr. Strange? I promise it won't go beyond these walls."

Adele nodded dismally. "But he doesn't remember me or any part of our life together. To him it's as if it never happened."

"If he's legally your husband, why do you have to work at all? The Carrolls have been one of the richest families in California for over twenty years. According to the law in this state you're entitled to half of everything he earns."

"You've known Blair Carroll a long time, haven't you, Mr. Donelli?"

"Yes. Ten years I've been his tailor."

"What is his opinion of women? It's pretty low, isn't it?"

Donelli agreed.

"Now, can you see me walking up to the Blair Carroll you know and saying, 'Excuse me, sir, you barely know me, but we've been married for almost two years and we have a baby girl you don't remember.' He'd think I was some kind of fortune hunter. He'd resent my presence. He'd hate me for putting him in such an awkward position. Undoubtedly he would do his legal duty by me, but I've seen how he does his duty by his son and I wouldn't wish such emotional neglect on a rabid dog. I have some pride. I've been working all my life. I don't need or want his money unless I have the man I married to go with it." Adele paused, embarrassed at her outburst. "I'd better leave now. I appreciate your giving me this commission. I know you aren't obligated to me in any way after so few months of employment."

Adele took the package Donelli wrapped, along with her smock and sewing kit and left the shop. She went upstairs to her room and threw herself on the bed and cried for more than an hour before she fell into a disturbed slumber.

She came fully awake suddenly. It was after five and darkening outside.

"Stephen. I've got to talk to Stephen. He'll know what to do," she said aloud.

Susannah was on the front stairs coming in as Adele rushed out. "Take care of Beatrice. I'll be back soon."

"Wait a minute, Sissy. Where are you going?"

"Up the Hill," she said, "I've got to talk to Stephen," she finished as she hopped on the cable car.

"Sissy, come back!" Susannah called after her. "Stephen will be here in less than an hour."

But Adele was already beyond earshot.

It was more than an hour before Adele got to the bottom of Nob Hill and walked up California Street to the Carroll mansion. Jennings answered the door.

"Please tell Mr. Stephen that Mrs. Strange needs to speak to him. It's very important," Adele requested, breathless both from nerves and the incline.

A familiar voice from the staircase replied, "Stephen's not here, Mrs. Strange. I don't expect him until late."

It was Blair. He had obviously just come from the office. He was still fully dressed in a blue-black cashmere frock coat, trousers and vest. His blue paisley tie was in stark contrast to his snow-white shirtfront. Adele knew the suit. She had put practically every stitch lovingly in place. Its cut emphasized his musculature and great height.

He looked so intimidating and yet so handsome that emotion overcame Adele, who collapsed in tears in the doorway.

Blair was down the stairs in seconds. Brushing aside the astonished Jennings, he picked Adele up as if she weighed nothing and carried her into the parlor, setting her down on the settee. He walked over to the gas jets and lit up the parlor and then sat down beside her. He barely touched Adele to gain her attention when she collapsed against his chest, sobbing uncontrollably.

Telling himself he hated such displays, Blair stiffened uncomfortably, then slowly—and astonishingly—drew his arms around her shoulders and held her while she cried. Amazingly, as he held her, it became more and more natural to him and he gently tightened his hold, raising one hand to cup her head to his chest. The man who hated women didn't even notice that her tears were dampening his shirtfront. Her hair felt so soft under his hand; her slender body seemed to melt into his as no woman in his memory ever had. It seemed so right it surprised him.

Finally, Adele's sobbing diminished and she became aware of her position. She bolted upright, wiping her cheeks with her hand. Blair handed her his handkerchief to finish the job.

"Now, suppose you tell me what's happened," he said.

She told him about Donelli. Blair swore violently at the news.

"Why come to Stephen?"

"Uh, because he's a lawyer. I thought maybe he'd know what I could do."

"It's plain what you need is another job."

"But what? After what's happened my reputation is worthless, even if Donelli writes me a glowing recommendation. Besides, I can't work as a dressmaker."

"Why not? I've never had garments better made than these. Antonio himself doesn't sew this well."

"And you've never seen me in anything except ready to wear. Mr. Carroll...."

"Now that you've cried all over my shirt, I think it's time you started calling me Blair."

"I come from a farm in Wyoming. I've never made anything but patchwork quilts, serviceable, plain dresses and men's clothes. I've never used silk for anything but a lining. I've certainly never owned or even tried on a silk gown. I know very little about the mode in women's fashion. How could I possibly compete with experienced ladies' dressmakers? And why would I want to make dresses for women who would accuse me of accepting indecent propositions from their husbands? I'm a respectable woman. I've always prided myself on my integrity."

"Somehow, Mrs. Strange—Adele, isn't it—it doesn't surprise me in the least. You are a very unusual woman, I've found," he added uncomfortably.

"I'm not so unusual where I come from, Mr. Carroll—Blair."

"Do you like children, Adele?"

Adele smiled. "Why I love children, Blair!"

"Maybe I've another solution. Stephen tells me my son is afraid of his governess. She is an old battle-ax. But he says all he talks about after you come here with clothes for him is 'Miss Adele' this and 'Miss Adele' that. Why don't I let her go and you be Joshua's governess?"

"I can't do that."

"Why not? It seems simple enough."

"I wish it were. First, I'd hate to be the cause of another person's losing her job...."

"I was probably going to have to do it anyway."

"Second, I have a family. I have an eleven-month-old baby, an adult younger sister and a tomcat. I can't leave them in a boarding house while I take care of someone else's child. Third, I have very little education beyond what my father and mother taught me themselves. I'm hardly governess material."

Blair frowned. "You can keep your baby in the nursery with Joshua. Stephen would probably approve of the boy having a playmate. And I suppose the cat will own the house within ten minutes of moving in. How old is your sister?"

"Eighteen. And she works."

"This house isn't exactly full, what with two bachelors and a child. I'm sure we can find an empty room for your sister. You probably make a sufficient chaperon for her. Is she seeing anyone socially?"

"Yes." *Good, he doesn't know.* "She's being courted by a very nice young man. I think they're serious about each other."

"Well then, she'll be married and out of the house soon anyway. What's her young man do?"

"Actually, he's an attorney."

"Does my brother know him?"

"Stephen knows him as well as anyone would."

"And as to your education level, what the boy needs is an adult supervisor until he can start school. Nursemaid is too condescending a title. While governess isn't exact, it will do for now." Before Adele could make another objection, he slapped his hands on his thighs and said, "Good, then it's settled. How soon can you start?"

Adele frowned suspiciously. "Mr. Carroll, why are you being so nice to me? You don't even like me."

"What gave you that impression?"

"You don't seem to have much regard for women in general."

"Most of the women I've met have been largely ornamental. I can't stand anything useless. Most women aren't bred for productive pursuits. They're a complete waste of time."

"And I'm a woman...."

Blair picked up her hands and held them palms up. "Look at your hands, farm girl," he said with surprising tenderness. "Your hands show that you've worked hard all your life. I'd be willing to bet you were never an ornament to anyone, not even your husband. I'll bet you walked behind the plow spreading seeds behind him...."

"When I wasn't pushing the plow myself."

"That's just it. You've earned these hands. There's strength in every inch of you. You're the most interesting woman I've ever met."

Adele slid her hands under his. "Your hands show the remains of calluses and scars. You're a businessman. You wear custom-tailored suits and sit behind a desk. How do you explain *your* hands?"

Blair stiffened. He pulled his hands away, stood up and walked toward the French doors that led to the outside of the house. "I can't explain them, because I don't know how they got that way. I've been able to speculate about how I came to lose my finger, but the remainder is a mystery."

Adele looked at him. His gray eyes were dark with misery. Her arms ached to gather him to her, but she knew the timing was wrong. He would not be likely to accept comforting in his current incarnation. Hastily, she said, "I must go. I left my sister with the baby. I've got to get back home."

"When can you start?"

"You tell me and I'll give notice at the boarding house and start packing."

"Three days, then. Let me get Lopez to take you home."

WHEN ADELE GOT home, Susannah and Stephen were waiting in the parlor, having forgone going out until she got back. Adele ran to Stephen and threw her arms around him.

"Oh, Stephen, I'm so happy."

"What's happened, Sissy?"

"Susannah, I've got a new job—and you're not going to believe it."

"What is it?"

"I'm going to be Joshua's governess. We move out of here in three days. Blair's going to put us all up, even Little Gent. Oh, go, have a nice evening. I'll explain everything in the morning."

Once outside, Stephen looked at Susannah. "Did you understand any of that?"

"Not really, except it sounds like we're going to be living under the same roof."

Stephen closed his eyes. "Oh, God, no."

Susannah got defensive. "What's the matter with you?"

"With you so close by, I'll never be able to keep my hands off you."

Susannah pulled him into an embrace. "I'm not going to complain, my darling."

He bent down and crushed her lips with his. His kiss was demanding and possessive. He pressed her against his length; she could feel the hard ridge of his desire building in him. Mischievously she slid her hand between them.

He released her with a gasp.

In the gaslight, her brown eyes were smoky with desire. "Just think. Once I'm living in your house, I can finally get a look at that."

"Oh, you'll get more than a look, I assure you."

"I can hardly wait."

Chapter 14

THREE DAYS later, Adele, Susannah and Bea took up residence in the Carroll mansion. Adele moved her things into the nanny's bedroom adjoining the nursery. A crib last used when Stephen was an infant was brought down from the attic, thoroughly cleaned and put in place for Beatrice to use.

Adele went into this new living arrangement with a great deal of foreboding. Though it seemed to serve the purpose she, Susannah and Stephen had discussed in the Chinese restaurant of putting her where she would be more in Blair's company, Adele was far from certain this would work. Independently, however, the idea of taking care of Joshua Carroll pleased her enormously. She thought he was a bright and delightful boy who had suffered a tremendous amount of upheaval in his very short life. She was willing to love and care for him merely because he was Blair's child. She quickly found herself loving him for himself.

Joshua was overjoyed. He was already more than a little bit in love with Adele from when she was fitting his new clothes. His former governess had stifled him with her overbearing strictness. Now he laughed, sang and chattered merrily. He tried to take possession of both Beatrice and Little Gent as his own. Beatrice loved his tickling and teasing and silly little songs. She followed him around as fast and far as her toddler's legs would allow. Joshua was so happy to have a playmate, even one who was still a baby, he purposely slowed down so he could keep Beatrice's hand in his as he walked her around the house. When she would plop down on her bottom and laugh, Joshua would find himself laughing with her, sharing her delight at her newly developing skill.

Little Gent was having none of it. Children were, after all, far beneath his feline dignity. He did, however, decide to adopt Blair, who would often unceremoniously carry him by the scruff of the neck and deposit him back in the nursery, only to find the little tom sleeping on his bed when he would turn in at night. Blair did not know what prompted Little Gent's behavior, since he could not remember that in Wyoming the cat often curled up on his lap when he read and would sleep in whichever bed in the house suited his fancy. Little Gent had always been partial to the scent of Brian Strange and this was the same man with the same scent as far as he was concerned.

Susannah blossomed. She set up in the little servant's room in the eaves like it was her own private atelier. She left every day with her easel and workbox to the railroad station, the square or the park where she would sketch people for a fee for hours. She started wearing her hair up. She began to spend the money she earned from her drawings on fashionable clothes that made her look so sophisticated that Stephen began to take her places where he could show her off.

She usually met Stephen outside the house and entered separately when they returned. They decided not to spring their growing relationship on Blair for fear of complicating matters.

About a week after they moved in, Susannah visited with Adele in the nursery, joining Bea and Joshua in play and then wished them goodnight. As she walked down the hall toward the back stairs, she checked to see if the coast was clear. Then she knocked twice on Stephen's closed door. He opened it and swept her in, locking the door behind him.

"Did anyone see you?" Stephen asked breathlessly.

"No," she responded confidently.

"Adele?"

"In the nursery with the kids, sewing Joshua's clothes. Blair?"

"Blair's out with business associates. He'll probably come home too drunk to hear anything."

"Then we're alone."

"Good." His arms were about her, crushing her to him. His mouth slanted against hers as he plunged the depths of her mouth, tasting her overwhelming sweetness. Her tongue dueled his, twisting and caressing. She nibbled on his lower lip and trailed wet kisses across his five o'clock shadowed cheek.

"It's been a long day," she said, stretching. She was well aware that reaching back thrust her full bosom into greater prominence.

Taking the hint, Stephen swept her up and carried her to his bed. He fell with her into its soft feather mattress and she wrapped her arms around him, feeling his whipcord leanness through the fine linen of his shirt. Susannah had grown up in the presence of work-muscled farm hands; first her father, then the reapers, then the massive musculature Blair had developed during the two years he lived with them in Wyoming. It often amazed her that she was so aroused by his reed slender younger brother. She pulled Stephen's face down to meet hers and plundered his mouth as he had done hers.

Stephen's hands roamed along her sides. Pulling her upright, he quickly undid the buttons down the back of her basque and pushed it down about her waist. Her chest heaved, causing her full breasts to strain against her muslin chemise. He bent down and began to suckle at her nipples through the thin fabric, feeling them tighten into hard buds.

"Please," she gasped, "I can't breathe. Let me up."

He did. She slid off the bed and turned to face him. With a wanton smile on her lips she pulled her arms out of her basque sleeves and dropped it to the ground. Untying the tapes that held her skirt and petticoats she slid them off her hips. Then, with agonizing slowness, she unhooked her corset hook by hook and dropped it on top of the pile. As she watched, she saw Stephen's desire growing harder by the minute beneath the meager protection of his trousers.

Susannah took a step towards the bed and Stephen grabbed her by both arms and pulled her on top of him. She kissed him full on the mouth and then drifted down to kiss the hollow at the base of his throat. Stephen yanked the hairpins out of her hair and put his fingers through the thick sable mass until he'd spread it out over her back. She began to undo the small bone buttons on the front of his shirt, following the opening with nips and kisses, nuzzling her nose in his thick wiry mat of black chest hair. She thought briefly in passing that the Carroll men were both finely furred—and that she liked it in Stephen—very much indeed. She felt no guilt whatsoever at these thoughts. She was an artist—a creature of the senses. Such observations were her nature.

Susannah reached the waistband of Stephen's trousers and began to pull his shirttails out of his pants. She spread his shirt open and followed the path of her hands to one of his flat copper paps. She nibbled on the sensitive bud until he nearly screamed.

In a quick move he had her on her back. Sitting beside her, he pulled open the buttons on her boots and drew them off. The misshapen boot that protected her clubfoot was harder to remove, but he gently pulled it off. Her stockings followed. He kissed her legs, beginning behind her knees and working his way down each calf as he uncovered it. He then positioned himself to sit between her thighs and bent her knees so her feet rested on his chest. He slipped his hands between his chest and her feet and laced his fingers between her toes, using his thumbs to massage her soles. Susannah moaned in her desire as he continued to massage her feet. A languid heat flowed through her starting at the base of her womanhood that lay partially open to him through the unsewn seam of her pantalets.

Stephen again shifted until he straddled her. He loosened the drawstring that held the top of her chemise and the waistband of her pantalets. He pulled both garments off so she was naked to his gaze. He shrugged off his shirt and reached for her. He ran his hands up her ribcage from her hips until he hefted the weight of her firm, full breasts in his hands. She was soft and gently round—almost plump—and it drove Stephen wild to touch her. As she had done to him, he took one pale pink nipple in his mouth and suckled possessively, raising the nipple to a hard pebble. Susannah moaned as lightning shot through her again and again. Stephen shifted to the other nipple and Susannah was sure her body would explode with sensation.

With his hands still caressing her breasts, Stephen once more took possession of her mouth, then lowered himself so his chest flattened her breasts against him. Both of them were breathing raggedly, unconsciously grunting and groaning as they caressed each other. He rose slightly and looked at her eyes. They were smoky with desire. She stared back at eyes dark as steel yet almost glowing silver.

"I know you're a virgin, Susannah," Stephen rasped. "I've never been with a virgin before, but I need you desperately. This is your last chance to say 'no,' Susannah. If you do, I'll stop right now, even if it kills me. But from this point on there's no turning back."

"I love you, Stephen. I don't ever want to say no to you," she murmured.

"It may hurt some," he warned.

"I can bear it."

Stephen rose to his knees and unbuttoned his fly, then slid his long legs out of the trousers. His manhood sprung out—long, thick and blood-engorged with need for her.

"Oh, my!" she gasped. "You are so beautiful!"

"Open for me, Susannah."

Her thighs parted and he touched her dark mound. She was moist and open as her hips rose to meet his hand. Stephen knew she was never so ready as now and he thrust home with one powerful stroke, piercing her fragile maidenhead as she bit her lip to keep from screaming in pain and pleasure. She was small, tight and wet inside and the rubbing of his engorged organ within her small passage raised both his arousal and her sensation. She wrapped her legs around his hips as he thrust again and again. Her nails dug into his back and she moaned more and more, her vaginal muscles trying to draw him further inside her.

Suddenly, wave after wave of powerful explosion crashed through her. Her body became covered with a sheen of perspiration and her eyes closed as her climax shattered her. With a groan, Stephen released his seed deep inside her until he collapsed, spent and sated, on top of her.

She held him in her arms, hardly feeling his weight on her, and stroked his coal black waves, lacing them through her fingers. His breathing evened out until she knew he had drifted off to sleep. She nudged him until he rolled off her and covered him with the sheet and coverlet, with her snuggling beside him until she, too, closed her eyes for the night.

When Stephen woke up the next morning, Susannah was gone, having gathered up her things and sneaked up to her room to avoid suspicion. The only hints to her presence were a few hairpins in the bed, a trace of blood on the sheet and—he saw later in the mirror as he dressed—some very noticeable love bites on his neck and shoulders.

Touching the marks she left on him as tenderly as he would have touched her, Stephen said aloud, "Soon, beloved, you won't have to leave before dawn. Soon you will be mine forever."

A FIRE CUT down the March chill, but did little to warm the atmosphere of the office Blair kept at home. The furnishings were heavy and Victorian; mahogany desk, bookshelves and filing cabinets; dark leather wing and desk chairs; dark wood paneling; heavy curtains. The overall impression was oppressively somber. It was a room fit for an individual who was trying very hard to keep contentment and happiness out of his life.

Blair sat at his desk, reviewing some documents he had not finished at the office. A steel pen poised in his hand, he made sketchy, scrawled notes on a separate page with quick dips into the inkwell. Occasionally he stared at the page, noting the change in his script that adjusting for his lost finger caused.

He closed his eyes trying to squeeze from his brain a memory that simply was not there. Did he know how he had lost the finger? Was that part of the lost time? Who was the woman who haunted his dreams? What kind of life had he been living that had changed his body so drastically? He had nobody he called friend, but his acquaintances and business associates commented, often snidely, about his tanned face with the pale forehead scar, his callused hands and the laborer's muscles even the best tailoring could not disguise.

Shaking his head, he resumed his review, trying to force his concentration to focus. In the four months since his return from God knows where, he had been unable to focus on this work he had hated but had managed so skillfully for so many years. Too many people relied on him to be what he had mandated himself to be: the stern, hard-driven entrepreneur. To keep wishing to return to his foggy idyll, his dream world of dark angels and open spaces was foolishness.

Unexpectedly, a light knock at the door served as a vaguely welcome interruption. Blair looked up to see Adele leaning in from around the door.

"Good afternoon, Blair. I hope I'm not disturbing you."

Blair put down his pen. "Not really. The words are swimming around tonight anyway. Why don't you come all the way in, Adele? I don't bite—much."

Adele stepped inside the room. Blair noticed she was wearing her usual modest white cotton shirtwaist with the tiny tucks in the front and an unassuming ruffle trimming the high collar, above a plain navy blue skirt of lightweight wool. As plain as the garments were, they perfectly suited Adele's tall, slender form. Blair thought fleetingly that he could not imagine this woman in frills or frivolous laces or pastel colors. She was a practical woman who wore practical clothes. Her hair was drawn back into a braided chignon at the nape of her neck.

For a moment Blair found himself wondering how long her hair was and what it might look like unbound. He then put the thought forcefully out of his head. It would not do for his dream world to intrude on reality anymore than it did already. It was folly to mistake this flesh and blood woman for the dark angel of his dreams.

"Is there something I can do for you?" he asked.

"Have you made any dinner plans?"

"Actually, I hadn't thought about it. Why do you ask?"

"Well, the cook has the night out and Stephen is taking my sister out for dinner and the theater. I was going to make something light and I wondered if you might be interested in joining the children and me for dinner in the nursery."

"Why would I want to do that?"

"Joshua was telling me he hasn't seen you for the longest time. I realize for a six-year-old 'the longest time' could be two or three days, but I think he would enjoy having dinner with his father. He tells me he hasn't done that in the three months he's been here. You really ought to get to know him better. He's a wonderful boy."

Blair stared through Adele. She could not tell what he thought of the idea.

Suddenly, he leaned forward as if better focused. "Are you a good cook?"

Adele looked down. Blair noticed how long and thick her lashes were. As he had the night Donelli fired her and she cried against his chest, he felt oddly drawn to her. If he did not know himself better, he would have sworn it was sexual attraction. But that was ridiculous. He did not even like women that much.

Adele's response brought him back into focus. "I guess the best compliment you could give me is to say that I'm a competent but indifferent cook. Susannah is the family cook. She loves cooking. I just make simple fare, filling but not too exciting. But you won't get sick from my cooking," she added hastily.

Blair chuckled. "Sounds just like you, Adele. Always practical."

"I make do; I always have. Being fancy doesn't get you too far on a farm. I suppose my only real talents are with a needle."

"Ah, but in that you're prime stock. I've never had clothes that fit so well as the ones you made for me. What's your secret?"

Adele blushed to her roots. *How can I tell you it's because I've had intimate contact with every part of your body? I probably know your body better than you do yourself.*

Instead she answered, "Just years of making everything my father, and then my husband, wore."

"Like that sacque suit you lent me until some of my order from Donelli was finished."

"Yes, only that suit was special. We couldn't afford new fabric very often, so before that suit I usually had to make over my father's things for him. He never criticized me for it, but it never stopped me from wanting to make him clothes that were just for him."

"How recently did your husband die?"

Adele started, a shudder running through her, "I never said he was dead."

Blair sat upright. "Is he still alive?"

"More or less," she said sadly. "He no longer recognizes me as his wife, nor is he aware of our marriage."

Blair had been under the impression that Adele was a recent widow. That she was still married was a shock to him. Even more shocking was his assumption now that her husband was insane to the point where he no longer recognized his wife.

If she were my *wife,* he found himself thinking, *I would never forget her.* Somehow, the idea of being married to this woman was not as repugnant as the thought of marriage had always been to him in the past. He frowned slightly. Since he had known Adele Strange, extraordinary thoughts of that sort had begun to bang around in his brain. "Is there no hope of his recovery?" he asked with mixed feelings of concern.

"While we're both alive, there is always hope, but I get discouraged," she answered. "He doesn't know I'm his wife, but he acknowledges my existence as a person. When I see him, he's generally nice to me, but not with any depth of feeling. Not like we had. I feel sorrier for my baby. She was truly Daddy's girl, but she's too young to explain to her where her father has gone. I'm so glad to have Joshua as well as my Beatrice to care for. It gives me something to keep from brooding about the past. I must get back to them now. Will you come tonight? Seven thirty?"

"Why not? It might be amusing."

Amusing was not what Adele had hoped for, but it was better than nothing. Adele turned and headed out the door.

"Adele—"

Adele poked her head around the door again. "Yes, Blair?"

"What are you making?"

"Oh, baked chicken, green salad, cooked carrots...."

"Do you like sweet wine or dry wine?"

Adele shrugged. "I don't know. I've never had wine before."

"Can you taste us?" he had asked that morning.

"Um-Hmm," she had responded. "We taste good together."

"Sweeter than wine."

"I wouldn't know. I've never had wine...."

With a smile, she added, "Surprise me."

For a minute, it seemed to Blair that the office lit up with her smile. Then she shut the door behind her as she left and the lightness faded.

A light knock bade him answer.

Adele pushed her head in again. "I forgot. Don't dress for dinner."

"Beg your pardon?"

"Shirt sleeves are okay. Dinner with a six-year-old and a baby is hardly the most formal dining. Until later," she finished and the door closed again.

SUSANNAH TWIRLED around in front of Adele in the bedroom just off the nursery. She was wearing a brand-new dress of lavender silk trimmed with silk violets and a ruffle-trimmed bustle. The gown was cut off the shoulder and lower in the décolletage than any gown she had ever owned, showing off her full bosom and pale skin. Her sable hair had been pulled up with sausage curls dripping down over one shoulder. The cut of the bodice combined with a tightly laced corset made her waist look small. Her face was rouged with excitement and her eyes shone. She looked a strange combination of sophisticated lady and wide-eyed country girl.

"You look like a princess tonight," Adele admired. "Like Cinderella going to the ball."

"You don't think this dress is too racy, do you? Do you think Stephen will like it?"

"I'm not expert on racy dresses, but I think it will drive him crazy. If you're not careful, you could wind up in bed with him. If it's not already too late."

Susannah blushed beet red. "Do you mind?"

Adele laughed, the first honest laugh she'd had in months. "Mind? Sweetheart, what kind of question is that from the girl who gave me a lover as a Christmas present?"

Soon both women were laughing uproariously at the joyful memory. They hardly heard the knock at the bedroom door.

Stephen strode into the room, looking like Prince Charming to Susannah's Cinderella. His long, lean frame was adorned in spotless white tie and perfectly cut evening clothes with a pearl gray waistcoat that turned his gray eyes silver. A rebellious curl of his raven hair fell over his brow despite the conservative cut of his hair. Although he was two inches shorter than Blair was, his slimness made him seem taller in these fine black clothes.

It was a toss up who gasped louder, Susannah at seeing Stephen or vice versa. Stephen took Susannah's hand and pressed the back of it to his lips. Susannah glanced downward, suddenly shy. The intensity of Stephen's gaze melted through her and turned her knees to jelly. She started to lose her balance, but Stephen caught her in his arms and pulled her towards him. Their arms slid around each other as Stephen pressed his lips to Susannah's.

"Excuse me," Adele interrupted, "but if you keep that up you're never going to get to the theater."

Stephen colored slightly, pulling away from Susannah and meeting Adele's steady gaze with a questioning one of his own.

"If you're concerned about my reaction, don't be. I'm all in favor. Just please be careful here in the house, for my sake. Blair knows you're going out tonight, but I'm afraid it wouldn't do yet to let him find out it's gone that far."

Stephen smiled at Adele, then turned to Susannah. "My brother is still cloistered in his office. Maybe you should get downstairs now and get your cloak and gloves. I need to have a few words with Adele in private before we leave."

"*I go, I go! Look how I go! Swifter than an arrow from the Tartar's bow.*" Susannah quoted. "See, I even read the play in advance. Meet you out front." She stepped out of the room, shut the door behind her and headed down the hall.

After Susannah left, Adele said to Stephen, "I casually let Blair know you're taking Susannah out tonight. But I didn't make it sound like anything particularly important except that you would both be out of the house. So I guess you two can stop acting like you don't know each other."

Stephen sat down in a chair next to Adele's.

"I know I don't need your permission, but I'm asking anyway. I'm in love with Susannah."

"I know."

"I think it was love at first sight."

"I know how that is."

"I want to marry her. I'm going to ask her tonight."

"You don't need my permission, but you certainly have my blessing. Do you enjoy each other?"

Stephen blushed. "You mean—um—you know, it all sort of just happened. But God, yes, we do have fun." His occasional fluster at the discussion of intimate subjects was endearing to Adele.

"Stephen, you're the only one I can tell," began Adele, tears blocking her throat. "This all is getting beyond my bearing it. To see Blair day after day and not be able to touch him or tell him. Stephen, we were always touching each other, teasing each other. It was like making love twenty-four hours a day. Just watching his muscles move when he worked could arouse me. This Blair Carroll is so stern and stiff and unhappy. Sometimes I see more of Brian Strange in you than in him."

Stephen was silent a moment. "I don't think Blair has been truly happy since he was sixteen. Before that he was a hell-raiser—well, maybe not a hell-raiser, but carefree and friendly and always finding things to laugh about. In those days, Blair was my best friend and protector. Our mother was not a very strong woman but she listened to us. It was Blair who wanted to be a lawyer, but when Mother died, Dad, in his grief, pushed Blair behind a desk at the company and didn't let him go to college like he wanted. Then, after Blair worked and waited two years for our father to get over Mother dying, he showed up back in town with a mistress barely older than we were and dumped the business on Blair to run for good. Alabama Dodge is pretty and I'm sure Father loves her to distraction, but she's silly and gushing and stupid and all the characteristics Blair has no patience for. I think Blair saw for the first time an example of a frivolous woman stealing his life from him. Then I went away to college. I can only assume he found more examples during those years. By the time I got back from college myself, Blair had built a shell around him. He'd had some quick affairs, including with Joshua's mother, but he expressed the opinion that all women were as useless and ornamental as Alabama and as much a waste of time. He was willing to marry Julia Longridge because she would look good on his arm and not intrude on his business nor his thoughts any more than necessary.

"By the time we went to Milwaukee two and a half years ago to get custody of Joshua, I think he'd developed such contempt for women that he'd virtually stopped having sex altogether. The funny, friendly big brother I grew up with made himself into a dour, hard-driving, misogynistic cynic. I think that blow to the head those bushwhackers gave him wiped the slate clean. The cynic was driven out of his brain and what was left for you to find was what was there before disappointment changed him."

"Stephen, I was his lover, then his wife. I'm still his wife. Our marriage was legal because he was using Brian Strange as his legal name when we got married. It was the only name he had. I love him with all my heart and I think that my heart will break if I can't get him back. I'm going to do something I never thought I would ever do. I'm going to attempt to seduce a married man—who happens to be my own husband. It may not work. He thought I was a widow. Now he knows I'm not. But I can't bear this much longer. If I can't help him fit the puzzle pieces together again by the time you and Susannah get married—and I know you will—I will take Bea and go back to Wyoming where I belong and file for divorce from 'Brian Strange' for desertion."

Stephen kissed his sister-in-law's cheek and rose to leave. "I love you, Adele. I don't want Susannah or myself to lose you. I'll help you in any way you want."

As Stephen reached for the door, Adele called, "When you come home tonight, do you think you can manage to convince Susannah not to visit my room as camouflage to conceal her going to yours? I may need this room to myself tonight."

Stephen's silver eyes sparkled. "Well—I can give it a try. But you know, the bed in Blair's room is larger."

"That may be, but I don't want this to seem too planned."

"Understood. Good night, big sister."

AS THE LAST half hour ticked down on the little mantel clock atop the nursery fireplace, Adele hurried to complete the finishing touches on the most important evening of her life.

Joshua sensed the importance to himself as well, as he insisted on wearing the new blue suit Adele had made for him, the small sacque coat and ankle length pants, with a light-blue dutchboy shirt. Fully dressed, he was helping out by arranging the silverware on the table that doubled for meals and lessons. His face was serious, concentrating on the task as if it were the most challenging campaign a general ever mounted.

Adele glanced over at the serious-faced little boy and her heart caught. His curly black hair and dark gray eyes were the image of the Carroll brothers. Blair must have looked so at this age. Joshua's uncanny ability to focus on a new task and learn it the first time was every bit like the father he, as yet, barely knew. He may have inherited his mother's gentle nature, but in that he was his father's son.

She then looked down at Beatrice, who was fussing tiredly in her arms. It was apparent she would sleep through the dinner and, with luck, the whole night. Like Joshua, Bea had the Carroll looks, baby soft black hair and eyes like silver velvet. Despite having different mothers, these children were as plainly sister and brother as the Carroll brothers themselves were. If Blair saw her, would he see it? Beatrice had none of Adele in her features, but everything of Blair.

"Is Bea coming to dinner?" asked Joshua.

"No, sweetheart. It looks like she's going to sleep now."

"That's too bad."

"Why so?"

"She's so funny when she bangs with the spoon and tries to talk."

Joshua ran over to Adele. "Miss Adele, can I kiss Bea good night?"

"May I...."

"May I kiss Bea good night?"

Adele stooped down to Joshua's height. The little boy threw his arms around the baby and kissed her on the cheek.

"Good night, Bea. Sleep well," he said, then added in a whisper in the baby's ear he didn't know Adele could hear, "I wish you were my sister."

Adele's eyes filled with unshed tears. *God, how I wish I could tell you that she really is your sister. There's so much love in this little boy. He needs so much in return. I only hope his father can see it.* She stood up and put Beatrice in the white painted crib in her bedroom. She brushed her hand up the baby's cheek and smoothed her fine curls. Bea made contented gibberish noises, which became less frequent until replaced with the even breathing of slumber.

Returning to the nursery, she said, "Joshua, how are you doing with the table?"

He took her hand and led her to the table. "See, all done."

"Indeed it is, and it's all correct." She drew her arm around the boy's shoulders and gave him a quick hug. "Can you sit over there and look at your picture book for a few minutes while I go downstairs and get our dinner?"

Joshua nodded his accord and went over to the rocker near the fireplace. Adele quickly ran down the back stairs and loaded the freshly cooked food on a silver serving tray Bertha had set up for her before leaving for her night out. She grabbed the tray by its handles and carried it upstairs to the nursery, the smell of freshly baked chicken drifting along behind her.

At 7:20 she went into her bedroom. Taking off the shirtwaist and navy skirt, she put on the muslin dress she'd worn on her wedding day and pinched her cheeks and glanced in the cheval glass. Something was not quite right.

"Not exactly the seductress type, are you?" she said aloud.

In a final gesture, she reached behind her head and systematically pulled every hairpin from her chignon. Unpinned, her braid unrolled down her back, ending as it did just above her knees. She said a prayer that the dress and braid might jog a memory.

Her heart pounding, Adele went back into the nursery, leaving the door ajar so she could hear Beatrice if need be. She stood over by the table and waited as the seconds inexorably ticked toward 7:30.

Chapter 15

AT PRECISELY 7:30 the nursery door opened and Blair walked in. He was dressed as he had been in his office, dress shirt, suit trousers and matching vest. He had left off his jacket, but had retied his necktie. A corkscrew stuck out of a vest pocket and he carried a bottle of white wine and two glasses in his left hand. His tall, muscled frame filled the doorway. In shirt sleeves there was no mistaking the breadth of his shoulders for padding. Adele was struck, as she always had been, by how unbearably handsome he was.

"Daddy!" came a musical voice from the direction of the fireplace as the black-haired little boy climbed down from the rocking chair and ran over to his father. Joshua threw his arms around Blair's leg and looked up at this giant more than twice his size. "I'm so glad you came!"

Blair stared down at the package of love and energy wrapped around his leg, then up at the woman who stood observing them. His eyes reflected fear, confusion and discomfort.

He should not be afraid. He was Blair Carroll. He was afraid of nothing. Nothing ever touched his soul anymore. He had long ago willed away his vulnerability. Why was it since returning home did he feel so changed? What had happened during those two missing years that made him react with emotion and need? The thought made him shudder inside.

He again looked down at the child and stiffly touched the little raven head with his right hand. He marveled at how soft Joshua's hair was and how worshipful the gaze. His face reddened with embarrassment at how little he deserved this unabashed show of affection. His touch on Joshua's hair relaxed and he stroked the dark curls with an awe he rarely felt in anyone's presence.

Quietly, Adele closed the distance between them and took the bottle and glasses from his hand and returned with them to the table. Joshua took his father's right hand, completely oblivious to its mutilation, and pulled Blair to the table.

"Look, Daddy, I set the table all by myself. Miss Adele taught me. She says it's a special occasion."

Blair looked at Adele. "Is it a special occasion, Miss Adele?" He could not avoid the upward turn of his lips at adding the *Miss* to her name.

"Joshua's first dinner with his father; I would think so."

"And your daughter? Will she be joining us?"

Adele looked in the direction of the bedroom. "Sound asleep. You'll have to meet Beatrice another time, I fear. It's a shame. She learned a new word in honor of the occasion."

"Miss Adele," Joshua put in, "Bea is learning new words every day. Daddy, you have to meet her. She's so smart and pretty. Almost as pretty as Miss Adele."

Adele felt a rush of color flood her face. Blair saw it, too.

"Well," Blair responded, "if she's almost as pretty as Miss Adele she must be very beautiful indeed."

Brian Strange often told Adele he thought her beautiful. With him, she had come to believe it. Brian was gone, but if it was not an idle compliment in response to Joshua's comments, than Adele could retain hope of winning the man who stood before her.

"Dinner smells wonderful. I could smell it in the hall as I came up from the wine cellar. It's a German Rhine wine, called Riesling," he added, indicating, "A little on the sweet side, but good for someone's first taste, I think."

ALL THROUGH the dinner, Joshua did most of the talking, Blair did most of the listening and Adele did most of the looking.

The eating itself was largely a formality. As Adele had warned, she was only an adequate cook, but the fare disappeared anyway.

Joshua assailed Blair with stories about the train ride from Milwaukee and all the things that he had seen in San Francisco and the park where Uncle Stephen had taken him and Miss Susannah's pictures and did Blair want to see the pictures Miss Susannah had drawn of him and Uncle Stephen the day he arrived in San Francisco. And Miss Adele: He talked over and over again about the wonderful things Miss Adele showed him, like how to tie his shoes and set the table and write his name, Joshua Leval Carroll and...and...and....

At the name *Leval*, Blair started a bit. He had been listening and nodding before that, wondering to himself in passing where he had acquired the patience to listen to a six-year-old. It was not in his experience or nature to do so. All the while he concentrated on the face of the dark-haired lady in the modest ecru muslin gown who sat across from him, earnestly returning his gaze over her still nearly full wine glass.

The sound of Cherry's last name reminded him that Joshua was a mistake, the result of a short term, meaningless affair he had conducted because there could be no repercussions. How wrong Blair had been about that! Joshua should never have been born, and yet, here he was, a perfect miniature of his reluctant father. Blair felt suddenly embarrassed at the ego of thinking he could have tried to swoop down and take this little boy away from his mother, even if she was an actress and a harlot. For a moment, he felt sorry that Cherry was dead, even though he could not begin to dredge her face up in his mind. She had raised a smart and enthusiastic son without anyone's help.

Blair had not wanted to like Joshua. He thought it would be easier that way, less complicated to just do his legal duty without getting emotionally involved. Now he knew that would be impossible. If he was not very careful, this little charmer would draw him in and force him to care about his new son. He was afraid he would begin to like it.

Adele had said next to nothing since they sat down to dinner. She watched as the emotional distance between her beloved and his miniature narrowed. This was not the emotional closeness of which Brian had been capable, but it was a start. It was every bit as important for these two to become truly father and son as it was for her to get her husband back. She didn't know whether to laugh or cry.

"Daddy, can I ask you a question?"

"*May* I," Adele corrected and Joshua repeated the question properly.

"What do you want to know, son?"

Joshua put his little hand on Blair's right. "Miss Adele told me that a bandit cut your finger off to steal a ring from you. Is that true?" Curiously he touched the small, thin, white scar.

Blair closed his hand over his son's. "Yes, I suspect that's true, but your Uncle Stephen got my ring back for me," he replied, showing Joshua the signet that he now wore on his left little finger.

Joshua touched the ring in wonder.

"When you're twenty-one years old, I'll buy you one. It was a tradition in your grandmother's family for at least four generations to have worn a ring like this one. Your grandfather gave me this one and one day you'll give one to your son."

Joshua's eyes brightened. "I have a grandfather?"

Blair shrugged. "Yes. He lives in Europe. Do you know where that is?" Blair tried very hard to keep his distaste for Oscar out of his comment. One day Joshua might have to make up his own mind about his grandfather if he ever met him.

Joshua nodded. "I can find it on the globe. It's a long way from San Francisco."

Blair nodded. "Yes, a very long way." *In more ways than one, eh, Oscar?*

"You're wearing two rings, Daddy. What's the other one for?"

Blair glanced down at the horseshoe nail band he wore on his left ring finger. "It's to remind me of something I've forgotten."

"I don't understand."

"I'm not sure I understand myself."

I understand, thought Adele. *I may be the only one who does.*

"Can—may I ask you another question, Daddy?"

"Of course. I'll answer it if I can."

"I was in the park with Miss Adele a few days ago. I was chasing a ball when I saw a family. It was a man with orange hair, a lady with yellow hair like Molly has and a little boy as big as me with orange hair, too. He picked up the ball and I asked him to give it back. The lady looked at me like she didn't like me. She took the ball out of the boy's hands and said, 'Stanley, you mustn't play with that boy.' The boy asked her why and she said, 'Don't you know who he is? He's Blair Carroll's bastard.' Then, she dropped the ball on the ground and the family walked away....'"

Adele gasped. Joshua had not told her of the exchange before now. As for Blair, the color drained out of his tanned face and he looked as if he had been struck by lightning.

"What's a bastard? The lady made it sound like something awful. Is something wrong with me?" he finished with a frown.

Blair stiffened noticeably and his hands fisted until the knuckles were white. "Absolutely not. There's nothing wrong with you. I'm the one with whom something is wrong."

"Then what's a bastard?" Joshua repeated. "Am I a bastard?"

Blair looked to Adele for help. How could he answer this question simply?

"Sweetheart," Adele said, "*bastard* is a not very nice word to call a child whose mama and daddy weren't married when he was born. You lived with your mama alone because she and your daddy weren't married, but when she died you came here to live with your daddy. There isn't anything you did except be born, but some people treat a little boy like you as if it was your fault you were born."

"But I didn't know those people who called me that. How did they know who I was?"

"News travels fast in San Francisco," Blair put in. "That family must have heard about you from someone. And you look so much like I did when I was a boy that there is no mistaking that you're my son."

Joshua frowned. "When Miss Susannah first saw me, she asked Uncle Stephen if *he* was my Daddy."

"Honey," said Adele. "I don't think she'd make that mistake again."

DINNER ENDED, and Joshua pulled Blair over to the rocking chair to show him his storybook while Adele cleared the table and brought the dishes downstairs for Bertha and Molly to attend to in the morning. The half-filled wine bottle and glasses she left on the table. When she turned around and saw father and son huddled together she was sure she had done the right thing for both of them. A jealous pain shot through her heart, as she realized that Beatrice deserved the same opportunity and might not ever have it again unless Blair regained the memory of his time as Brian Strange.

As Blair read Joshua a story from his book, the little boy's head began to nod and he was asleep before the tale was told.

"I think it's time for bed," whispered Adele, reaching for Joshua.

Blair usurped her duty, rising from the rocker with Joshua in his arms and carried him into his bedroom adjoining the nursery. Together they undressed him and got him into his nightshirt. When Adele had him all tucked in, as she had done to Beatrice, she ran her hand along his cheek and through his black hair.

As she looked up, her brandy brown eyes met Blair's steady gray gaze. Silently, she walked back into the nursery, Blair following behind.

"What a change you've wrought," he said. "When he first came here from Milwaukee, he was scared to death of me."

"Not as scared as you were of him," she observed. "You didn't stop being scared until tonight."

Blair looked pained. "You're right. He loves me."

"You seem amazed at that. You're his father."

"You loved your father, didn't you."

Adele sighed, "I truly did. I would have cut off my arm if it meant he hadn't had to die in such slow agony. He gave us everything he had without hesitation. But you and your father are at odds and have been for years."

Blair responded bitterly, "I sometimes wonder if he ever loved me as much as he loved the *idea* of me, oldest son and heir and all. It was so convenient for him that I was the right age when he decided to go gallivanting around the world and leave me with the business and Stephen to raise. You know, I purposely changed the company name from Carroll and Sons to Carroll Enterprises just to spite him."

"You know, history doesn't have to repeat itself. You're not your father. You don't have to treat your son like your father treated you. Give him a fair chance to be himself and give yourself a fair chance to love him."

"Joshua isn't even your kin, but you seem to care about him so much more than just a governess."

Adele shrugged. "I'm a mother first and a governess because it suits me to be one. Joshua has enough love to go around and some to spare. One day you'll see him with Bea. He's so bright and inquisitive. He learns things so quickly. I seldom have to teach him anything twice. He has a memory like I've never seen. You read him something once and he can recite it back to you exactly. If I ever have a son, I would want him to be just like Josh. I hope Bea grows up to be like Josh."

"I don't deserve him, you know."

Adele put her hand over Blair's mouth. "Don't you dare say that! What makes you think you don't deserve love?"

Blair took that hand in his. He looked right in Adele's eyes as he had over Joshua's bed. She felt the heat of his gaze and gave as good as she got.

"The first time I meet someone I could possibly love and she's not available." He pressed her hand to his lips.

Adele closed her eyes. An electrical shudder ran through her. "Maybe she's more available than you think." She pulled away suddenly and walked away from him toward the nursery window.

As she stared out the window at the March night, she felt the heat of his presence behind. He lifted his hand to the nape of her neck and ran it under her braid.

"You wore your hair down. I wondered how long it was."

The air was charged with electricity. Without warning, Blair spun Adele around and crushed her along his length. Her tall body fit his taller one perfectly. He lowered his lips to hers and gently kissed her.

To him it seemed that they were built to be each other's complement. To her, it was like they had always fit together, no matter what he was calling himself. She slid her arms around him and parted her lips.

His kiss became more possessive. His tongue probed, dueling with hers. She could feel the rising hardness of his maleness through her skirts and warmth began to suffuse her, burning up from her secret core. He nibbled on her lower lip and drifted up, kissing her jaw and nibbling her earlobe.

She shuddered a little. This was not her gentle Brian sharing his love with her. This was Blair Carroll taking what he wanted. She told herself it was the same man, then refuted it. He was a different man with different ways. She told herself this man shouldn't arouse her this way, then realized this lovemaking was every bit as exciting as the other. She barely noticed the slight tugging at her scalp as Blair pulled the binding from the bottom of her braid and began to unplait it. Neither did she feel his fingers on the bone buttons on the back of her bodice, buttons he himself had made for her.

Blair ran his fingers through her hair as he held her against him. "So soft," he murmured. Desire seared through him as it had never done before—at least to his memory.

The cold feel of her hair on her back reminded Adele of her goal for the evening. Taking Blair's hands in hers, she backed into her bedroom and guided him to the bed. She dropped her slippers from her feet as she allowed him to press her onto her back on the bed.

Blair swung one knee onto the bed and eased Adele's bodice off her shoulders and below her bosom. He unbuttoned her chemise and unhooked her corset, revealing her small firm breasts with the aureolae darkened from lactation. The nipples were already hardening into hard buds as he worried them with his thumbs. Adele noticed his hands were nearly as smooth and callus-free again as they had been when she had first found him. Four months of care had all but erased two years of hard labor. The thought saddened her and she sighed.

Blair mistook the sigh for a sign of arousal. He quickly pulled his own clothes off and, returning to the bed, pressed his lips to one dusky nipple. As he laved at the bud, to his surprise he tasted mother's milk.

"You're still nursing?" he said in amazement.

"A bit. She's nearly weaned now. Do you mind?"

His answer was to taste another sample. The action and taste aroused him to a hardness he never expected. He reached for the tapes closing her skirt, petticoats and pantalets and slid them down from her waist, across her firm, flat stomach and down her long legs.

Starting at each knee, he released her garters and rained kisses on her shins as he peeled off her stockings until she was naked and revealed to him. He drifted his trail of kisses back up from her toes to the sensitive flesh of her inner thighs. He found her pulsing bud with his tongue. His mustache grazed the aching flesh, increasing the sensations. Using his tongue, lips and teeth Blair visited exquisite pleasure pain on Adele.

Her response was to cry out mindlessly as he drew her higher and higher; her hips rose to meet his ministrations, she rained her desire in sex-scented fragrant flow. She could not be calculating. She needed him too much.

"It's too much," she gasped.

"Should I stop?"

"Oh, no, don't stop, don't stop."

"You're so ready."

He returned to his task. Her heat rose higher still, her moans more emphatic until, suddenly, she exploded in wave after wave of fulfillment, her whole body shaking, tears flowing from her eyes.

Her climaxes barely were stilled when he rose above her and plunged his sex like a sword into her sheath. Childbirth notwithstanding, her muscles drew him in tightly, holding his increasing arousal, which was hardening more and more. Wrapping her legs around her hips, she tried to pull him inside her more and more deeply as he thrust himself harder and harder.

His own release brought a shattering moan and near convulsive shudders as his seed spilled inside her. He collapsed on top of her; she barely felt his weight on her although she could feel the dampness of his perspiration on his back and fur pelted chest. For the first time in four months, she felt whole. Tears welled in her eyes as he rolled off her and fell asleep next to her. Not knowing what else to do, she cuddled up against his side and drifted off herself, her hand on his chest.

ALONG ABOUT two a.m., Beatrice woke up and began to cry. The sound slowly roused Adele, but as she moved to respond, her partner opened his eyes and rolled out of bed. Still naked, he walked toward the crib. He leaned down into the crib and picked up the little girl, holding her to his bare chest.

"Don't cry now, sweeting, Daddy's here," he crooned, smoothing her curls.

The words brought Adele to immediate attention. In the dim light she saw him approach the bed again and sit. She took a good look at his eyes; they were cloudy and unfocused in a way she had never seen.

She took a deep breath and a big chance. "Brian?"

"I think she may be hungry." He held Beatrice out to her.

Adele held Bea to her naked breast. The baby rooted a moment and found the familiar tap and began to suck contentedly.

She took another look; her gaze was not met. Brian was looking in her direction but not really at her.

"Brian, I'm so glad you're back. I missed you."

He cocked his head slightly and grinned, "Green River's not so far away. Did Susannah enjoy her paintbox?"

"Brian, what date is it?"

"Silly girl," he said kissing her forehead. "It's December eighth, Susannah's birthday, unless it's after midnight already."

"What do you remember last?"

There was a pause. His brow furrowed. "Thunder was screaming, spooked at something. He must have kicked me; I don't remember getting home tonight."

Brian stroked Adele's hair. "I love it when you unplait your hair. It's like a satin curtain." He pressed her head against his shoulder; Bea wedged between them. "It's so right, the three of us together. I was right that first day. You are an angel."

He took the sated Beatrice back into his arms and rising, brought her back to her crib. Adele saw the outline of his magnificent body, still hard with muscle even if his hands were now smooth, as he moved back to the bed. She held out her arms, welcoming him back into that intimate space.

"Brian, I love you so much."

"Ten times your love wouldn't equal mine for you."

She sobbed. "Make love to me, please darling."

His old crooked grin appeared, seeming strange under the well-trimmed mustache. He pressed his lips to her shoulder and blew against her skin like a trumpet. Adele squealed as he moved his hands to her taut belly and began to tickle her mercilessly with the backs of his fingers. She laughed and tickled him back, teasing his ridged stomach as his hands drifted down to her sable thatch. His tickles turned to caresses as he manipulated her throbbing bud with his fingers.

For her part she found one of his flat copper nipples and began to lave it with tongue and teeth.

"You undo me," he groaned hoarsely.

Shifting in the bed, she responded, "I haven't even begun to undo you."

Rising to her hands and knees, she pushed Brian back in the bed. Using her own fingernails, she drifted lines of heat down his belly to his own protective nest. Gently she slid her hands under his scrotum and around his manroot. She lowered her head to its iron length and velvet tip. Brian gasped as she moved her tongue around the underside of the ridge where tip joined shaft. She bit slightly, not to cause pain, but to tease and arouse.

Brian's breath ragged, he reveled in sensation as she slid her fingers and tongue up and down his sex. He hardened beyond standing.

"If I'm not inside you in two seconds, I'm going to lose control completely," he groaned.

"Do your worst, sir," she challenged with a laugh.

He sat up, pushing her flat on her back in return. Straddling her, he parted her legs and plunged into her. He began to move slowly, taking his time, playing with her. Adele was already so aroused by having him back that his release signaled hers. In two years as lovers and spouses they had never come at the same time although before it had usually been one following closely on the other. Tonight they came together, crying their mutual release before drifting off into sated slumber.

MORNING FOUND Adele alone in bed, the sheets cold, but smelling of sex. She knew for certain she had made love to Blair that night, but had she dreamed about Brian, or had it happened?

The door opened a crack. Susannah peeked in. Seeing Adele alone, she came in. She was clad in her chemise and pantalets and Stephen's dressing gown. Her gown, petticoats and corset were folded over her arm. Susannah entered briefly and came over to the bed. She held out her left hand to her older sister. On her ring finger was a small gold and turquoise ring, her birth stone. She mouthed the word "June" and disappeared again.

BREAKFAST DOWN in the kitchen alcove was a chorus of odd notes. Susannah came down from the third floor humming snatches of the incidental music Mendelssohn wrote for *A Midsummer Night's Dream,* which she'd heard played the night before. "Good morning, Bertha. Isn't it a glorious day to be alive?"

Adele came down. She was serious looking, but to Susannah's

eyes, her mouth showed definite signs of having been thoroughly kissed the night before.

"Good morning, Sissy," Susannah sang out, planting a kiss on Adele's cheek. "Did everything turn out as you planned?"

"More or less," she sighed, "I'll tell you about it privately tonight if you remind me."

"Okay, got to run. Sissy, will you have time to make me a dress for that date in June I told you about or should I go to a dressmaker?"

"I should be able to pull something together for you... I'm really very happy for you."

"Gosh, I'm happy, too. I don't think I've been this happy in my life—even drawing."

Stephen came down next. He was dressed in the suit she recognized as the one he wore to court. It was his most sober suit, but the satisfied grin on his face was at odds with his costume.

"Good morning, Adele, Bertha. I need a cup of coffee and some raw eggs. I've got to eat some defense attorney's *cojones* for breakfast but I'm in too good a mood to be bloodthirsty. Oh, Bertha, you might as well scramble those eggs. I could never eat them raw. I'll just have to chew on the carriage reins to get good and deadly this morning."

"Well, Lord above, Mr. Stephen, what's got into you?" asked Bertha.

Stephen grabbed the plump old cook and spun her around, then pulled Adele into his grasp and danced around the kitchen.

"Bertha, my love, I'm getting married. I'm in love and getting married as soon as possible. I'm going to have the most beautiful wife and the most beautiful sister-in-law and the most beautiful niece in the world."

He continued to dance with Adele, singing the wedding march he'd heard the night before.

"I feel like playing hooky today and spending the day in the park with the woman I love...."

"Well, I feel it would be a better idea if you went to Superior Court and won Carroll Enterprises v. Bosworth Lines instead."

At Blair's sour voice, Stephen stopped swinging Adele around. His smile faded and he looked from his brother to his sister-in-law and back. Adele shrugged her shoulders and went back to the table where she swallowed her lukewarm tea and picked up a tray containing cooked cereal for the children.

Bertha served Stephen his eggs and he bolted them down,

followed with a swallow of scalding hot coffee. Casting a sidelong glance at Blair, Stephen declared, "Now I'm feeling aggressive. Better, big brother?" With that he stormed out of the kitchen.

"What happened," asked Adele, "wake up on the wrong side of the bed this morning? Or was it just the wrong bed?" she added in a harsh whisper as she headed upstairs to the nursery.

Adele was feeding cereal to Beatrice when Blair opened the nursery door. "My office, ten minutes," he snapped and shut the door. The door immediately opened again and Blair took a long look at Beatrice and shut the door again without saying a word.

Josh's eyes widened. "What's wrong, Miss Adele? Is Daddy angry with you?"

"I don't know, sweetheart. I guess I'll find out in ten minutes."

"Did you have a fight last night after I fell asleep?"

"No, sweetheart, anything but."

Joshua ran over to Adele and hugged her. "You're not going to leave me, are you?"

"I'm not planning to leave, but if I do, I promise I will tell you before I go. Is that a deal?"

"I love you, Miss Adele."

"I love you, too, Josh, almost as if you were my own little boy."

"I hate him."

"Don't say that. Your Daddy is a very sad man who can't always remember how many people really love him. I'll bet if you continue to love him like you love Uncle Stephen and Beatrice and me you'll help him to love you back. It's like someone cast a spell on him so he would be mean and stern. We'll have to love him an awful lot to break the spell. Can you do that?"

"Yes, Miss Adele."

WHEN ADELE entered the office, Blair was standing at the large window, looking out. She couldn't remember seeing the drapes drawn in the room so the brightness was surprising. She quietly walked over and sat in one of the wing chairs.

"I'm afraid I did you a disservice last night," Blair began.

"In what way?"

"I've had more than my share of women in my time, but I've never seduced a married woman before. I feel damned wretched about it."

"Don't. You didn't exactly take me against my will."

"That concerns me, too," he added sternly, still looking out the window.

"Sit down, Blair," Adele demanded carefully. "I can't talk to your back like this."

He sat down in the chair opposite her. "How much are you aware of my history?"

"Well, I don't know where you were born, but I have a pretty good idea about the rest. By the way, where were you born?"

"That's not important now...Baltimore as it happens."

"Really? Me, too. That's peculiar."

Blair ignored her response. "What do you know about the last two or three years of my life?"

Adele stiffened. "What do you want me to know?"

"There are two years missing from my life. Traveling home from Wisconsin, I left the train I was on and was riding to a small town to pick up a spur line. On my way there I was assaulted by bandits and remember nothing else until I showed up on my own doorstep this past December, two years after I left Milwaukee. Everything else about that time is gone. The only clues I have are the clothes I was wearing, a horseshoe nail ring and changes in my physique. Before then, I was built along Stephen's lines. I don't even have the train ticket to know if or where I picked up the train."

"Do you have dreams you can't explain?"

Blair started. "Why would you ask that?" he asked suspiciously.

"Well, um, I've heard that people who've lost their memory sometimes have dreams where they see clues about the time they've forgotten. Do you have those kinds of dreams?"

"Yes, I keep seeing a woman I call my dark angel. Usually we're either outdoors or in a roughly built cabin. But last night I had the strangest dream yet."

"Tell me."

"Usually the dark angel is either reaching toward me or is weeping. Last night in my dream I made love to her. She had a baby—I knew it was our baby—the angel's and mine. I held it in my arms and it knew me. It seemed so right. But it was like it wasn't me, it was someone else."

"Could you see any faces or recognize where you were?"

"No, I never can see any faces, but yesterday the place seemed more familiar, more civilized somehow. And the angel spoke to me. I couldn't understand what she said, but her voice was soft and her skin was so white...." He buried his face in his hands.

Adele dropped to her knees before him. Softly she said, "If you think it's not right to have made love to me and you don't want to do it again, I'll understand. But I don't regret having done it. I wanted it every bit as much as you did, maybe more—and I'd welcome you to my bed again anytime you want...Blair, your family has become very dear to me...You've become very dear to me in spite of yourself."

"You don't understand. I think the angel in my dreams is a woman I married during the time I can't remember. I think that's what this ring means. I've never worn a ring on my left hand before. The signet is from necessity now...but the other...Somehow I believe it's a wedding ring. I'm married and have a child other than Joshua somewhere. If I can't remember who my dark angel is I can never go back to her, nor will I ever be free to be with anyone else. I'm married to a stranger who cannot let me go."

Adele reached up and brushed his hair with her hand. "I do understand. Remember, I'm married to a man who disappeared on me and when I located him again he didn't know who I was. I may never be free either. Please, Blair, let yourself love. Someone very special gave me that advice once and it changed my life. If not me—or your angel— then love your son. He's more adrift than either of us because he's completely helpless. If he grows up without love he'll grow hard and mean—and that would break my heart."

"You mean, don't let him grow up like me."

"Blair, the sins of the fathers don't have to be visited on the sons. You're not Oscar and Joshua isn't you. He can overcome his bastard birth and his mother dying if he has an anchor. You're his father; you can't afford to leave it to anyone else to do for you. You're capable of raising your son—look at the job you did with Stephen—how fine a man he's turned out to be. If he hasn't told you yet, your brother is getting married in June. He'll be raising his own family. Joshua's anchor has to be your love."

She rose to leave.

"Adele, what happens to you?"

"I don't know. I have my daughter and my memories. I'll make do. I always have and I always will. It's the way I was brought up."

"Adele, who is Beatrice's father?" Blair asked suddenly.

Adele answered stiffly, "Brian Strange."

"She doesn't take after you, does she."

"No, she takes after her father, like Joshua takes after you. Before all this happened she was Daddy's girl, but then, he brought her into the world. Susannah drew a beautiful sketch last fall. I remember when she drew it. I was at the frame working on a quilt. Brian was lying on Susannah's bed in the main room of our house reading a dime novel. Beatrice was lying on his chest, sound asleep. Every so often she'd stir slightly and Brian would stroke her hair and then return to his reading. On that evening I realized that I had never felt so safe and secure before, that everything in my life was as it should be. When Brian disappeared, I felt like someone had torn my beating heart out of my chest and crushed it in front of me...Last night I felt safe and secure again for the first time since then."

Blair stood up and walked away. "What we did last night, Adele, it was wrong," he said stiffly. "It was unfair to the husband you know you have and unfair to the wife I think I have. You should hate me for it."

"Don't manipulate me into hating you, Blair Carroll, you won't be able to do it."

"Can you disregard your husband so cavalierly?"

"Are you making this my fault alone, Blair?" Adele retorted. "Both of us are adults. *No* is part of both of our vocabularies. I invited you into my bed because I wanted you there. You came because you wanted me. Had either of us not wanted it, last night would not have happened."

Blair folded his arms defiantly. "You're not the woman I thought you were."

Adele gritted her teeth. "Oh, no, Blair Carroll. I'm exactly the woman you thought I was. You always know what you're getting with me. If you don't want what I have to offer, then don't take it."

"I won't," Blair shouted petulantly.

"Fine," Adele snapped back. "But think twice before you make any decisions regarding me. If I leave this house, I won't come back."

She stormed to the office door and turned back to him. "What made you so hard and mean, Blair? You couldn't have been born that way."

"You wouldn't understand."

"Maybe not, but maybe you ought to look into it yourself before you drive everyone who loves you away."

Blair watched her as she turned and walked out of his office, shutting the door hard behind her. He walked over to the sideboard to pour himself a drink, but realized it was not even nine in the morning.

Throwing himself into a chair, he began to think about what Adele had said as a parting shot. It had been a long time since he thought about the day that changed his life forever.

Unlike his father, Blair would never drop all his responsibilities on a son of his for a woman, any woman.

Maybe Adele was right. He could be a better father to Joshua than his father had been to him.

Adele. Like his father's mistress, she too had a husband somewhere. Blair could not let history repeat itself.

Chapter 16

THERE WERE NO repeats of dinner in the nursery after that. Blair left for the office earlier and returned later. If he did return early, it was usually to change into evening clothes and meet with business associates. Although he had never resumed smoking after coming back in December, he usually smelled of other men's tobacco and whisky. About the only thing he didn't smell of was perfume.

Having decided his dream of his dark angel and a baby meant he must have married during his lost years, he made the decision that he owed his unknown wife his fidelity. He might be falling in love with Adele Strange, but he could not have her again.

Falling in love? No, it couldn't be. Blair Carroll didn't fall in love—couldn't fall in love. He didn't even *like* most women—but he did like Adele Strange. He liked her enough to want to spend his life with her. He could see her sharing his home, sharing his bed, sharing his life.

But it could never be. She was married and he probably was, too. A man of honor would give her up, even if he loved her.

He did. No debate. He loved her as he had never thought he could love.

If he was going to have to give up the woman he loved because of a woman he did not even know, he determined to remain celibate rather than hurt either Adele or his anonymous wife. Having Joshua around, even though he didn't see his son often, also served to remind him of the perils of injudicious sexual relations.

What did disturb him was his attraction to Adele seemed to grow exponentially. He couldn't reconcile his decision regarding abstinence and the fact that just being near her aroused him beyond standing. Thoughts of her invaded his concentration. The desire to carry her into his bed and make love to her until his pain went away was overpowering. Knowing she would willingly accept his attention made things worse. He was in love with Adele and suspected that she might feel the same towards him. Love scared him to death.

The only solution was to keep his distance, stay away from the house as much as possible, try to pretend she was one of those women he disdained. He tried to fortify his decision with whisky, but the hangovers did not help his mood. He could not know Adele Strange and mistake her for a frivolous, ornamental woman. She was not Alabama and she was not Julia. This woman gave, not took. Trying to lessen her quality in his mind because of her willingness to be his lover simply did not work. He could not make her less than she was. He had met his equal, not in wealth or education, but in strength and resolve, and that very equality made him love her more.

Neither did the whisky make his dark angel dreams go away. She cried more now, his angel did. They were the tears Blair himself wanted to shed, but would not. He woke up at dawn with a pounding head and an empty feeling in his gut, like a starving man. He responded by being cynical and sarcastic with everyone, as if he just did not care what anyone thought of him. He thought even less of himself.

For her part, Adele felt as if someone was stomping on what was left of her heart. Every time she got anywhere near Blair he either made a cynical comment about women in general or walked in the opposite direction. Yet she could feel his eyes burning into her back as she walked away from him. She watched his increasing pain and his concerted efforts to deny his feelings. She saw in his stormy eyes the vulnerability of the man who had admitted, to his shame, that he didn't know how to chop wood. She suspected Blair was falling in love with her again but trying very hard to deny it. Adele had never stopped loving this man, even when she realized he did not know her. She felt empty and lost in her lonely bed.

She tended to the children, sewed and repaired their garments and read more than she ever had the opportunity before. Occasionally, Molly would agree to watch the children and Adele would meet Susannah or Stephen or both for lunch, usually in Chinatown. It was a good break from the tension, but she wasn't really good company.

As for the lovers, Stephen and Susannah got more bold in their attentions. Having made the decision to marry, and realizing that keeping their relationship a secret from Blair was no longer necessary, they were often caught kissing on the stairs and went on their dates openly. The only thing they kept secret from Blair and the household staff was that they were sleeping together almost every night—the hardest part was Susannah having to wake up at four to get back to her room before anyone else woke up. Fortunately, she never did get caught, because things being the way they were, Blair would have been unlikely to forgive her as his sister-in-law-to-be and think it some kind of manipulation on the part of Adele.

One day, in frustration, Adele even sought out a doctor. What he told her wasn't encouraging. Although there was archaeological evidence of brain surgeries being performed in Ancient Egypt, modern medicine knew very little about the real operations of the brain. What multiple head trauma had done to Blair Carroll's memory was not unheard of, but the length of the amnesias was unusual. The doctor did affirm that amnesia victims did sometimes have "dreams" of the seemingly forgotten memories, and that this was a good sign, because it meant the memories were buried, but not truly lost and therefore might return.

"I guess my question is; will I get my husband back?"

"Mrs. Strange, my best guess is that eventually the demeanor you identify as your husband and that of man you see now will merge into a whole. What you will likely get is a man who remembers nearly everything, but is a combination of the two men. With any luck, you will get the best of both. All it will take is time."

"Doctor, can I do anything to speed up the process? This is slowly driving me mad."

"Well," the doctor chuckled, "Short of hitting him in the head again and hoping for the best...I'm sorry, no. You can encourage him to talk about his dreams and prompt him to fill in the blanks himself, but his memories are going to have to come from him; time is the only cure—if there is one."

Not encouraging news—to say the least.

"WHAT DID THE doctor say?" asked Stephen over lunch.

"He said I could hit him over the head again...No, I didn't laugh either. He said I could talk to him about his dreams, encourage him to fill in the blanks."

"How are you going to do that? He's barely speaking to you."

"I know. It seems that my little seduction plan didn't work. Now he thinks I'm some kind of unfaithful hussy. I'm probably the first woman in history to cheat on my husband by sleeping with my husband! None of this makes sense anymore. Maybe I should just take Bea and go home. I don't belong here."

"Don't do anything rash."

"Stephen, the last thing I'm being is rash. I've been trying to deal with this since December. All I've succeeded in doing is making Blair angry, myself depressed, and throwing you, Susannah and Blair's little boy into the mire. Maybe if Bea and I go home now, Blair will stop avoiding Josh in order to avoid me, you and Susannah can get married and start your life together and Bea and I can have a happy life."

Stephen reached across the table and took Adele's hands in his. Looking evenly into her sad brown eyes, he said, "I love you, big sister. If you're going to leave, do it quickly and quietly as soon as you can make the arrangements. I'll make sure Carroll money supports you. Don't refuse it, it's your right as well as Bea's even if you deny it. You have a valid marriage and California law will support your claim."

Adele frowned. "Do you want me to leave?"

Stephen's eyes widened. "Of course not. But I can see that this is tearing you apart. Going on like you have been will kill you and what good will that be for Bea?"

"What do I tell Susannah?"

"Don't tell Susannah, send her a letter. I love her dearly, but she can be less than judicious. If she tries to talk you out of it, word will get around to Blair before you want it to. Include me in that letter as if I didn't know. Don't tell Blair either, just go back to your home in Wyoming. Send any correspondence to my office. I'll make sure Susannah and Joshua get anything for them. I'll arrange with Jennings and Lopez to get your trunk downstairs and you to the station, just let me know the date you're leaving."

"I may go back to using Stoddard."

"That's up to you. Just take good care of my niece and let her know that her Uncle Stephen loves her."

As Adele left the restaurant, she kissed Stephen on the cheek. "If anything good has come out of this debacle, it's knowing you, little brother. What a wonderful father you'll make."

"Believe me, Adele, I look forward to the opportunity."

A FEW DAYS after that, Adele sat down in the rocking chair and lifted Joshua onto her lap.

"Joshua, I made you a promise once that I would tell you if I was going to leave this house. I can no longer remain here. I want to go home to my farm in Wyoming, so I'm taking Beatrice and going home tomorrow."

Big, tear-filled gray eyes looked up at her. "Why do you have to go? Don't you love me anymore?"

Adele put her arms around Joshua and held him close to her. "Of course I love you, darling—and I always will. You're as dear to me as my Beatrice—but there are a lot of reasons why I have to go."

The little boy sat there for a while. Then he asked, "Miss Adele, do you love my Daddy?"

"Yes, honey, I do."

"Does he love you?"

"He did once. I don't know for certain now."

"You could marry him. Then you wouldn't have to leave."

"Your daddy doesn't feel free to ask me, even if he wanted to. And don't ask me why because I can't tell you simply enough for you to understand.

"Now, Josh, you mustn't tell your daddy, but Lopez is taking me to the station tomorrow morning after he comes back from taking your daddy and Uncle Stephen to their office. I want you to be a good boy for your daddy. Help him so he won't be so sad and alone. He's going to need you much more now...."

THE NEXT MORNING, Adele bathed, dressed and packed the remainder of her things in her old trunk. Some things didn't seem to be where she remembered putting them, but Adele assumed that in the wake of her strong emotions she had just forgotten exactly where she put them when she packed the night before. The last thing she packed before locking the trunk was the *Wedding Morning* drawing. Closing the trunk was like closing a chapter of her life, except that her book of life would be very empty from now on.

About ten that morning Lopez and Jennings loaded the trunk and the cat basket in the carriage and Adele and Beatrice got in for the ride to the station.

"*Señora* Estrange, I think you make a big mistake to leave like this," said Lopez, surprising Adele, since the stocky driver had never really spoken to her before.

"It's possible, Mr. Lopez, but if it's a mistake, I'm prepared to live with it."

"*Señora*, I am the driver for this family twenty-five years. I know *Señor* Blair and *Señor* Esteban since they are *muchachos*. *Señor* Blair, he is change since you come. I think he is in love with you. *Señor* Esteban, he shows how he feels too easily. With *Señor* Blair, he is confuse. He has hidden how he feel about things for so long he does not know how to show them."

"Mr. Lopez, if Mr. Carroll is in love with me, he has an awfully hateful way of expressing it. I know you think highly of your employers, but remaining here is killing me. I can't be good for my daughter if I am dying inside. I don't wish to speak of this anymore. I appreciate your taking me to the station."

"I CAN'T BELIEVE she did it."

"What are you talking about, Susannah?" asked Stephen.

Susannah walked into the parlor carrying a letter that she had found on her dressing table, when she'd gotten home from drawing in the park. "Adele—she's gone home."

"Home?" echoed Stephen, as if this was a surprise.

Susannah held out the letter. "Read it, darling. It's addressed to both of us. I'm going back upstairs to the nursery. Joshua must be beside himself. Molly said he hasn't been out of his room all day."

Stephen sat down on the settee, his long legs stretched out in front of him.

He read:

Dearest Susannah and Stephen,

I have decided enough is enough. I must release Blair to live as he would have had our paths never crossed. I must accept that Brian Strange was nothing more than the dream of a lonely, too tall, old maid who never really believed love would fall into her arms. It seems I was correct in the first place. But as with all dreams, I have awakened.

I will make do—I always have and I always will. Beatrice will know her mother loves her and that she once had a father who loved her dearly.

I had a dream that Brian returned the night you became engaged. For a few precious hours I was happy again, but in the morning he was gone. All that was left was Blair Carroll, who will never allow himself to love anyone as much as my Brian loved me.

Stephen, be good to my sister. I have tried to bring her up to be a loving woman. When she loves deeply it shows in her art. Cherish her and encourage her.

Susannah, you have found yourself a treasure beyond price. Fill your life with his love. Cherish him and hold him close. I'm sorry to miss your wedding. I suppose you'll have to go to a dressmaker after all. But then, you're marrying one of the San Francisco Carrolls. You deserve a wedding gown that will make the society column of the Chronicle, *not a homemade gown from your rustic older sister.*

Please watch over Joshua. He is a beautiful child who deserves better than fate has dealt him so far. More than anything I will miss watching him grow. Give him freedom to dream.

I ask only one additional favor: Don't tell Blair where I am. If he finds his missing years, he will know where to find me himself—if he wants to.

With all my love,
Adele Stoddard.

SUSANNAH CAME downstairs, her brow knit with worry. "He's not in the nursery. No one has seen him all day."

"Who hasn't been seen all day?" Blair stood in the doorway.

"Joshua. Molly thought he was hiding in the nursery, but I just came down from there and he's not there."

"Maybe he went shopping with Adele," Blair suggested.

Stephen took a quick glance at Susannah. "I doubt it, big brother."

"I'm sure he'll turn up when he gets hungry—unless he's in my office chasing after that benighted tomcat. I'll get him out of there before he knocks over something," and Blair headed up the stairs.

Stephen drew Susannah into his arms. "What do you think?"

"You don't think Joshua tried to follow her to the station, do you?" Susannah continued tearfully, "She didn't even tell me she was leaving. Oh, Stephen, I've been so selfish. I've been so happy about us lately I've barely noticed how hard things must have been for Adele."

Stephen stroked Susannah's back. "She doesn't begrudge your happiness, sweetheart. I think she remembers what it was to be happy in love."

JOSHUA WAS NOT in the office, but on the seat of a wing chair was an envelope addressed to Blair. He sat down and tore it open.

To his surprise, along with the stationery a small iron circlet fell out, a ring wrought from a horseshoe nail. He held it in his palm like an alien thing as he read:

Dear Blair,

I had a dark angel of my own once, with laughing silver eyes and hair like midnight. He gave me this ring because sometimes an axle is more valuable than gold. My angel is gone now, so I no longer need to wear his ring.

You once told Joshua that a ring could remind you of what you had forgotten. I can only hope for your sake that you were right about that. If this ring answers those questions, you will know what to do.

Be good to your son. Cherish his love and try to return it. You will

receive more than you can ever hope to give.
   Adele Stoddard.

A pounding began in Blair's head. He squeezed the little circle until it left an indentation in his palm.

"Did I know you before, Adele? God damn it, why can't I remember?" he groaned.

"Blair, he's nowhere in the house." Stephen was standing at the office door.

"He?" Blair asked absently.

"Your *son*," Stephen emphasized, annoyed.

Blair threw open his office window and bellowed, "Lopez!"

From the carriage house, the stocky Mexican came out, "*Sì, Señor* Blair."

"How did Mrs. Strange get to the train station?"

"She ask me and I drive her, *Señor*."

"Did you take Joshua with you?"

"No, *Señor*, only her *hija* and the *gatito*."

"Lopez, get dressed and get a policeman here immediately. My son has disappeared."

SPRING HAD COME to the mountains. The snow was all but gone and green was rioting everywhere.

Beatrice was staring out the train window, completely fascinated by the brilliant display passing before her. She kept tugging on her mother's sleeve and pointing. The train had left Carson City at dawn and would soon be entering the desert, where the scenery would change from green to gold.

Adele barely noticed. Heartbroken, she stared unfocused at the empty seats facing her, glad no one was there to chatter and demand her society. She could discern the baby words of her daughter and the unhappy protesting of the imprisoned Little Gent, but responded to Beatrice by rote. The stern-faced conductor had to shake her shoulder several times to get her attention.

"Are you Mrs. Strange?"

"Yes, sir; is there a problem?"

"Will you accompany me to the baggage car at once, Ma'am?"

Adele picked up Beatrice and followed the conductor back several cars to the dark railroad car, piled high with trunks and crates.

"There is a strange sound coming from your trunk, ma'am. I need your keys to investigate."

Adele fumbled in her pocket for the key, hampered by the squirming of the baby. She handed the key to the conductor, who unlocked the trunk and lifted the lid. The contents were moving!

"All right, come out now," commanded the conductor, "and don't try anything funny."

A little hand pushed aside a quilt in the trunk.

"Joshua! What in heaven's name are you doing in there? You can't come with me. You're supposed to be with your father."

Joshua glared at the conductor and then at Adele. The conductor pulled him bodily out of the trunk, dripping clothing behind him. The minute the conductor put him down, he ran to Adele and buried her face in her skirts.

"Oh, Mommy," he cried, "please take me with you."

Mommy?

"Joshua...."

He sobbed, "Please don't make me go back to Daddy. Please take me with you, Mommy."

The conductor looked at the two children clinging to Adele. Both had the same black curls and gray eyes. His eyes softened.

"Your man divorce you and decide to keep the boy, ma'am?"

Adele shrugged. She would never be able to explain.

The conductor shut the trunk lid and locked it again, handing Adele back her key. "I don't hold much for divorcing, ma'am, but it seems a shame to separate a brother and sister like this."

"See, Mommy," said Joshua, "The man says I should go with you."

"Ma'am, there's a telegraph and ticket agent in Eureka. I'm afraid he's going to be a half fare at his age—can you pay the fare?"

"Yes, I have enough money—and to telegraph his father to tell him where he is."

The conductor stooped down and looked Joshua square in the eye. "Now you see here, young man, that was a very foolish thing you've done. I'll bet your Pa is scared to death wondering where you are—not to mention the scare you've given your Ma here. Don't ever let me catch you sneaking onto a train again."

"I won't, sir."

Adele grabbed Joshua by the hand and pulled him back to her seat. Seating him opposite her, she fumed, "Where did you learn to be such a liar?"

Josh ignored the question. "Don't you want to be my mommy?" he asked.

Of course I do, Adele thought. "That's not the point. You're not supposed to be here. As much as I might want to be your mother, I'm not. Honey, your daddy could accuse me of kidnapping you and I could go to jail. Then what would happen to Beatrice?"

"I'd take care of her," he answered gravely, "and I'd tell them you didn't steal me."

"Why did you tell the conductor I was your mother?"

"I don't know."

"Well it's too late now. You'll just have to keep pretending until we get to Green River. By then I'll figure out what to do."

THE POLICE officer took down the information in a small notebook as he asked his questions.

"Who was the last person to see the boy?"

"It had to have been my sister," said Susannah. "She was his governess."

Molly put in, "Last night when I brought their dinner up to the nursery, Joshua was there. So were Miss Adele and little Bea."

Blair added, "My driver said Joshua was not with them when he drove Mrs. Strange to the station. I can't believe Adele would want to do Joshua any harm."

"The letter Adele wrote to Susannah and me didn't sound like she had anything to do with Josh disappearing," Stephen commented.

The police officer looked skeptical. "Do you have a theory, Mr. Carroll?"

"Yes. If my son knew Mrs. Strange was leaving—and I doubt she could have hidden her packing from him—I'm afraid he might have tried to follow the carriage to the station on foot and gotten lost. Officer, I want you to proceed on that basis. I simply do not believe Adele Strange had anything to do with my son's disappearance, at least not actively."

"As you wish, Mr. Carroll. If you hear anything or if the boy returns, you will let us know."

Chapter 17

STEPHEN FOUND the telegram on his desk the next morning. He tore into the envelope to read:

STEPHEN CARROLL
CARROLL ENTERPRISES
EMBARCADERO
SAN FRANCISCO, CALIFORNIA
JOSHUA STOWED AWAY STOP I AM NOT RETURNING STOP WILL NOT SEND HIM UNACCOMPANIED STOP IF BLAIR WANTS HIM COME GET HIM CARE OF DUNEAGAN GREEN RIVER STOP WILL NOT SEND HIM HOME WITH STRANGER STOP ADELE.

"Thank God," he exclaimed. The past twenty-four hours had been terrible. None of them had slept more than a few winks while sitting in chairs in the parlor. Stephen had never seen Blair more worried, though the older man refused to discuss it.

Quickly he summoned young Todd to deliver a note to the police to call off their search. Then he brought the message into Blair's office and handed it to his brother to read.

Blair scanned the yellow paper. A frown creased his brow.

"She sent the telegram to you, Stephen. Why to you? Joshua is my son."

Stephen was angry but not shocked that Blair's first comment should be about the mode of address of the wire rather than any show of relief about Joshua's safety.

Testily he replied, "Because I told her before she left to contact me if she needed anything."

Blair looked up suddenly. "You knew she was leaving?" he responded.

"I knew she was considering it, yes. The only thing I didn't know was exactly when. I don't blame her, though. Staying here was killing her by slow torture."

"She never told me she was upset."

"Would you have listened? Would you have tried to stop her? You've spent most of the last few weeks going out of your way to avoid her. What happened the night you had dinner in the nursery?"

A deep flush suffused Blair's face. "That's none of your damned business," he bit out.

Stephen smiled enigmatically. "Just what I thought. You've thrown away the only woman you've ever met who doesn't fit your idea of what women are. Adele and Susannah Stoddard are a breed apart. But even a special woman like Adele can't live with constant rejection from the man she loves. It doesn't surprise me in the least that she left without a word to you. She's through with you, Blair. And I say it's about time."

"What the hell is 'Duneagan Green River?'"

"I made Adele a promise not to tell you. I expect she thinks you should know the answer. And don't ask Susannah. I had her promise me to stay out of this."

"Why do I feel that everyone around me knows more about this than I do?" Blair exclaimed.

"Probably because everyone does. You refuse to put the pieces together. You've buried yourself—in work—in your nightmares. Do you want your memory to come back or don't you?"

"Of course I do," Blair growled. "Do you think I like having a blank space in my mind?"

"Sometimes I think you do. It gives you someplace to run away to. It gives you a reason not to get involved with the best woman you've ever laid eyes on."

"What the hell does my amnesia have to do with Adele? I never met her before this past December."

Or did I? A nagging voice assailed him.

"Adele couldn't live with your brutal coldness anymore and I've had enough of it, too."

"You don't understand. I love her."

"Well you figured it out a little bit late. Look at yourself in the mirror, big brother; you've thrown away everyone in your life."

"Even you?"

"Blair, I'm marrying Susannah Stoddard in June. I've bought my own house and I'm moving in as soon as the sale is closed and the decorating is done. Now that Adele is gone, Susannah is going back to live at Mrs. O'Bannion's boarding house until the wedding. I'd love her to live with me, but she's concerned about her reputation. But one thing's dead certain: We're not starting married life in a house you've made so oppressive that your own son would rather live with a complete stranger than with you. But then, Blair, come to think of it, which of you is the complete stranger to Josh, Adele—or you?"

"Damn you, Stephen!"

Stephen's quiet reply shook Blair. "I'm not the one who's damned." He left the office quietly.

That night Blair came home drunk. The servants were long abed and Stephen was so angry that he rented a hotel room for the night where Susannah joined him. The quiet was eerie.

He went into his office and poured himself another whisky and collapsed in the wing chair. The taste of the whisky seared his throat. God, he hated the stuff! His aching eyes closed.

His fevered brain heard the sound of weeping. To his dying day, Blair never knew for sure if his eyes were open or closed, but he saw the dark angel on her knees, her hair loose around her shoulders, her face buried in her hands. But unlike his earlier dreams, the angel was dressed in a white—no, a colorless gown. He'd seen that gown before—but where?

Then he saw a shadow rise behind the angel and hand her a bundle. The angel rose to her feet, holding the bundle to her. The bundle was an infant and she held it gently in her arms. The shadow behind her materialized into a man—with long black hair and mustache—who drew the angel into his embrace.

"Don't cry, sweeting," said the shadow. "I'm here. I'll never forget you."

The faces became clear to him....

In the morning, Blair awoke to find both horseshoe nail rings in his hand, linked together like a chain, despite the fact that both had been welded into continuous circles when they were created almost two years before.

He had no memory of how they'd come into his hand this night.

But what they were was less of a mystery.

THE LATE SPRING was turning the prairie green and blue. Welcome rain washed the sky and the unplowed ground was covered in grasses and hints of wildflowers. The fields of the Stoddard farm were already budding with wheat and corn, promising a fruitful harvest.

Adele stood on the porch of her house, staring out beyond to the horizon. She felt a strange detachment to the scene. Her attention was recaptured by the high-pitched playful screams of children.

John Lawrence, once called Swift Arrow, was lying on the ground under a pile of teasing children. Sean Duneagan's half-Cheyenne son-in-law was doing his best against his own two red-haired hooligans, Tess and Aaron, aged seven and eight, and their guest, Josh Carroll, but seemed to be losing the wrestling match, which was dissolving into a tickling contest.

Following them around on baby round legs, fourteen-month-old Bea Strange had her arms locked firmly under the front paws of an excessively annoyed Little Gent. The poor tom did not know whether to claw his way down or just stoically endure the affectionate mauling Bea gave her "Lijen." Like the others, Bea was screeching and giggling as she tried to insinuate herself into the fray, tomcat and all.

From inside the house, Moira Duneagan Lawrence emerged carrying two cups of tea, one of which she handed Adele. Moira was red-haired, freckled and green-eyed—and well on her way to her third child.

"I can't tell you what being able to lease this land from you has meant to us, Adele. Arrow wanted to take me off the reservation and go back to my family, but we didn't have enough money to buy land. It was so miserable there. Sometimes I can't believe my husband's part Cheyenne, farming seems too much a part of his blood."

"It's so strange," Adele commented, "I lived on this land almost my entire life, yet it seems so alien to see crops growing I didn't seed and people and livestock I've never met. But when I walked out to see the fields, I could see that you've put as much love into this place as I ever did—and as much hard work. Your husband is a remarkable man."

Moira laughed. "Yes, indeed. Did you know, before I went to the reservation to be a nurse, I was thinking of becoming a nun, but one look at Arrow and my only thought was that my true vocation was going to be complete devotion to him. He was trying so hard to make that horribly barren reservation land arable. Da thought I'd lost my mind—not that he'd wanted me to take the veil." She sighed, "It wasn't my mind I'd lost; it was my heart, but in exchange I've gained so much more."

Adele rubbed her left hand with her right. Her hand felt naked with her wedding ring gone, the skin still white and rubbed smooth where it had been. Her eyes filled with tears.

I never used to cry, Adele thought, *the last few months I've barely stopped. Damn you, Blair Carroll! You stole my heart, then you took my strength away from me and left me nothing but tears.*

Moira put her hand on Adele's shoulder. "Da told me about your husband disappearing like he did—I think if anything happened to Arrow I'd wither away and die. It's so wonderful that you have two such beautiful children to remember him by."

Since Josh had been calling Adele nothing but "Mommy" since the train, Adele decided to just let him have his way than explain why he was with her. Sean Duneagan knew the truth, but agreed to say nothing. Either his father would come and claim him or she would be gone from here soon enough and explanations could follow.

"Moira, I'm so glad you let us stay the day...." she began.

"Adele, you must always feel that this is still your home."

"No, I can see now that this is no longer my home—your love and hard work has made it yours." She held up her hand to silence Moira. "I couldn't continue to live here. It would remind me too much of...." She hesitated on the name, not even sure to call him Blair or Brian anymore. Brian Strange had loved her. As for Blair Carroll, she was not sure he loved anyone, including himself. "I've changed since I've been away. That's clear. I'll just have to make my home elsewhere. If you're interested, I'd like to meet with you and Arrow and Mr. Duneagan and work out some kind of plan where you could buy the place from Susannah and me over time. I know she doesn't plan to come back here. Her life is now in San Francisco. I'm sure there's a lawyer in Green River who can work out the details so that it's fair to all concerned."

Funny, Susannah told me when we left in December that she felt she was never coming back. It's a good thing, since there's nothing left to come back to.

Moira suddenly embraced Adele, then ran down the porch step and called to her husband, "Arrow, Adele wants us to buy the place—what do you think?"

The half-breed came over to Adele. "If you're sure, I'm sure Sean can work out a deal. The first time I broke a plow furrow in the soil, I knew I was home." He laughed. "Some Cheyenne I've turned out to be! No matter. You go forward or you die."

His sentiments echoed Adele's perfectly. If only she had some place to go forward towards.

"Then it's settled," she responded. "We'll talk over the details with your father-in-law this evening."

Another chapter in Adele's book of life closed.

OWEN WINSLOW came into Stephen Carroll's office. The lawyer looked up from the file he was reviewing.

"Can I do something for you, Mr. Winslow?"

"I was hoping Mr. Blair was in here."

"I haven't laid eyes on Blair in over a week. I've moved out of the house temporarily. My brother has some things to work out in his mind that are better served by my absence."

"I was glad to hear the little boy is safe. I assume one of you will be heading east to get him soon."

Stephen sighed, "As much as I love that kid, it won't be me. Right now he's better off with Mrs. Strange—um—Miss Stoddard, wherever she is. When my brother decides what he wants, it will be for him to do."

"On another subject, Mr. Blair scheduled a number of appointments for this afternoon. If he doesn't return are you willing to see them in his stead?"

Stephen leaned back in his chair. "Of course. Just bring me the files and proposals beforehand. I've run this company before and I can do it again if I must. The only difference is, this time I know Blair will be back."

"Very good, sir," Winslow said and then departed.

Stephen closed his eyes painfully. "At least I hope so," he commented wearily.

"ADELE, IF YOU don't eat something, you're going to get sick," Mr. Duneagan chided, but his teasing tone only barely disguised his concern.

An almost ghostly gauntness surrounded her, making her usual slenderness seem almost plump by comparison. Her hair and eyes were dull, stealing color from her face. Her cheekbones were painfully prominent in her oval face and topped with the purplish bruises of one for whom sleep is a stranger.

In the four weeks since returning to Green River, Adele had been slowly withering away. There had been no word from anyone in San Francisco about returning Joshua—and now, for all intents and purposes, the farm was the property of Mr. & Mrs. John Lawrence. She weaned Beatrice, the little girl chattered new words to anyone who would give her five minutes and seemed determined to hug Little Gent to death—when she wasn't doing the same to Josh. Joshua took it better than the cat did. He hugged her and carried her around until she squealed with laughter. As far as he was concerned, Bea was his sister and no one could tell him otherwise.

The children were happy. Anywhere they were was home enough for them.

Green River had never been home to Adele. She had seldom gone into town more than three or four times a year in her entire life. After spending months in San Francisco, the town seemed too quiet. Somehow starting a new life in this little city made no sense. She could wire Stephen for money. She knew he would send it. She could start a small business. But could she pass the municipal building without remembering her short but ultimately sweet wedding day? Could she pass the hotel without remembering Brian slipping the horseshoe nail wedding ring on her finger? Could she go into the mercantile without remembering that it was in front of that shop that Brian Strange had been taken away from her so suddenly? She felt like a dry, brown leaf, ready to blow wherever the wind blew, but of no earthly use to anyone.

Duneagan sat down opposite Adele. His kind green eyes were empathetic. He ran his hand through his thinning grayish-red hair. He had known Adele Stoddard as long as he had been factoring crops on the prairie, nearly twenty years since he had pulled his family out of a starving Ireland only to discover that his love of the land did not include working it, but did include the commerce of it. He remembered the slender, solemn sixteen-year-old who grasped her little sister's hand so bravely at their mother's grave-side, who learned to plow and plant following her father behind a mule, who took the reins herself and become father, mother, farm hand, anchor, when her father began to waste slowly and painfully away. But he also remembered the radiant bride. Was it only two years ago that she asked him and Grace— as the only townspeople she really knew—to stand up with her at her wedding to the man who was responsible for breaking her heart?

No, he thought, the bastard had broken more than her heart—he had broken her spirit, her willingness to care. Adele's aloneness was shattering. She went through the motions of living in the world, but no longer really chose to inhabit it. Not the child she had borne, nor the handsome one who had adopted her, nor even her pugnacious feline was successfully penetrating her devastating solitude.

"Adele, you've got to do something about yourself. If not here, somewhere."

Adele sighed, "What do you suggest?"

"Right after your mother died you gave me a letter to post that you wrote to her parents to tell them."

"Yes, I remember doing that. I told them about Susannah and me and all sorts of things about Ma. They never wrote back, but their lawyer sent me a bank draft to buy Ma a headstone. Seems to me we used it to buy a new plow."

"Your grandparents would probably be in their sixties or seventies now, if they're still alive. Age can soften grudges. Maybe they would be more forgiving of their grand- and great-granddaughters now."

Adele shook her head as if to settle the notion in her brain. "Are you suggesting I take Bea and go to Baltimore? We left there when I was Bea's age."

"The way you're going now, one place is as good as another. I'd rather think of you as alive in Baltimore than dead in Wyoming. And if you don't pull yourself out of the hole you've dug for yourself, I'm fully afraid that's the way you're going."

"But I don't even know my Maxwell relatives."

"Even so. Baltimore's a big city full of possibilities. And I'd be willing to wager you could make a go of a tailor shop much better in the East than Green River or anywhere else."

"What would I do about Josh? I can't take him east with me if I don't know where I'm going and I've heard nothing from the Carrolls about what to do with him."

"He's your stepson, isn't he?" Adele had told Mr. Duneagan about Blair's amnesia and about Joshua and how he came to be with her when she arrived in Green River. "I don't hear him begging to go home. He's having a grand time playing with Beatrice and Moira's kids and getting his clothes dirty. And I don't hear you talking about divorcing your man, so I suppose the boy's as well off with you as with that bastard you married."

Adele ignored the last comment. "I wired Stephen that I wouldn't send him home with a stranger. Even if I broke that vow, I suspect he would try to escape the train and follow me and that would be more dangerous than keeping him with me. But before I go to Baltimore, I ought to make sure someone there wants me."

DEAR GRANDFATHER and Grandmother, Adele wrote.

I last wrote to you nearly ten years ago when your daughter, my mother, Beatrice Maxwell Stoddard, died. At that time you did not answer my letter.

I am still your granddaughter. My sister, your other

granddaughter, Susannah is living in San Francisco and is engaged to be married to a young attorney from a prominent family. He is a good man who will make her very happy.

I have recently returned to Wyoming with my daughter, whom I have named Beatrice after my mother. I am also in temporary, although indefinite custody of my stepson while I await my husband's decision regarding his return. For a number of reasons too complicated to go into here, my marriage of just under two years is over and I have resumed using my maiden name.

I have discovered there is nothing holding me in Wyoming and I am selling our farm to a young family. I also find that I cannot return to San Francisco.

I had hoped in the past ten years you might have softened your attitude regarding my parents' marriage and might be willing to accept Beatrice and me in your lives. I am more than willing to seek and accept employment and find my own living accommodations, but it would be very helpful to know that I have family of some sort nearby if I am to attempt to restart my life in a city where I have not lived in twenty-five years.

I can be reached by mail or wire c/o Mr. Sean Duneagan, Green River, Wyoming Territory, for the time being. I pray that I may hear from you soon. I remain,

  Your granddaughter,
  Adele Stoddard.

ADELE WAS actually surprised that a letter came back from Baltimore:

Dear Adele Stoddard,

Your letter was an amazing surprise. To introduce myself, my name is Darren Maxwell, and your mother was my younger sister. When your letter arrived in 1866, I was posted to the military government in Mississippi after the War. As a result, my parents did not let me know you had written. I discovered the letter in my father's papers when he died this past Christmas. My mother died not long after your first letter arrived. I wrote to you at once, but the Postmaster in Green River returned my letter stating you had moved and left no forwarding address.

I never agreed with my father's decision to disown Bea and drive her and Thomas away, but I was posted in Texas when it happened. Neither Mother nor Father would ever discuss it beyond saying that no daughter of theirs was going to marry a dirt farmer. I had no idea where you were living or I would certainly have maintained contact.

I am currently residing in Maryland just outside of Washington as I am attached to the War Department. I have recently been restored to the rank of Brigadier General (having held the rank temporarily during the War). My wife of twenty years passed away a year ago.

Since we were not blessed with children, you and your sister are my only remaining family. It would please me greatly if you and your daughter would join me in Washington. I will also gladly accommodate your stepson if you have not returned him to his father. In addition to a too long overdue meeting, I would value your services as my official hostess. In this Centennial year there are many functions with which you could assist me.

Please write or wire me with your decision and I will happily wire you the train fare necessary.

Your reluctantly long-lost Uncle,
    Darren Maxwell,
    Brig. Gen'l., U.S. Army

ADELE SHOWED the letter to the Duneagans as soon as she finished reading it. Her face glowed with the first genuine smile they had seen since she returned to Green River.

"It's amazing after all these years to discover I have an uncle I've never met—and who welcomes me just like that. I'm so glad you suggested I try to write again. Thank you."

"Will you go?" asked Duneagan.

"Right this moment I can't think of any reason not to. There's nothing keeping me here...."

"Except some vague hope your husband will remember you're married to him and will come looking for you here."

Adele's smile faded. "Yes, that. Of course I would write Susannah as soon as I was settled. She wrote me that Stephen bought them a house. At least I don't worry about her happiness with Stephen. He is the best thing that ever happened to her. But I really no longer hold any hope for myself. Bea will have a good life in Washington. From the tone of his letter, I have no doubt my Uncle Darren will spoil her terribly."

"Well, I guess that settles things," said Duneagan. "If you want, I have to go to telegraph office to wire my broker in Chicago. I'll take a telegram to your Uncle for you."

Adele's telegram to Darren Maxwell read:

HAPPILY ACCEPT STOP CAN TRAVEL TO WASHINGTON ONE WEEK FROM TODAY STOP UNLESS SOMETHING CHANGES IN NEXT SEVEN DAYS WILL BE MYSELF AND TWO CHILDREN STOP ADELE STODDARD.

DUNEAGAN'S telegram to Susannah Stoddard read:

ADELE LEAVES FOR WASHINGTON ONE WEEK FROM TODAY UNLESS THAT SORRY EXCUSE FOR A HUSBAND COMES FOR HER STOP DO SOMETHING STOP SEAN DUNEAGAN.

Sean Duneagan was not sure how long it took to get from San Francisco to Green River by train. He only hoped it was less than a week.

Chapter 18

"PENNY FOR your thoughts," commented General Darren Maxwell.

"I'm just thinking how exciting Washington will be next month when we celebrate the national Centennial, Uncle Darren. The children will love it."

"There'll be quite a social whirl, especially in government circles. Do you think you'll be able to handle everything?"

"I'll make do," Adele commented, "I always have."

She leaned back against the squabs in General Maxwell's carriage and closed her eyes.

It had been quite an unusual meeting—could it have been only a month ago? Darren Maxwell had been a revelation to Adele. Her vague memories of her mother's face were brought into focus in him. He had the same brandy brown eyes as Adele and Susannah. His hair, now liberally streaked with white at age forty-eight, had been the same sable color. He also answered the question of Adele's exceptional stature, since he was six feet eight inches of lean cavalry muscle, honed by thirty years in the saddle until his recent posting to Washington. In his dress uniform he was an imposing, impressive figure, exuding controlled power. He was bearded as was his commander-in-chief, President Grant, which only added to his magnificent image.

Ironically, privately Darren Maxwell was a jovial and compassionate man. He had risked his political career and had delayed his repromotion to General during Reconstruction by administering his district with a just hand rather than a punitive one. As a Marylander, he was aware of the divided loyalties of Washingtonians and border staters and had no use for extending the misery of the conquered South.

His only regret during his life was that his Lorena and he had been childless. If he was welcoming to the sudden existence of his sadly rootless elder niece, he was ecstatic about the presence of his little grandniece and her half-brother and delighted them with stories about his "adventures" in the Cavalry, although Adele was aware that these "adventures" were considerably expurgated to eliminate the death and destruction that are a soldier's constant companions.

Adele tried not to think in terms of time anymore. Since there had

been neither telegram nor letter with instructions regarding Joshua—
and the little boy did threaten to run away from anyone she might hire
to bring him home to San Francisco—Adele had brought him along.

FINALLY, SHE SAT Joshua down and told him about Brian Strange
and Blair's missing two years. She told him that Beatrice was truly his
half-sister, which pleased the little boy no end. Her only excuse to
herself was that she was his stepmother and had some right to keep him
with her, at least until his father decided to do something about it.

Joshua never questioned why his father did not send for him. He
was happy enough staying with Adele and Bea. And now he also had
Uncle Darren, who promised him a pony and a tutor. They were the
only family he wanted now. Even the lingering sadness over his
mother's death seemed to disappear in this happy house.

Adele maintained her decision to return to using her maiden name
of Stoddard. She felt no real right to call herself Adele Carroll and she
knew that she could no longer maintain the fiction of being Adele
Strange.

Stephen wired her money as soon as he had her address, but said
nothing about Blair or Joshua. He and Susannah both wrote to her, but
talked only of each other, their wedding plans and general news of San
Francisco. Of Blair, they wrote nothing.

From Blair himself there was nothing but silence. Not about
Joshua and not about anything else. Adele almost wished he would
write her and tell her to go to the devil. Missing him was marring her
chance at contentment.

Darren Maxwell's first action was to refurbish their wardrobes. It
was evident that the females' simple calicoes and Joshua's limited
choices were insufficient for Washington society. The expense was no
concern. The Maxwells were a very wealthy family and the general was
the sole inheritor of a huge estate. He also set up a trust fund for
Beatrice to educate her or dower her or support her in any way she
needed.

For Adele, who had never owned a store-bought garment until she
had gone to work for Donelli, to have a stylish dressmaker and her
assistants rush through measuring and stitching to make her gowns in
the latest fashions and in rich jewel colors and fabrics which made her
skin and eyes seem to glow was an unimagined luxury. House gowns,
day frocks, evening and ball gowns with custom-made shoes to match.
Little hats decorated with feathers and flowers and gloves that were

made to fit her long-fingered hands completed her wardrobe. It was coming summer—and Washington would be a steam bath soon enough, so coats and wraps could wait, but the image that stared back at Adele from the mirror was of a sophisticated woman. It is possible Adele was as shocked by her appearance the first time she saw herself fashionably dressed as Blair had been the first time he saw himself upon returning to San Francisco.

"So, the country mouse becomes a town mouse," had been Maxwell's comment on seeing her fashionably dressed for the first time. "This is how you should look all the time, Adele."

"I can hardly recognize myself," Adele commented.

"You're a beautiful woman," her uncle responded. "I can see it, even if that ne'er do well you married couldn't."

"Please, Uncle Darren. It was my mistake to fall in love with a man with no memory. I was a fool to forget he would have a life out there that had nothing to do with me. Then, when I could have easily told him who I was and what he was to me, I stood back and kept silent." Adele sighed. "I guess I brought on my own unhappiness. Still...." she trailed off.

"You love him."

Adele nodded. "More than my life, whether he deserves it or not."

ADELE MADE DO. She worked hard to adapt to the social life in the nation's capital. Even the first meetings were easier than Adele expected. General Maxwell was proud to introduce his soft-spoken niece to Washington matrons. She was a gracious, if quiet, hostess and a sought-after guest. Adele always figured it was because most of these women had never met a real pioneer woman and were interested in the details of farm life, because her private story she kept to herself.

Her skill as a hostess seemed to have been an inherent trait because she certainly had no experience. If people were expecting a rustic, she surprised. Some San Francisco must have rubbed off.

Adele was glad to find out she could do something besides sew. But even in that, she became a popular hostess and guest. Though the quilts they made were a far cry from the decorated but basically utilitarian quilts of her growing up, Adele's skills with a needle quickly allowed her to participate in the ladies' circles that made these beautiful covers. A new circle of friends developed. Adele realized how isolated her life had been and relished the camaraderie she was discovering.

The children were something special as well. Beatrice and Joshua were growing by leaps and bounds. Bea was toddling around and talking more and more. Joshua was Bea's constant companion, taking more time than would ever be expected of a six-year-old to play with her and talk to her. On more than one occasion, Adele would look into the bedroom that had been converted into a nursery for them and hear Josh singing lullabies to Bea at her nap time. His childish voice was sweet and clear and he loved to sing. The lullabies were his only inheritance from Cherry Leval and he shared them unselfishly.

Both children called her Mommy now—and although hearing it from Josh was a wrenching reminder of Blair, she did nothing to dissuade him. He was a symbol both of what she had lost—and what she had gained. She realized she could not love Joshua more if he was her own blood kin.

ADELE AND Uncle Darren were returning from a War Department reception committee meeting where plans for Centennial celebrations were in progress. Since military activity in the West fell under the War Department aegis, there was also plenty of gossip about recent Plains Indian hostilities. The general consensus was that the cavalry commands under such leaders as General Custer would make short work of these unlettered savages, and then Custer would use his glory to ride into the White House.

Adele was looking forward to getting back to the comfortable house her uncle owned. The gossip and chatter had given her a headache. She was still not completely comfortable in heavily perfumed crowds, though she was getting better at it daily. Even in San Francisco she had lived a quiet and isolated life. Her positions as tailor and then governess had pretty much mandated a quiet life.

All Adele wanted to do was get back to the children. A letter from Susannah had arrived in the post just as they were leaving. She and Stephen should have been married by now—Adele was sorry to have missed it.

The housekeeper answered the door as General Maxwell and Adele arrived home.

"General," she began, "there's a gentleman waiting in your study to see you. And a parcel came for you, Miss Adele. I took the liberty of putting it in your room along with your letter."

"Thank you, Mrs. Greene. Uncle Darren, I think I'll go upstairs and read the letter from Susannah, and see what that parcel might be."

"Of course. You've been thinking about that letter all day, haven't you?"

"Well, until we found each other, Susannah's been my only family. I've missed her terribly."

Darren kissed her on the cheek. "Go up and read your letter. I'll see what my caller wants. I know you'll probably want to spend some time with the children before you dress for dinner anyway."

Adele slightly lifted the skirts of her sapphire blue and white striped chintz day gown and hurried up the stairs.

General Maxwell unconsciously brushed down the front of his uniform tunic and opened the door to his study. He took one look at his nervously pacing visitor and immediately effected his command facade. The visitor stared at the first man ever to make him feel short and the color fled behind his bronzed face.

Darren walked over to the sideboard and poured two glasses of whisky. He handed one to his visitor, but noted that the man set the glass down untouched. He glared down at him and stated, "I am General Maxwell, Adele's uncle, and I believe I know who you are, sir. But perhaps you want to tell me precisely what you want...."

ADELE TOOK THE letter and the parcel from her room and went into the nursery. Josh was there, playing with Bea, trying to teach her, somewhat unsuccessfully, to count to ten on her fingers. Too young to comprehend, Bea merely aped, and soon both children were laughing on the carpeted floor, with Adele laughing along. Little Gent was curled up on the hearth. Occasionally he opened his eyes halfway and then returned to sleep.

"Kids, I've a letter from Aunt Susannah. You want to hear?"

Joshua immediately sat down at the foot of the rocking chair attempting to hold the squirming Bea in his lap and embrace.

"Josh, you'd better let Bea go. She's too little to sit still for long. She'll sit down eventually."

After sitting down in the rocking chair, Adele opened the envelope and read:

Dear Sissy,

I can't believe you've discovered Ma's brother like that! How wonderful to know she wasn't forgotten. I hope one day Stephen and I can go to Washington or Uncle Darren can come to San Francisco so we can meet. I also would love to get him down on paper.

"Of course," Adele interjected, "meet your uncle and draw him."

Speaking of drawing, I've started to take some lessons in painting with watercolors and oils. My teacher says I have plenty of talent—just need some experience. I like watercolors better; they are almost as fast as pencil and charcoal. He thinks once I've painted just a short while, he will be able to get me an exhibition. Of course, it won't hurt to be Mrs. Stephen Carroll to open a few doors. I've begun to fully realize the power this family has in business and social circles, even with the scandal involving Stephen's father and his mistress.

Our new house is almost ready, probably done by the first of July. We've decided to postpone the wedding until it is. I'm living at Mrs. O'Bannion's (for propriety sake) until we're married. I don't want to live apart from Stephen, but neither do I want to begin married life in Blair's house.

Things are very tense here between Blair and Stephen. They barely speak to each other these days except on business-related matters and even then they start sniping at each other. Blair doesn't talk to me at all—for which I am entirely grateful, because he is being entirely moody and unpleasant. Besides, I think when he sees me he is upset about your being gone—although he won't say it. He is spending a lot of time in Sausalito. Stephen says they used to go there as boys. Quite frankly, right now I don't miss him.

The house is very empty with Joshua and Beatrice gone—I hope they're happy with you. I for one am spending all my spare time drawing and painting in the park, although I am no longer doing it for a dollar per picture since Stephen is already supporting me in a manner to which I hope to remain accustomed. I just can't spend anymore time in the house than necessary. I eat supper with Stephen, then he escorts me to the boarding house. Blair is never home for supper. Where he goes, who can say?

We're thinking of getting married on July 4th. Somehow a Centennial wedding date seems like a good way to make sure we don't forget it in future. My wedding dress is beautiful, yards and yards of satin and lace. At my fittings I have felt like a royal princess. I only regret it being made by a stranger. I'd much rather have had a dress like your muslin if it could have been made by you.

There is still time for you to reconsider and return for the wedding. I will have no maid or matron of honor if it isn't you. And if you could convince Uncle Darren to come west, I would be honored to have him give me away. (Is he really six foot eight? I can barely conceive of it! Now I know where you got it from. I bet he's quite a sight in his uniform.) If you would agree to come, I would even *postpone the wedding again until you could arrive. Stephen agrees with me. He's really come to love you and misses you nearly as much as I do.*

I've run on so. Write back soon. Kiss Josh and Bea for me and tell them their Aunt Susannah misses them.

Love always,

Susannah.

"Do you want to go back to San Francisco?" asked Joshua.

"I would have liked to see my sister get married, sweetheart, but it's just too hard for me to see your father every day knowing I don't mean anything to him."

"You mean if he asked you to come back you might?"

"If he came to me and told me he remembers and loves me and wants me back—yes, Josh, I would go back to him."

Joshua crawled onto Adele's lap and rested his head against her breast. "If Daddy doesn't want you back, I'll stay with you. I'll never leave you."

Adele wrapped her arms around Josh. "Josh, I love you, and I'm honored you want to call me 'Mommy,' but if your father sends for you, I will have to let you go; you know that. I'm not blood to you and really have no right to keep you with me."

For a long time they sat there, not talking. Beatrice came over to the rocking chair and insisted on being lifted up. Both children sat quietly in Adele's lap with her arms around them. For the first time in months, Adele had no more tears. She just closed her eyes and let their loving warmth seep into her soul.

After a while, Josh shifted slightly. In moving to make him more comfortable, the small, previously ignored parcel slipped through the rungs of the rocking chair and fell onto the carpeted floor.

"What's that?" asked Josh, his eyes following the object to the floor.

Adele looked down. The small parcel was wrapped in brown paper, tied with string. The only mark on it was her first name hand written in India ink.

Joshua climbed down and retrieved the parcel and climbed back on Adele's lap, handing it to her.

Adele opened the parcel. There was a small box and a letter. She opened the box. In it were two gold rings, smaller and larger, molded to resemble horseshoe nails.

Adele gasped. She tore open the letter.

Dearest Adele,

You always deserved a gold wedding ring—and a man who loves you. I realize I've loved you since that first November morning when my entire world consisted of you. Without you it doesn't matter who I am—my world is empty.

B.

P.S. I hand delivered this parcel. With any luck, I'm waiting downstairs.

As quickly as she could, Adele lifted Josh and Bea from her lap and, holding the box, ran out of the nursery and bounded down the stairs.

She was halfway down the stairs when Blair emerged from Darren's study, tall and elegant in frock coat and striped trousers. Adele paused.

"Blair?" Her voice was barely audible.

"And Brian," was his husky answer.

He opened his arms. Adele tore down the last of the stairs and crashed into his embrace. His mouth came down on hers as he crushed her against his hard length. She felt his desire; hers was its equal. She gave as good as she got, tasting and nibbling his intoxicating sharpness as he tasted her sweetness, pressing her arms against his back as if to meld them into one entity. Their breathing fell into unison rhythm, ragged and rapid. He pressed her head against his chest and took a deep ragged breath. Adele felt something on her head. She looked up at Blair to see the track of a tear that had fallen down his cheek and landed in her hair. She touched her hand to that cheek.

"I've been in hell," he said.

"So have I."

"I was afraid your uncle would boot me out the door."

"He wouldn't have," she responded with a laugh. "He's just being protective. Come upstairs and see your children."

She grabbed him by his hand and pulled him up the stairs behind her. She led him into the nursery. Blair strode over to Josh and Bea and lifted them in his arms. Beatrice, surprised by the action, began to fuss.

"Don't cry, sweeting. Daddy's here."

Blair kissed Bea and then Josh and motioned Adele over to them. He put the kids down and knelt down, pulling Adele down to her knees and taking the box from her hand. He picked up the smaller ring and holding her left hand, he slid the gold band on her finger.

"With this ring, I thee wed. Now and forever, till death do we part.

Now you."

Adele stared at her left hand. These were the same words he had said after their wedding. She then picked the other circlet and pushed it onto his left ring finger.

"With this ring, I thee wed. Now and forever, till death us do part. You remember everything then?"

Blair put his arms around her and kissed her lightly on the forehead. "My memory came back in bits and pieces. It was agonizing. I'm so sorry, my darling, but I had to be completely alone for a while and sort out what was flooding into my brain. I couldn't deal with you or Joshua. I even left the business to Stephen for a while. I took the train to Green River. I even went to the farm. Slowly things began to fit together—faces, places. The only things I can't remember that I was conscious for are the faces of the men who ambushed me and how Thunder came to injure me. I'm told those will probably never come back. I couldn't come sooner, beloved. It took time for everything to come back to me. I just wish I hadn't been the cause of so much pain for you."

"Susannah wrote me that you spent time in Sausalito."

"I had to get away to think, to come to grips with who I am."

"And who are you?" Adele asked tentatively.

"I am Blair Carroll. Brian Strange was a temporary name you gave me until my memory returned, but I think the man I was able to be when I won you is an integral part of me. It took not knowing that I had intentionally suppressed that part of my personality to bring it out. I suppose I hid that part of me and hid from it as well because I never wanted to be hurt again the way my father hurt me. Now my question is, who are you?"

Adele shrugged, and then smiled radiantly, "I'm Adele Carroll, and I'm married to the most wonderful man in the world."

"Always remember that I love you," he added.

"I always will. And will you remember my love?"

"Always, my dark angel. Now, let's take our beautiful children and go home."

Home, Adele thought with a smile.

Home with Blair, where she belonged.

Epilogue

San Francisco, May 1877

AN EMERY BOARD tongue over his eyelids woke Blair from his contented slumber. He opened his eyes to stare into the iridescent green gaze of Little Gent.

"That damned cat is in bed with us again," he said amusedly.

Adele stirred. Sleepily, she responded, "That's all right. He doesn't take up as much room as you do."

"Or you, for now."

Adele rolled from her side where she had lain cradled in Blair's arms onto her back. Her abdomen was softly rounded with the promise of new life.

"It's funny," she said, "I never thought of Susannah as ever becoming a mother, but they had such a beautiful baby. And Stephen is acting like the cock of the walk. You'd think they were the first people ever to have a baby. I'm glad they decided to name their son Darren. The general was so pleased. Of course, it might have been more convenient if she hadn't gone into labor on the opening day of her exhibition."

"There are some out there who were shocked she would even appear in public so close to term," Blair observed.

"Fortunately, Mrs. Stephen Carroll can rise above public opinion." She put a hand on her own belly. "Of course, so can Mrs. Blair Carroll."

"Do you know what today is?" Blair asked.

Adele grinned. "Yes, of course. It's our third wedding anniversary."

Blair held her left hand in his. Their gold rings, shaped like horseshoe nails, gleamed together in the morning light. He threaded his fingers through hers and brought her hand to his mouth where he kissed it tenderly.

"What do you want for an anniversary present?"

"How about a whole day in bed with my husband."

"That can easily be arranged."

Her eyes sparkling, Adele raised herself on one elbow and retorted, "What! On a weekday? Carroll Enterprises won't fall to rack and ruin without you?"

Blair laughed. It was an honest, happy laugh, full of love and tenderness. "Oh, we'll be filing for bankruptcy tomorrow, I'm sure," he responded teasingly. He leaned over and kissed his wife on the lips. She reached for him and was returning his kisses when suddenly she gasped and stopped.

"What's wrong?"

Adele beamed. "Nothing," she said. "It moved. That's the first time. Feel."

Blair put his hands and his cheek on her swollen belly. Yes, he definitely felt a faint kick. His grin turned his gray eyes silvery with delight. Five years ago he would never have imagined that he would be finding pleasure in feeling his own child moving within his wife's womb. Five years ago he hated his life. But he had learned to find satisfaction in hard work. He had learned to temper seriousness with laughter. He had learned how to love. And the woman lying beside him had been the best teacher he could ever have imagined.

"God, I love you so much, Adele," he declared.

"And I you, my sweetest darling. I've been thinking about names."

"And...."

"If it's a boy, I want to name it after you."

"Oh, please," Blair groaned, "I wouldn't wish Blair Carroll, Junior, on any child of mine."

"Well, actually, I was sort of thinking of 'Brian.'"

Blair laughed again. "Have I told you lately that I love you?"

"Of course you have. I never forget that you love me."

"And, God willing, I will never forget again either."

Elise Dee Beraru

Elise Dee Beraru can't recall a time since she learned to read that she hasn't been a writer. She chooses to write romance because she believes love stories featuring smart, strong women who find true love with the men of their dreams without sacrificing their core selves are the ultimate empowerment.

When not writing, Elise is an attorney in solo practice in Beverly Hills, California. She is also an award-winning quiltmaker and public speaker as well as being active in promoting opera and the rights of injured workers. She is a member of Romance Writers of America, the Electronically Published Internet Connection [EPIC], World Romance Writers and Women Writing the West.

In addition to the honors garnered by *Remember My Love*, Elise was also the winner of the 2000 PASIC "Book of Your Heart" contest for unpublished manuscript proposals in the Historical Romance category.

If you enjoyed ***Remember My Love***,
you may enjoy our other historical romance titles.

Visit us on the web at:
http://www.hardshell.com

or send a LSASE for a complete book list and order form to:
**Hard Shell Word Factory
PO Box 161
Amherst Jct. WI 54407
USA**

Printed in the United Kingdom by
Lightning Source UK Ltd., Milton Keynes
141766UK00001B/8/A